JURY DUTY

by

daniel storm

daniel storm

JURY DUTY

By Daniel Storm

Copyright © 2006 By Daniel Storm

William J. Pulkinen & Associates
705 Sunny Slope Road
Elm Grove, Wisconsin 53122
Pulkinen@wi.rr.com

This book is a work of creativity, observation, research and experience. If any names, events and characters have any resemblance or similarities to actual persons, names, places or events in this story, it is purely coincidental, or the personal knowledge of the author.

ISBN # 978-0-9826782-3-7

COVER DESIGN

The cover illustration **"A Prayer for the Dead"** by *Eddie Mize* (Copyright) 2009-2011   http://eddietheyeti.deviantart.com

Cover art direction by *Tom Wilcox*

http://tomwilcox.deviantart.com

daniel storm

DEDICATION

This book is for all those who encouraged me, those who believed in me and those tolerant enough to understand me. The creation of *Jury Duty* was a labor of love for me and the convincing evidence of those who cared. There will be more stories to follow.

Thank you!

Books by Daniel Storm

Reaper's Gate

Jury Duty

Praetorian Guard

Surviving the Alphabet Soup

The Apostle (March 2012)

Mantis (May 2012)

The Prey (July 2012)

**Not Afraid to Kill, Not Afraid to Die
(September 2012)**

Malevolence (December 2012)

Masters of the Race (coming soon)

*Check for Our Books in Spanish!

Daniel Storm

Mr. Storm is Native American and ascribes to the Blackfoot heritage and ways. He grew up in Illinois and Wisconsin, where he attended the University of Wisconsin and ultimately studied law. After college, he participated in defending some of America's most notable crime figures, while associated with prestigious law firms.

As an author of numerous crime/fiction novels, he spends hours creating stories that compel readers to devote their undivided attention. Internationally, he is on the threshold of tremendous success, despite his retaining control of his stories, the production of his books and distribution.

He lives near Milwaukee with his German Shepherd, Merlin. He enjoys seeing the sites in Wisconsin on his Harley.

As a Viet Nam veteran, Storm works within the Wisconsin community to assist soldiers and military families, both of those in active service, and veterans and their families.

www.danielstormauthor.com

daniel storm

Chapter 1   Prologue

"Good afternoon, Edward. May I join you?" He always calls him "Edward," though J.D. Barnhill knew it annoyed Eddie.

"Of course, J.D." Everyone calls him Mr. Barnhill. Eddie evened the score by calling him "J.D."

It is a beautiful Southern Illinois afternoon, the gentle westerly breeze carrying the scents of wild flowers mixed with the typical farm community odors of freshly tilled soil, manure and fertilizers. Eddie enjoyed these smells, having spent most of his adult life in "the city," Chicago and its suburbs. There, he smelled exhaust from cars, buses, trains, planes and a million restaurants. He missed those familiar olfactory amusements at times, but today he was sitting on a concrete bench, soaking up the sun's energy and the scents that enveloped him.

J.D. would often visit Eddie. He found him smart and always quick with his silver tongue, quite unlike the others of their cloistered community. Sometimes they'd talk about current events, the change in Presidential administrations, business and even international conflicts. He sincerely enjoyed Eddie's company and wit. He looked forward to their little meetings.

J.D. is the same height as Eddie, 6'1", but only weighs one-hundred-eighty pounds, compared to Eddie's 230. J.D.

worked his way through college, earning a Bachelor's Degree in Criminal Justice from the University of Illinois at Urbana while working as a correctional officer for the Illinois Department of Corrections at a facility in Lincoln. He continues to enlarge his education through extension courses in criminal law, human services, psychology and management from various universities. He has achieved accolades from numerous community groups for his intense interest in juvenile justice, deferred prosecution programs and Big Brothers. His mantra is that "there is no such thing as a bad kid." For being a mere forty years old, he has accomplished monumental strides. Of all the people in his professional life, Eddie is the most interesting, an intellectual in his own right. They've known each other for over six years now and respect each other immensely. In another world or life, they'd be real friends, sharing families and maybe fishing trips to far away places. But that cannot happen as they are today. A bright line must separate them, as one may have to kill the other and emotions have no place in such decisions.

Eddie and J.D. exchange pleasantries, how absolutely perfect the afternoon weather is, the sparrows spinning and frolicking in play, the rustle of broad leaves on the trees in the distance and how peaceful one can be on such days.

J.D. asked, "Is there anything you'd like to talk to me about, Eddie?" He'd been asking this same question lately. Eddie suspected that someone or a number of people are urging him on with this line of questioning, including Eddie's own attorney.

But Eddie is a stoic man. He speaks when he has something on his mind, but reserves that right, holding his thoughts and emotions close to the vest. When he does speak, he is very straight forward and not worried in the least about being offensive.

Eddie avoids the inquisition and changes the subject by asking, "J.D., have you ever considered the impact of magnetic resonance on low frequency microwave transmissions?"

J.D. said, "What?" Knowing that this question was meant to derail his line of questioning, he abandoned the quest and asked Eddie if he ever thought about an afterlife.

Eddie responded, "J.D., there is no God, no deity or supreme icon. You know I'm atheist and have no religious preferences." Eddie realized that J.D. had good intentions and means to console him. But, the icy hand of death separates them. One meant to kill the other, no hard feelings. Eddie wondered how J.D. will take it when the time comes. One dies, the other lives on. Deciding who lives and who dies was nothing new to Eddie. Although he was no mercenary or soldier, he made those fatal decisions and has paid for them ever since.

"Edward, you are the most unique man I have ever met, more facets than a diamond and a genuine pleasure to talk to.

I'll be damned if I can figure out why you got into this kind of trouble." J.D. is sincere, the expression on his face is earnest, his brow furrowed, eyes locked on Eddie's and lips pursed in a grimace.

Eddie likes this man. In another time they could be friends, but they must remain adversaries. It could only make their lives complicated. So Eddie replies, "J.D., everything a man does is for a reason. Why, you came outside here to see me for a reason. We do nothing without a reason. Perhaps one day you'll understand." With that, Eddie rose from the bench, stuffed his hands in his khaki pants and turned his back as a signal that the conversation was at end.

Despite J.D.'s numerous attempts to discover why it happened, Eddie would always dodge the question. It frustrated J.D. because over the years he had become adept at reading the men around him. Eddie was his greatest challenge and he was determined to find out the motive in Eddie's case. He needed to know why this otherwise compassionate man could be so ruthless.

Eddie on the other hand, used this quiet time with nature as a tool to pry the silent screams of agony from his mind. At first, those screams were exquisite, like a toast to his success in imposing justice over them. There is no God, there's only Eddie.

Chapter 2

It's a typical day in downtown Chicago, winds whipping along at 30-40 mph, the gas and diesel fumes still managing to cling to every molecule of oxygen and the customary masses of people shuffling to and fro to their respective destinations.

In the Sun Times Building, on the 20th floor, a covey of reporters and interns churn into news the day's tidbits of gossip, police and fire reports, press releases from organizations and hungry. At six feet, 160 pounds, he fills his Brooks Brothers suits handsomely. He attributes his white hair to his Jewish ancestors, and the adage of white hair representing intelligence. He radiates confidence and his feature articles are respected and read by power brokers, politicians and the elite.

His current dilemma involves an unprecedented crime and the possible motivation for the murders of a dozen people. It seems untenable that powers could align to save the life of a serial killer, now due to meet his end in a more merciful way than his victims. To do so could impinge the justice system and strike fear in potential jurors. What would these people do if they discovered the truth about the system's failure to protect an entire jury of innocent people who did their civic duty and paid with their lives. It was preposterous to even consider saving a man of that evil caliber! The calls started arriving, then e-mails, letters and faxes, after Mort announced evidence linking a convict on Illinois' death row to numerous killings in several jurisdictions. He raised the question as to the convict's imminent execution and should it be delayed to prosecute him on these other offenses. It seems like Mort's whole career has been spent in relation to this case, in one way or another. So far, Mort has refused to disclose the true motive for these crimes or the utter ferocity in which the perpetrator sought his victims' blood and pain, like ingredients of a five star recipe.

"Mort!" some pesky bitch who interns with the reporters hollered out, "You're wanted on line five. Some guy named Foreman wants you."

Without answering her, he proceeded to his cubicle to take the call. Mort doesn't like this Foreman guy one iota and thinks he's a privateer from the grief and shame of his vulnerable clients. Besides, he's flashy and the veneer of his attitude is far too transparent. However, Patrick Foreman is one of the most powerful and respected criminal defense attorneys in the country and Chicago is his strongest front, so it pays to schmooze a little and get along.

"Good morning, Patrick, what can I do for you?"

On the other end of the line, sitting in his plush office on Van Buren Street, a corner suite filled with trophy pictures of victories in courts and in the political arena, Foreman stares at the document before him. "Mort, I'd like to buy you lunch and get your perspectives on the Veins case."

What he really wants is to see what side Mort was taking in the debate, so he could muster his troops to try to bully Mort into helping him, or welcome him into the fold. It was Mort who finally pieced together the totality of the crimes Veins committed, the utter disregard for human life and the forces which drove him on his insatiable thirst for vengeance. Therefore, Mort was the prominent voice in how future matters were viewed, as thousands of readers were fascinated at the story he had unearthed.

"Patrick, you know where I stand on this Veins character. He is an 'oxygen thief' and has no reason to steal good air. He deserves to die a thousand times," Mort replied.

"I don't doubt the sincerity of your feelings, Mort, but journalism should be practiced sans emotion and based on facts. Let the people draw their own conclusions."

"Bullshit, Patrick, that cretin murdered an entire fucking jury, because his bitch sister decided to take matters into her own hands."

To this Foreman retorted that "The law, Mort, states that the jury which sentenced Veins to die, should have heard the motive to determine the mens rea, state of mind, at the time of the offense, as a mitigating factor." Mort knew this, as he had witnessed several murder trials in his tenure and every time, defense counsel was given the opportunity to present mitigating evidence in an attempt to avoid the death penalty.

"Listen, Patrick, I am about to meet with the Editor. I'll listen to what you have to say, but I am inclined to rally support against your play for clemency."

With that, Foreman knew he had one last shot at convincing Mort it was the right thing to do, given that a federal court could overturn the sentence altogether or the conviction itself and another jury could find Veins insane and send him off to a mental institution and someday he could be free again. Shit!

"OK, I'll meet you at the Chancery at 12:15 for your free lunch, but you're wasting your time and money." With that, Mort cradled the phone and sat back in his chair.

What began as reporter gossip between "brother" and "sister" reporters from surrounding states and even some competitors had turned into a manifestation of evil upon which not even he could fathom. Never before in American jurisprudence has a jury been annihilated by some maniac bent on his personal agenda of retribution. This story was likely to propel him and all the ancillary players into the throngs of national and international news. Mort's career was sure to shine as the reporter who broke this story and his legacy of authoring real news that others overlooked a certainty. A Pulitzer Prize assuredly bore his name now.

However, Mort must still be careful until the Editor and the *Sun Times* gave the signal on which slant he was to take. Newspapers sell a product, which oftentimes responded to public opinion. Become a pariah among readers and your competitors bury you. This story required heavy thought. Attorneys for the paper were consulted for the accuracy of the law. Pollsters were called in to glean insight into contemporary thoughts on capital punishment and how this story would play to those passions. Would it benefit sales to reveal Veins as a monster and demand his death or assume a more compassionate approach, embrace the love motive, the depressed state-of-mind, the loneliness Veins felt and the rage that drove him in unfortunate times?

Mort lost control of his story now. The powers above him would decide how this story would be told. Mordecai did not like that fact, either.

So Mort would attend this luncheon and listen to this pompous ass who will strut like a Banty rooster before the media like he gives two hoots about this guy Veins, but merely seeks the fortunes which follow from the limelight. Mort might have to join this dago bastard and force a smile doing it. Marketing should not control the truth. He has to figure out how to get his perspective into the story.

Chapter 3

Benedict Ori is a veritable mountain of a man towering six feet-six inches, at 350 pounds, with jet black, oiled hair, long arms and size 15 Width 5E feet. Ben, as he is called by everyone except his superiors when he's in trouble, has a reputation for his great sense of humor, often interjecting a barrage of jokes to break up the doldrums of his squad room. He is also known for his uncanny attention to detail. Ben, who has been a Detective First Grade for over ten years, heads up the Homicide Division at Police Headquarters at 11th and State Streets. He dropped out of law school in his second year for financial reasons, having graduated from "Podunk U" in a federally funded, minority recruiting program.

His family hoped he would become a big attorney, be something more than a cop like his father! But when the money ran out, Ben reached for the only thing he knew, the Chicago Police Department. His father retired as a vice cop, even through the protestations of his mother that his father loved his work with the whores, prostitutes and pimps more than his family. His father prided himself on never being on the take or accepting free sex for passes on arrests. Ben hoped his record ended in the same fashion. Although he has never taken a bribe or even considered it, he was accused a couple times of roughing up perps. This was later cleared by Internal Affairs, but it was well known around the districts that Ben never took any crap from anyone and despite his unusual size, he was agile and strong.

On this particular afternoon, he planned to get his squad together to brainstorm the case of a murdered child found in an alleyway stairwell, bound, but otherwise untouched. They found bright line ligature marks around the neck and no trace of a weapon or perpetrator. The case perplexed these veterans, as the child was not molested, robbed or harmed in any other fashion. Motive escaped them. Either the kid saw something and was killed for silence or perhaps other kids did it as payback for some reason. Either way, Ben decided what they needed was a brainstorming session to produce some fresh ideas.

Ben's afternoon was disrupted when his partner told him Patrick Foreman, the Patrick Foreman of numerous televised cases of high profile defendants, wanted to talk to him. A bad feeling returned to him. "Mr. Foreman, Benedict Ori returning your call. What can I help you with?"

Foreman answered that he'd like to buy him lunch and needed to talk to him about the Veins case. Everyone was hopping over the Veins case! Two years ago the masses clamored for his death and today Ben was getting calls from the Police Commissioner to the Mayor, to newsies, to watchdog groups. Hell, he even got a call from the Governor about Veins, which resulted in a meeting scheduled with aides to discuss how it should be handled. Veins! Everybody wants to talk about Veins. Even his wife. But Foreman represents the guy, so he gets the edge on information and appointments.

"I can't get away until 1:30. Where do you want to meet?"

"How about the Chancery on Wabash? They have great Philly Steaks and brews," Patrick said. He knows this giant cop loves both, so he'll treat him like royalty today, as he may have to bash him in the press later. Patrick sincerely likes this cop, though, and respects his reputation, which would prove formidable to attack.

"Ah, you tempt me with peasant fare, knowing that I cannot resist. Of course I'll be there. Besides, I can't wait to hear your carnival pitch for your client's life." With that, Ben trudged off to get ready for the meeting of the minds after lunch. He hoped it wasn't a small puddle.

At 1:28 that afternoon, Ben parked his "plain wrapper" in front of the Chancery, lowered his visor with the "official business" card so it wouldn't get ticketed and went inside. Immediately, he spotted Foreman wearing an impeccably tailored Seville Rowe suit of deep blue summer wool blend with the inch of white cuff and diamond links. He was no match in his off-the-rack Big & Tall special, a medium gray with lots of wrinkles from sitting in the squad car and a few telltale stains from hurried lunches. Definitely a cop's attire.

As Ben approached, Foreman rose, hand extended and that million dollar smile for which he was famous. If Foreman wasn't a lawyer, he could have made millions as a fashion model.

"Ben, I'm glad you could make it. I know you're busy. Care for a beer before we order?" Ben enjoyed his beer, but never to excess and never while on duty. Not that he couldn't handle just one beer, but the appearance of a police officer drinking while on duty was bad for the department. Ben ordered iced tea with lemon and sat down. Foreman ordered two Philly Steak platters and he had another beer.

"Ben, I am filing a 'Petition for Executive Clemency' with the Governor's counsel and I want to know your perspective." Ben's eyebrows raised at that remark, as he believed the whole frigging world knew how he felt about Veins.

Foreman saw the facial expression and interjected, "I know what you're thinking, but hear me out first. That's all I ask."

Ben couldn't resist the smile as he pictured Foreman at a carnival game ring toss or at the baseballs, three for 50 cents. "Step right up, get that pretty lady a teddy bear. You love her, don't you?" Oh, yes, he could picture Foreman pitching his game.

"Mr. Foreman," Ben began, "with all due respect, the man is a killer of such magnitude, surely his legend will walk tall as an ancestor for future generations for ages to come. What can I do for you? I am just the arresting officer!"

"Ben, since Mort Habush put the whole Veins case together, I've done some soul searching. I questioned whether my legal ethics should take precedence over my humanity."

Ben knew this was all lip service, but made no comment. The pitch was going to be better than expected.

Foreman continued, "I don't make this decision lightly, but I sincerely believe Veins should not be on death row. The statutes provide, in pertinent part, that the jury was entitled to consider all mitigating factors before rendering the death penalty."

"Mr. Foreman, I am well aware of the law. Please cut to the chase and explain your argument."

Their meals arrived and between bites, Foreman said that he actually had two arguments to spare his client. "First, Ben, is his mens rea at the time of the commission of the offense, or offenses we should say."

Ben was tired of hearing whiney defendants claim insanity trying to save their miserable hides and this smacked of yet another one.

"Ben, Veins never disclosed any of this to me, never appeared other than what he was, an articulate, professional engineer, who seemed the epitome of mental health. But, had he discussed any of this with me, I'd have had him examined by experts."

Ben had watched Foreman at trial and had no doubt about that statement. Foreman was thorough. So, he remained silent and let Foreman continue while he savored his food.

Foreman was on a roll now, arguing before a virtual jury which happened to be Ben.

"I think I could have presented a good case of insanity to a jury, but for me to see a new trial now at this stage, I damn near have to prove that the jury would have acquitted him had I done so and there's no way I can do that." Foreman let that tidbit sink in. "However, I have no such burden of proof for the Governor." This, too, Ben knew was true. The Governor could consider anything.

"Second, Ben, I'm not sure that the jury would have returned with a death verdict had I been allowed to present this evidence from Habush."

Ben's mind tried to recall the jurors, their faces and comments post-trial, but instead of those faces in the jury box, he could only recall those horrible crime scene photos, depicting these civic minded people in death, some so utterly destroyed that they were mere globs of flesh and blood.

"Ben, he lost his sister and to him, the justice system cruelly failed her. Veins acted in rage and not from rational thought."

Ben had worked a number of "crimes of passion" to understand the lengths people will go to for love and he had to admit that since Habush disclosed the other offenses, he had not uncovered a scintilla of evidence to refute Foreman's contention that Veins deeply loved his sister and assumed a different psyche after her death. Co-workers stated that he seemed displaced, often found staring out office windows. They all thought that with time, he'd recover, but he just was not the same.

Ben could see where this was leading and he had to admit that it was persuasive and not just because it came from the great Patrick Foreman. It's because good people can react wrongly after suffering a grievous loss.

"Goddamn, Ben, the jury should have heard that evidence. It quite possibly would have resulted in prison, not death."

"Mr. Foreman, I agree that the jury could have been swayed by all this, but Veins chose not to tell anyone, including you. I don't see how it matters now as his time draws near. I haven't decided if I'll attend the execution, but I have been officially invited as a witness," Ben said.

Foreman was obliged to do his best to get Ben on his side. It would be a quantum leap in convincing the Governor if the arresting officer agreed. "Ben, I'm only asking that you consider the notion that Veins was ill at the time and it's more prudent to spare his life and err, if at all, on the side of caution."

There it was, Ben thought, the whole argument like Cliff's Notes; let's spare the sonofabitch because none of us was smart enough to figure it all out in the beginning.

"Besides, Ben, if we do the Clemency route on a single case basis, sealed of course, I don't have to file a 'Petition for Post-Conviction Relief' in the trial court and set out all of the facts of this case." Touché. Point, game and match. Either Ben plays along or the whole world learns that he and the entire law enforcement community let a frigging madman murder an entire jury. Ben did not want to see that happen, not only for himself, but for the sake of his sovereign, the Chicago Police Department.

"Mr. Foreman, I agree that the information you and I now possess may have had an impact on all of us, including a jury. Given that, I will agree to an official position of 'no objection,' if or when the Governor considers your Clemency Petition, *in camera.*"

There you have it, friends, the greatest game in town: power, politics and death. Foreman loved the game. He had already calculated the risks that the C.P.D. would take in burying the whole story and the math paid off. Officially, the C.P.D. was not going to fight him in the press or elsewhere to save their execution. The Department was willing to let the Department of Corrections tuck Veins into some maximum security cubbyhole and die of old age. That way Veins' story, his legacy of being the ultimate vigilante, would die with him. Only a few people needed to know.

"I met with Habush today and he said the *Sun Times* hasn't decided what position they will take on this case."

Foreman let Ben digest that statement and its implications. Although the paper had already published articles that a convict on death row appears to be linked to several murders in numerous jurisdictions, it hadn't disclosed the hows and whys. There has to be a really good reason the paper has not reported this. What is it? Something personal? Maybe the Editor realized the dramatic impact it would have on future venires or they were planning to milk it for everything it was worth. For whatever reason, the proverbial cat was not yet out of the bag and for individual reasons, everyone was being cautious about it all.

"Habush says he's meeting with his superiors on this. With your permission, Ben, I would like to tell him the official position of the C.P.D. and yourself.

Ben had already discussed this case with his superiors and the top brass had already directed him to take prophylactic measures to put this debacle to rest.

"You will have the Department's official position on your fax this afternoon," Ben said. In fact, the letter, on C.P.D. stationary, was sitting in the middle drawer of his desk, waiting to put the last nail in the story's coffin.

With business done, Ben and Patrick Foreman finished their lunch discussing other current events. Not one patron of the Chancery was aware that a major step had been taken in their presence, to conceal the slaughter of an entire petit jury.

Having called Mordecai Habush and informing him of the luncheon revelations regarding the Chicago P.D., Foreman settled into his office to finish off the Petition for Executive Clemency he would file on Veins' behalf. Foreman loved his job. He loved the way he pranced before juries, the way his kids would hug him at the door after seeing their father on the evening news and he especially enjoyed a courtroom victory. To him, the latter was like medieval combat, mounted knights jousting for honor and their cause. How noble. But, there was no nobility in this cause. No victory dance to savor. They were all covering up the vile acts of one of America's most calculating killers, far above Gacy or Speck. No, this bastard had intelligence, method and a coolness that chilled the spine of the great Patrick Foreman, a man who routinely represents the most notable killers and drug kingpins in a multi-state area.

Veins had touched a vulnerable spot in Foreman's soul, which the masses deny that he even possessed. What bothered him was the question, whether Veins was content with the jury's demise or were other targets in his sights, like the judge who presided over his sister's case and even her attorney as well? Foreman did not represent her, or she would have gotten off, he boasted, but an acquaintance of his did appear for her.

Contrary to public opinion, lawyers are not amoral, totally void of emotion while worshipping the dollar and it's not true that "sharks don't bite them because of professional courtesy." Somewhere inside, Foreman realized for the first time, he could be touched by evil. He had some emotional reaction to the thought of Veins hunting the cloistered community he cherished so much. Could he be suffering from some virgin ethic he overlooked all his years in practice?

So, here he sits behind his ten thousand dollar cherry wood desk, in his thousand dollar black leather wingback chair, looking at the draft of Veins' petition before him - and he suddenly felt cold. He took an oath to defend his clients within all constitutional parameters, to subject prosecutions to adversarial processes and do so without personal involvement. Everyone was entitled to the best defense possible, for if emotions ever played a role in defensive tactics, clients would never get fair trials. An attorney who did not like a client might be tempted to overlook a viable maneuver and that is totally unacceptable in Foreman's world.

With the emotional side suppressed, Foreman began the final draft of the Petition. He could now include the official C.P.D. position and incorporate the letter he received from Ben a short time ago. In pertinent part it reads:

"In re: **Petition for Executive Clemency**

Now comes the Petitioner, by and through his counsel, Patrick Foreman, pursuant to Illinois Revised Statutes, Chapter 38 and petitions the

Governor, the Honorable James R. Thompson, to exercise his executive authority and to commute the Death Warrant, now scheduled for execution on September 29, 1987, at 12:01 a.m. by the Warden at Thames Correctional Center, pursuant to a finding of guilt in Circuit Court of Cook County, *People of Illinois v Veins*, 82 CF 122, to life in prison. In support counsel states as follows:

1) That at the time of the commission of the crime, Petitioner was incompetent, as is defined in Ill. Revised Stats. Chapter 38;

2) That during sentencing, certain facts in mitigation were omitted which renders the jury's verdict of death as unreliable and unjust;

3) That the above are contrary to those rights guaranteed by the United States and Illinois Constitutions, Amendments Four, Five, Six and Fourteen thereof.

Wherefore, Petitioner prays that the Governor exercise that executive authority vested in him by law and affixes his hand and seal upon a Clemency Order, attached and incorporated herein by reference, thereby commuting Petitioner's sentence to life without possibility of parole, instanter.

Submitted this_____day
of_____20_____.
By_____
Patrick Foreman, Counsel for Petitioner
Foreman & Hansen, S.C.

Foreman then began to skim through the brief attached thereto, which he hoped the Governor's counsel would comprehend and explain to the Governor. He started reading:

"In **Lowenfield v Phelps**, 484 U.S. 231, the Supreme Court discerned the qualitative difference between death and other penalties, calling for a greater degree of reliability when death is imposed. *Id*. 238-39. It is such a heavy burden which brings this eleventh hour Petition to Bar. Under Illinois statutory scheme, the Petitioner opted to be sentenced by the trial jury, rather than the Court or impaneling another jury for the sole purpose of the death sentence imposition.

The State, in its Notice to seek death, relied solely on the heinous circumstances which resulted in the victim's demise. The State conceded that Petitioner lacked any prior criminal history whatsoever, that he acted alone and not in concert with others. The State successfully argued for death, without this Petitioner's *mens rea* or motive being considered by the sentencers, the jury therefore not having a full and fair accounting.

In **McClesky v Kemp**, 481 U.S. 281, the Supreme Court reiterated the gravamen in capital cases, when it held that when considering the taking of human life, there is a need to minimize the risk of an arbitrary or capricious action."

Foreman skimmed over the boilerplate wording about the Eighth Amendment prohibition on cruel and unusual punishment, the Sixth Amendment right to effective assistance of counsel, and finally, the Fifth Amendment Due Process guarantee in capital offenses. The crescendo of its closing rolls like the kettle drums of the Chicago Symphony Orchestra:

"In sum, the Petitioner's conviction and sentence was imposed contrary to law and the United States Constitution, requiring equitable relief to serve the spirit and our Framer's intent, when they included that *'no man shall face a capital crime without Due Process of law.'*

Wherefore, Petitioner is entitled to the Clemency he seeks as a matter of law."

Foreman sounded authoritative enough, burying the true components of Veins' offenses within the dicta of the Petition, while saying just enough to warrant relief. Besides, election time was on the horizon and the Governor did not want the innocent blood of a jury on his hands during his watch. Who said politics never plays a role in judicial areas? That whole separation of powers nonsense is for the common man, not the power brokers who operate behind the scenes. Not for Patrick Foreman, Esquire!

There it is, the instrument to save his client's life, the final draft, exhibits attached and ready for filing. All Foreman needed was a decision for Mordecai Habush and the *Sun Times*, because if they published the truth, all bets were off and Veins was set to die. Once everyone knew of the "system's" failure, there was no reason to spare Veins unless the other jurisdictions wished to prosecute him, which was unlikely since he would soon die anyway. If Habush agreed to withhold the link to the jury, the Governor was a cinch to sign the Clemency Order. All he had to do now was to wait for Habush and the small detail of getting his client to approve the Petition. Foreman saw no problem there.

Chapter 4

"Gentlemen, I've gotten you all together because of an impending execution and we need to review the protocol," the Warden began. "As you know, this will be the State's first execution since the death penalty was reinstated and our first by lethal injection."

The Warden looked at the somber faces around his office. Each man was selected by him from the entire employee pool of the Department of Corrections. None of these men looked forward to killing, but each swore to fulfill their duty with utmost professionalism. Furthermore, each was given the option to decline this service. His Captain, a stern religious man with more than 20 years of service, would carry out the execution and the measures up to and after that point.

"Gentlemen, this is not the Green Mile or some Hollywood production. I expect each and every man to follow protocol to the letter." With that, he quietly sat down and Captain Greer assumed control of the meeting.

"Guys, you've each received the 'Lethal Injection Protocol' manual, which you cannot photocopy, make notes from or remove from this building, so I suggest that you memorize it as quickly as possible." The manual for executions has long been sought after by ghouls, reporters, collectors and the curious, so the Department keeps close watch on it.

Greer continued after a brief pause to sip some tepid coffee he always seemed to have in hand, saying they would begin rehearsal the following day, three times per week for the first two weeks, and once a week the other two weeks, with the final run through the day of the execution.

"Men, let me briefly discuss the procedure we'll follow and some specifics will be left to medical professionals." Everyone settled down now, giving complete concentration on the Captain's every word.

"Thirty days prior to the date, we'll move Veins from his current cell to the 'death cell' adjacent to the room where the procedure will take place. We'll issue new bedding and a jumpsuit uniform. His property will be thoroughly searched for weapons, narcotics and other contraband. He will be allowed minimal property, his legal materials, his Bible and one paperback book, which he can exchange for another from our library whenever he desires. He will be afforded extended periods of time on our segregation recreation yard. He will be escorted in waist, hand and ankle restraints to and from the yard by three officers. He will remain under constant observation by at least one staff member at all times. He will also be given unlimited access to the phone next to his cell for collect calls. He will also be permitted daily visits between the hours of 8 a.m. and 10:00 p.m. in our Visitors' Room, where at least one staff will observe at all times. He will be strip searched after each visitor has left and a clean jumpsuit issued to him. There will be no food brought in on these visits, but we will provide common fare meals and beverages from our kitchen. Visitors will not be permitted to carry any items into the visit and their personal property will be stored in a secure locker and then they will submit to electronic and pat-searches. We will have female staff on hand for all female visitors. Is everybody with me so far?"

Greer swallowed his now cold coffee and with a simple nod, asked for a refill.

"OK, three days prior to execution, prison clergy will be on-call and will routinely visit, as well as medical and psychological staff. At 10 p.m., medical staff will enter the death cell and shave Veins' right leg from the crotch to knee. I guess they're worried about infection." This brought a few smiles around the room and Greer said this to break the unholy air that seemed to take over the room. After his fresh coffee arrived, he continued.

"At 11:45 p.m., Veins will be restrained at the waist, hands and ankles and moved by wheelchair to the execution room. He is not to walk there. We will not have him fall down or have problems with executing an unconscious man. Once in the execution room, he will stand with two officers on each side of him. I'm not concerned how you divide yourselves. You can work that out among you. The fifth officer in that room will be armed with a Taser. In the event Veins begins to fight or struggle, he will immediately discharge that device, so be aware of that and don't get in the way."

Greer drank some hot coffee for the first time that day and savored the hot liquid going down his throat. "Any questions? No? Then let's continue. Once Veins is standing next to the table, one officer on each side will unfasten a handcuff, while the second officer firmly holds onto Veins' arms. Veins will turn and sit on the table and the officers holding the arms will lay him back, while the first officer begins tightly applying the leather restraints. Once his arms are secured to the table, two officers will begin the body restraints. Only then will you remove the ankle chains."

At this time Greer took a ten minute break, so things weren't so guarded or intense. Just thinking about taking Veins' life was unnerving to most of the fellas in the room. Over the years he had been on Death Row, he had been a model prisoner, never complained, always greeted the staff with a smile, was quiet and played an excellent game of chess, as some of even the most talented staff discovered. Veins was a likable guy, basically, and no one looked forward to killing him.

When they all returned, having made for the restrooms or outside for a smoke, Greer began again. "Alright, once Veins is strapped down in crucified position, medical staff will enter the room. The three chemicals which will kill him will be underneath the table in a sealed compartment, along with the pumps which will push them into Veins' femoral artery, through a single puncture. The doctor will insert the I.V. and tape the needle and hose onto the shaved leg. That's why his final jumpsuit will have only the left pant leg.

At precisely midnight, we will open the security curtain for the witness gallery to view. The Warden will remain next to a phone bank in case of last minute stays or clemency from the Governor. On the Warden's signal, I will approach Veins and read the Death Warrant aloud and ask him if he has anything to say before the sentence is carried out. After a brief moment, I will signal the doctor to begin. You will then hear the pumps begin. The first chemical, sodium pentothal, will be employed is an anesthetic, like in a normal surgical procedure. The second, potassium chloride, will stop his nervous system, including the brain and heart. The third, pancuronium bromide, will cease respiration. The doctor will monitor Veins until pronounced dead. The curtain will be closed and Veins will be removed from the table, placed into a body bag, which will be brought in along with a gurney for transport to our sally port to await the approved funeral home director to receive."

By now Greer's coffee was cool, but still a welcome taste to his pallet, as his stomach was not interested in food and he needed something. "Any questions?"

One of his guys shyly raised his hand shoulder high. When Greer pointed to him he asked, "Why do they give him anesthetic? Isn't it supposed to hurt?"

Chance knew the answer, as the ACLU had argued "cruel and unusual punishment," due to the intense suffering when the condemned was administered Sodium Amytal. So, the procedure was changed to where it was truly painless, except when the needle was inserted, which appeared to be about the size of a pencil. So, Greer explained this to all of them and asked if anyone had any more questions.

"Sir, what about the last meal? Will Veins get his choices?" This question was not from any morbid curiosity, but because they liked Veins and would want to see him treated as well as one could be under the circumstances.

Greer, on the other hand, could never understand the fascination with what a dead man soils himself with, but plans had been made for Veins to select his final meal. Reporters always asked what the dead men had to eat and it made for some interesting fodder for readers. For example, Bundy wanted just ice cream, Gacy a cheeseburger and fries, and seldom did they see the steak or lobster. Greer acknowledged that Veins would be given a menu to select from and cooks would do their utmost to prepare it to perfection.

With this all said, the men broke for lunch and were to report to the Death Cell for their initial practice. Greer didn't think he would bump into any of them in the mess hall. They did not look very hungry.

"Warden, these guys are professionals and I assure you that the procedure will be followed to the letter and this execution will come off without a hitch. But, I've got t tell you that even my callous heart is not happy killing Veins."

The Warden understood this emotion all too well, as he had come to like Veins himself and enjoyed their weekly chess game outside on the yard.

"Captain, I don't like this either, but remember, he is a convicted murderer and that thought may help you through it." Not even the Warden himself would be able to use this tactic, but it's all he could think to say, without parroting Greer's own sentiments. On that woeful note, the Warden and Greer departed separate ways.

Chapter 5

Florence Veins is an L.P.N., a licensed practical nurse who worked hospital med-surg floors, third shift, so she could take care of her kids during the day. Her husband, Clay, worked in a printing plant as head of maintenance. At night he operated the projector at a local theater. Together, he and Flo made more than enough for their lifestyle in a three bedroom, one bath home, with two children, Edward, the oldest, and a girl they took in when Florence's sister and husband were killed in a traffic accident.

Elizabeth Conly was affectionately called Betty, as Florence always loved "Betty Boop" in the old cartoon strip. Betty came to them as a gift from their Creator, as Florence could not have any more children after her son was born, due to clamps and a subsequent tubal ligation. Betty's arrival, even under the cloud of her sister's untimely death, was a bundle of joy.

Betty was gone from this world now, taken to wherever souls go that take their own life on earth. But Florence prayed every day that God would forgive her that suicidal sin, as she was not the same after that horrible experience and could no longer bear the pain.

Now her son was about to directly leave this world. The State of Illinois was going to kill him like some rabid animal and she and Clay would be alone. No grandchildren to call her "gran-ma" or to babysit for while her own children were either working or at college. That part of their dreams would never happen now. Instead, they received angry mail, had their little home vandalized with obscene graffiti and the constant flow of reporters seeking interviews, which is obscenity as well. At first she and Clay refused to answer their phone or the door, but then their family attorney thought that if they were very careful at what they said, they could help their son in the media and public opinion. So they would say things like, "Our son does not deserve to die. Before this he was a model citizen and we're sure they have the wrong guy."

It's true that the State's case was pitched on one witness who identified their son as her abductor, just prior to her mother's murder; ergo it must be the same guy who killed her mom. It's also true that "eyewitness testimony" is usually the least credible and there is a "Pattern Jury Instruction," crafted by the Justices of the Illinois Supreme Court that warns of that inherent danger in relying solely on such testimony.

Their son was never in trouble. Not one police officer ever brought him home or called her. He was never arrested. He was a Catholic like his parents and even served as an altar boy for a time. He was smart and after high school, went to DeVry Institute of Technology, for electrical engineering. She was so proud of him on that stage, accepting his diploma in that cap and gown. She was proud of Betty, too, when she was studying hospital administration at Northwestern University. Florence took solace in knowing that her children would never have to work the long, tedious hours she and Clay did to support their families. Both children would earn handsome salaries after college, get married and make Florence and Clay grandparents.

All of those dreams are erased now. Gone. Her God had imposed a heavy cross for Florence to bear. She quit going to church, not solely because God had forsaken her, but she was pretty pissed at Him right now, and the reporters, and those dreadful people who called them names. There were some who took the time to paint signs and strut back and forth in front of their home. One said "An Eye for an Eye, Exodus 21:24," as though they were religiously righteous. Florence wanted to remind them of "Judge not, that he not be judged, Matthew 7:1," since those who thought they knew the Bible enough to spout that often used quote, often took it out of context. Her rage seethed, like a cauldron of toxic waste.

Clay, on the other hand, plodded to work each day. His head, which was generally carried high and proud, hung like a bobblehead doll with a broken spring. His co-workers were mostly considerate and respected this gentle giant, who kept their presses operating in top flight form. But a few of the more abrasive types talked behind his back. They never had the courage to confront Clay with their tasteless quips. They feared the strength that lay beneath those well-defined biceps.

Clay used his work more to divert his sorrow, than for money. He could not stand to sit in that lonely house, his world destroyed, his son about to die at the hands of those bastards who wrongly convicted him. His wife a shambles. She puttered around the house doing nothing except mumbling incoherently. It wasn't bad enough when several years before, they endured a nightmarish ordeal with Elizabeth, his little girl, who went through another sham trial for avenging herself and then took her own precious life. "No, God, that was not enough pain on my plate, give me more," he said to himself sarcastically, as now he was about to lose his only son.

Clay thought about the time after his son is executed and how unbearable life will be. So, he planned to blow out the pilot-lights on the stove in their little kitchen, turn on all the gas jets to the burners and oven, with the door open, and trod off to bed with his wife and hold her until they fell asleep and the gas took them to their kids again. He was not a violent man and he had no guns, so the gas seemed the best way. He loved his wife too much to watch her suffer like that and quite frankly, he figured this would be the only way that God would let them all be together again. He had made up his mind. They already had wills made, where the Catholic Church would receive their estate and hopefully Florence's life insurance, as the cops could figure out it was murder/suicide and not a double suicide. But, that didn't really matter to Clay any more. He just needed the pain to stop.

Chapter 6

"*People-versus-Veins*, 82 CF 122," the bailiff called and the attorneys made their appearances for the record.

"Your honor, Assistant State's Attorney Christian Schroeder for the State."

"Your honor, Mr. Veins appears in person and with counsel, Joshua Carlin."

The Honorable Earl Strayhorn presided over the trial and as he did in all his trials, he never lost control and attorneys knew who was the boss.

"OK, this case is continuing from yesterday, when we empanelled the jury and had opening statements. Mr. Schroeder, call your first witness," Strayhorn said.

With that the State called Melissa Kilponen to the stand. She was sworn in by the bailiff.

"Miss Kilponen, I'd like you to recall the evening of January 10, 1982. Did you call the police?"

"Yes, I did, after I regained consciousness in some alley," she answered.

"When you say 'consciousness,' was that due to alcohol or an accident you suffered?" Schroeder asked.

"No, sir, a man grabbed me from behind when I left a small shop near my home, dragged me into the alley while covering my mouth with some oily rag with something that smelled like ether or chloroform," she stated, with just a hint of moisture in her eyes.

"When the man grabbed you, did he say anything? Ask you anything?"

Melissa demurely said that the man said hello to her by name, as if he knew her personally and told her to be quiet and she wouldn't get hurt.

"And then what occurred, if anything?" the prosecutor asked.

"I was handcuffed, my mouth was taped and I was locked in the trunk of a blue Ford Crown Victoria."

"And what happened then?"

"Well, the car drove about an hour or so, went over a bumpy road and bounced to a stop."

Schroeder approached Melissa and with a wave of his arm, like Moses pointing to where God spoke to him, asked, "Melissa, would you tell these ladies and gentlemen of the jury, what, if anything, occurred then?" He knew what was coming and he played an Oscar winning role.

"The man got me out of the trunk and said that he had no choice, that justice demanded that I die and produced a chrome-plated, straight razor. Then he removed the tape and asked me if I knew why he was doing this. When I told him he must have made a mistake, he asked me what the 'C' stood for in my name. When I said there was no 'C' in my name, he went through my wallet and took my driver's license."

"What did he do then?" the prosecutor asked.

"Well, he got real upset, taped my mouth again and pushed me back into the trunk, slammed the trunk and we left again."

"Melissa, you said you regained consciousness in some alley. How did you come to be there?"

"When he stopped after about another hour, he opened the trunk and put the same oily rag over my face and I passed out. When I came to, I was in the alley."

"Melissa," Shroeder began, "I want you to look around the courtroom and tell us if you recognize the man you've been referring to? Please take your time."

Melissa immediately pointed to the defense table and said, "That's him in light blue shirt, gray slacks, thick glasses and sitting next to the man in the suit."

"Your honor, I ask that the record reflect that the witness has identified the Defendant." While looking at the jurors, Schroeder paused to let that identification sink in.

"Let the record reflect the identification," Strayhorn said.

"One last question, Melissa," Schroeder said. "How did you know the car you were locked in was a blue Crown Victoria?"

She began, "Well, at first I didn't," then went on with, "but I found a sheet of paper in the trunk, stuffed it down the front of my jeans and it was still there when I came to, in the alley. It was an 'inspection sheet' from a car rental agency and it had the make and model. I knew what blue looked like."

"Melissa, I'm showing you what's been marked as 'State's Exhibit No. 1' for identification. Is that the sheet you found in the trunk and hid?"

"Yes, sir," she answered.

"Nothing further," and with that, Schroeder returned to his seat and glowed with confidence.   Melissa was the link between the defendant and her mom, who was "C. Melissa Kilponen." She was the "C" in the Defendant's question. He'd hammer that home at a later time, though. Perhaps the defense missed the significance? Melissa's testimony, though vehemently objected to by Mr. Carlin, was permitted for two reasons: a) Rules of Evidence, Rule 404(b), "prior bad acts or wrongs," and (b) because of the Offer of Proof the State made with regard to the defendant inquiring if the victim knew him and why he was there displaying a straight razor, her release and ultimately her mother's ghastly murder by what the Medical Examiner would testify to as a razor, with about a 4" blade. The oddity here that Veins was charged with abducting Melissa, along with several other related counts, but the State opted to try the murder first.   Carlin could not figure out what flaw existed in their case against Veins, if the "evidence" was so overwhelming.

After perfunctory questions about her education, relationship with her mother and father and if she had seen a psychologist for the trauma of being kidnapped, he noticed a tick in one eyelid. He realized he was in a sensitive area here and that the reaction could indicate recollection or something more valuable. He didn't notice the usually implacable prosecutor, tense under the table. Carlin pondered whether or not he should risk a violation of the law school maxim, "a lawyer never asks a question that he already doesn't know the answer to."

One thing about high profile cases, where lots of cops are involved, each of them generates a report and before you know it, you have reams of discovery material. One could easily miss something, artfully placed in stacks of paper. When an attorney reads medical records, for example, it appears nothing more than a compilation of Greek letters and symbols. He would need some formal education in medical areas to be of some proficiency.

The paralegal employed by Schroeder to copy and compile the file for discovery purposes, along with *Bates* stamps at the bottom for numerical reference, included a copy of the "Chem.24" report among the reports from the Medical Examiner. If one failed to notice the "C" missing in the name, they would miss the significance of trace elements of fentanyl in the blood obtained after she was taken to a local hospital, to determine if toxins or other chemicals were used on her during the abduction.

Schroeder anguished over this report, whether it was discoverable at all or protected by some patient/doctor relationship. They decided to slide it among the mother's volumes of medical records and see if the defense caught it. Evidently, the maneuver worked. Carlin left it alone, when one glance at a Physician's Desk Reference, or PDR, would have informed him that fentanyl, a synthetic opiate, was stronger than heroin.

"The State calls Detective Benedict Ori to the stand," Schroeder announced and Ben entered the courtroom, as witnesses had been excluded from the trial, on defense motion.

"Was there a time, Detective, when you became aware of the defendant here?" the prosecutor asked after running through all the customary and required questions.

"Yes, sir," Ben replied, "our division was contacted by officers who investigated the abduction of Melissa Kilponen and that they were then working a lead to locate her assailant. We all agreed that the questions asked by her assailant during that offense, directly implicated and connected to the perpetrator of this offense. Simply stated, we were convinced that whoever abducted Melissa, most likely committed the murder of her Mother."

"Objection!" Carlin shouted, "The witness is not testifying about facts, but emotion and is irrelevant, incompetent and immaterial."

Strayhorn considered this for a moment and then overruled the objection as the witness was able to testify about investigative techniques and purpose.

Schroeder continued, "Detective, the lead you testified to, what was it?"

"Well, Melissa had an inspection form from a national car rental company. It's a common form used when lot attendants clean and service cars before being re-rented. It had no specific location identifier, so officers had to go to every office and satellite office to find the origin of that form, and possibly the rental records."

"And did there come a time when the form, which I've handed you, marked State's Exhibit No. 1, was identified and the origin determined?"

"Yes, sir," Ben answered proudly, as it took many officers to canvas the city like that.
"Detectives from Area 5 located the office and records relating to a rental of a blue Crown Victoria, to Capital Construction of Oakbrook, Illinois."

"How did you proceed from there?"

Ben was matter-of-fact now, almost as if logic would be apparent. "We inquired of the company's accounting office, who had access to this vehicle, received a list of names, obtained photos, mostly from the Secretary of State Driver Services, and presented a photo array for Melissa to review."

Schroeder walked towards the jury when he asked the next question. "Did Melissa positively identify anyone?"

"Yes, sir," Ben said, looking at the woman in the first chair of the jury box. "She identified Mr. Veins as the man who abducted her."

With that, Mr. Carlin requested a sidebar. When he and Schroeder were there with the court reporter, Carlin objected to the State trying his client for one crime, when charged with another. "Your honor, I want the record to reflect my continuing objection to all of this. Its prejudicial effect far outweighs the probative value. The Defendant is charged with murder, yet all we've heard thus far relates to an alleged abduction which occurred months before what he is on trial for today. I also move for a mistrial at this time, as my client's rights to a fair and impartial jury have been compromised by this testimony."

"Your honor, we covered all this when we gave notice to the defense. Mr. Carlin filed a *motion in limine*, which was heard and denied. This testimony is admissible," Schroeder insisted.

"Mr. Carlin, the record will reflect your ongoing objection to this and you are free to bring it up on appeal. Motion for Mistrial, denied."

With that, everyone returned to their seats and the prosecution continued.

"Now, Detective, what, if anything, did you do after Melissa identified the Defendant?"

"We impounded the car, had it transported by C.P.D. flatbed to our secure storage for the forensics people, and prepared an affidavit for the search of the Defendant's home, office and vehicles, along with obtaining a Warrant for his arrest."

"And was there a time when you and other officers executed those warrants?"

"Yes, sir," Ben beamed brightly, as solving a case and removing a violent offender off the streets is why he was a cop. "We entered his home at 4 a.m. the following morning, arrested the Defendant in his bedroom and searched his home, impounded his personal vehicle and transported him and his vehicle to the station."

The search of Veins' home was a hotly contested issue during pretrial motions and, quite frankly, disturbed Strayhorn, as the defense argued that the search was pretextual and clearly violated the Fourth Amendment. It is well settled law, that law enforcement cannot obtain a search warrant based on one crime, while it is really meant to gather evidence of another.

On the other hand, officers searching who come across evidence of another crime are not required to overlook that evidence, and that is exactly the position the State took on the legality of the search.

The trouble came from a tactical briefing, where a squad leader advised his men that Veins was the primary suspect in a murder and gave them a short list of evidence to watch for, including "records which indicate the whereabouts of Veins on the night of the murder" of Melissa's mother. What permitted Strayhorn to deny the *Motion to Suppress* was the similarities of the crimes, Melissa seeing a razor and the need to show that Veins operated this particular Ford and the best way would be through credit card or cash receipts for gas or service.

But, Strayhorn admonished the prosecution it was a very close call and might be reversed on appeal. Naturally, Carlin had a continuing objection on this as well, which meant that he didn't have to object every time a question is asked, but that he objects to the whole line of questioning.

"Were you present during the search?"

"Yes sir."

"Detective Ori, did you personally observe items being located, tagged for evidence and taken into custody?"

"Yes sir."

"I show you what has been marked as State's Exhibit Number 21 for identification. Do you recognize that?"

"Yes, sir, my signature is on the evidence tape and tag," Ben replied.

"And can you identity what that item is for the jury?" At this, the courtroom became absolutely silent, while every eye was on the clear, plastic envelope, for it held a shiny object, about six inches long, by about 1 ½ inches wide.

"Yes, sir, it's a straight razor," Ben answered.

Chapter 7

The significance of the straight razor found at Veins' home, although such shaving devices are not uncommon for men to have, was that it was all chrome and did not have wood or bone handles like most, just chromed steel. The forensic people examined the razor with every test available to them and nothing was found by way of blood, tissue, D.N.A., fingerprint or even evidence that it was used to cut tape, which would leave traces of adhesive behind. However, over Carlin's lame objection, which he knew would fail, the razor was introduced because Melissa said it was similar in shape and design to the one she'd seen him with and the killer used a razor to murder her mother. It showed that Veins had access to a razor.

"Has the jury reached a verdict?" Strayhorn asked as a deathly hush fell over the gallery.

The foreperson, who now sat in the first seat on the left hand side of the jury box and closest to the Judge, rose to answer the question. "Yes, Your Honor, we have." With that he handed the form to the uniformed deputy who handed it to the Judge. After noting the verdict, he returned it to the deputy, who gave it back to the foreman, who remained standing.

"Will the foreperson read the verdict, please?"

"We, the jury, as to Count One of the Indictment, for the offense of murder of Catherine M. Kilponen, find the Defendant guilty."

Carlin and his client, who were standing for the reading of the verdict, faced each other, eyes locked, and an unusual look appeared in Veins' eyes. Carlin had seen plenty of defendants who had been found guilty and the dire expressions that creased their faces and the despair that reached their fears of going to prison. What Carlin saw in Veins' eyes had no traces of fear or despair. It was something other than that. He might be mistaken, but he believed he saw relief and some twisted form of satisfaction. Could that be?

"Your Honor, since the State seeks imposition of the death penalty, state statute provides that the Defendant has this jury decide his fate, or the Court, or impanel a new jury. At this juncture, having discussed this with my client thoroughly, it is Mr. Veins' desire for this jury to make that determination."

"All right, we'll adjourn for today and resume tomorrow morning. In the meantime, I want an Offer of Proof from the State setting forth all relevant factors it believes supports imposition of death. In the Offer, I want explicit statutory provisions upon which the State relies, a list of witnesses it intends to call and any additional information it intends to introduce. I want that Offer in Mr. Carlin's possession by 2 o'clock this afternoon. It's only 11:15 now, so that'll give you time to get it to him. Mr. Carlin, you will file any objections you have to the Offer by 8:30 tomorrow morning, along with mitigating factors you intend to introduce, along with your witness list. Anything further?"

When no one responded, Strayhorn banged his gavel on the bench and said, "Court's adjourned," rose and left the courtroom.

The next morning, the sun shone brightly across Lake Michigan, lighting up the mirrored, kaleidoscopic shrouds of the heart of Chicago. The jurors were seated and the defense table was surrounded by uniformed deputies. The Defendant was sporting the latest in restraint technology, a shock-belt, capable of delivering fifty thousand volts at the push of a button on the remote control in the possession of one of the deputies. Security in the courtroom was usually tight, with every person who was not a sworn officer being pat searched as an added measure.

Everyone rose when Strayhorn entered and seated himself behind the bench.

"Good morning everyone. This is the penalty phase of the trial in **State v Veins**, 82 CF 122. As per my instructions, the parties have submitted their pleadings regarding the Offer of Proof and Objections thereto, in a timely manner. I find the Offer of Proof within the statutory scheme and spirit of the law and overrule the Objections. The Court will file its Findings of Fact and Memorandum of Law with counsel, in camera. I see that everyone is here, so let's begin. I want to give each party as much time as possible, but I do not want to turn this into a dog and pony show with repetitious witnesses."

"Good morning, Your Honor, ladies and gentlemen of the jury. We're here to determine if circumstances exist to warrant the Defendant be put to death. You've heard the evidence in this case and have found the Defendant guilty of premeditated murder. Now, you'll hear why the State believes that the Defendant deserves nothing less than death himself."

Schroeder left the podium and said, "State calls Melissa Kilponen."

Melissa approached the stand wearing a gray business suit, impeccably coifed hair and nails, with a subdued look across her face.

"Melissa, you're still under oath, you realize that?" She nodded and the reporter silently entered a "yes" in her notes.

"Melissa, I want to ask you about the night you found your mother's corpse. Would you tell us, in your own words, what happened?"

The Rules of Evidence are relaxed for sentencing hearings. Besides, Carlin wouldn't object too much or risk making her a living martyr in front of this jury and Schroeder knew it. So, he set her free to tell the story of a gruesome discovery.

"When I returned home that night, I called for my mother, but got no answer, yet I knew that she should be home. So, I went looking in the bedrooms to see if she was asleep. When I didn't find her, I went looking everywhere, the garage, back yard and finally, the basement. That's where I found her."

At this, Melissa began to tremble as though she should register somewhere on a Richter scale, yet not a tear. Just an inner quake.

"When I started walking down the stairs, I remember smelling feces and I thought our dog messed on the stairs or floor. When I got to the bottom, I saw a light on in my Dad's workshop, so I went there first. When I entered the shop, that's when I found my mom." Now tears began and that quake registered in Melissa's voice.

"That's when I saw what that sonofabitch did to her!"

Strayhorn immediately admonished her about her cursing, but you could sense the empathy in his every word, like a father scolding a child.

"I apologize." Melissa took a minute to ready herself. She and the State's Attorney had discussed this, the inner strength to recall that morbid scene and describe it for these people. How do you describe the complete insanity imposed upon her mother to sane people and expect them to understand? But, she had assured Schroeder that she possessed that willpower, as he could have called a detective or the M.E. to describe the carnage that remained, from a once vibrant, healthy mother and the passion of a daughter describing that macabre sight was priceless towards his goal of killing Veins.

They all waited for her, and then she began again. "My mother's naked corpse, was hanging from a floor beam." She began sobbing, but pushed herself to get past it. "Her hands were nailed to that beam and she had a towel over her eyes, but I knew it was my mother. There was a short noose around her neck, which actually supported her body." The last part came in a gush of tears, her shoulders racked and she slumped forward.

"We'll take a short break so she can gather herself," Strayhorn said, when Melissa burst out with, "No! I need to get this done. My mother will give me the strength!"

"Go on, Melissa, we're with you," Schroeder said, more for the emotion than the witness.

"My mother was skinned like some fur bearing animal, her blood pooled beneath her and her tongue was cut out." There it was! The worst was over.

Strayhorn said, "Now we'll break," banged his gavel on the bench and exited quickly. It appeared that even he was struck by the heinousness of the crime, the impact forever etched in this girl's mind.

When they returned 20 minutes later, Schroeder chose to forego any further details of the discovery of her mother, instead going into how the crime impacted Melissa.

"That cadaver in my basement was not my mother. My mom was a homemaker, the one who sat with me when I was sick, took me to school and picked me up, with a freshly baked cookie for me. Mom was the nucleus of our home. She never hurt anyone. The only place she felt safe was in her home and that monster over there slaughtered her like an animal in it. I ask God each night, why he would let this happen, why this demon walks among us, but God never answers me."

By now, even jurors had Kleenex and handkerchiefs in their hands or to their eyes.

"Melissa, is there anything you wish to say to the Defendant?" the prosecutor asked.

"Yes." Then Melissa squared her shoulders, raised her head and looked Veins in the eyes. "I wish the laws of this State permitted the punishment be the same as the crime. I would take great satisfaction in watching you butchered like you did my mother. You killed the greatest person I have ever met. I hope you rot in hell."

Veins sat there totally void of emotion, not a flicker of reaction, as if he were the world's greatest poker player. Almost statuesque.

After a moment, Strayhorn asked Carlin if he had any questions and Carlin declined.

"The State calls Thomas Dorf," Schroeder said and watched as the Medical Examiner took the stand. The man who was seated in the witness box had a very familiar face, as he was always in the news. If it wasn't part of an investigation, it was some high profile death. When famous people died, "Tommy" performed the autopsy himself and filed the reports.

"Mr. Dorf, I remind you that you're still under oath." Tommy nodded and replied, "Yes."

"Sir, you've testified already in this case, but I need to review some areas and get opinions in others. You were called to the scene by investigators of Chicago Police Department, is that correct?"

"Yes, the detectives believed the killing was symbolic in some fashion, that the crime was atypical and unusually gruesome, so I came there."

Schroeder wanted to mill this witness's testimony and the popularity he possessed, for the jury and the media which filled the room. He walked to the far end of the jury box, leaned backwards against the rail, enjoying all eyes on him and asked, "When you arrived, what was the condition of the victim?"

"She was suspended from a floor joist in the basement. There was a noose around her neck, which held the bulk of her weight. Both hands were nailed through the palms, to the same joist. About 90% of her epiderma was removed from the neck down, leaving only her breasts and feet untouched. Cause of death was due to exsanguination and laryngeal ligation, simultaneously."

"Sir," Schroeder began, "those medical terms you use, could you translate them for us, put them in simple words?" Schroeder knew exactly what the words meant, having taken pre-med courses himself, before law school. But he needed to appear as a common man with a difficult job, if he intended to be governor some day.

"The poor woman was initially suspended, pulled up to the joist by the rope, while she stood on a sawhorse we found lying beneath her. The noose choked her if she tried to move or look down. I believe she was crucified next and that probably sent her into shock. That's when the defendant began using a razor, with a blade of 4 inches long, to cut, slice and peal the victim's skin from her body, from the neck to her feet. He left the breasts, but removed the outer genitalia and stopped at her ankles."

There were murmurs in the jury box and throughout the courtroom, which the Judge quelled with a simple look around the room. Veins' counsel bowed his head, wondering how his client could have done such a thing. Carlin looked at Veins, who sat inches away, ramrod straight, looking direct at the M.E. as if challenging him to explain the superb job he did on this woman and how the end finally came.

Dorf continued. "She died of blood loss and the strangulation, almost simultaneously. As she was bleeding out, the muscles could no longer get enough oxygen and the noose closed her trachea or windpipes, suffocating her."

"Sir, in your expert medical opinion, how long would it take to remove the skin as this defendant did and in the fashion he used?"

"I believe about four hours!" There it was, the mental picture Schroeder needed for the jury. However, that paled, when Melissa fainted in the front row and people were gathering around her.

Strayhorn recessed immediately, directed security to remove Veins quickly and summoned medical personnel. Schroeder couldn't have planned this better, if he could, as he moved to appear sympathetic to Melissa's situation.

The state rested. Carlin had no intentions of asking Dorf a single question. He knew the trap that lay ahead. Pain. If Carlin probed much, Dorf would probably relate that this woman died in excruciating agony. Visions of her pleas to stop the carnage that was once a human being would be indelibly etched in the jurors' minds. Dorf would probably include that the skin which was sliced from this woman's body, was never found. God, he hated his job at times.

Carlin called on both parents and co-workers, all who had laudatory feelings for "Mr. Veins," parental love and a stipulation that the defendant lacked any prior record or even an arrest. Carlin argued to the jury that the case was circumstantial, giving rise to an element of mistaken identity. He also argued that life in prison was no vacation itself and that "Mr. Veins," trying to give his client some form of human identity, would still suffer immensely. He closed with the logic that the state failed to substantiate the special circumstances upon which to impose the death sentence.

Schroeder approached the podium, where he turned to face the jury and in a baritone voice began his final scene in this mortal production. "Ladies and gentlemen, on behalf of the people of this state, I want to thank you for the time and effort you've expended in doing your civic duty. But, that duty is not over yet. When you were selected to serve, you were asked if you would have a problem meting out a death sentence if this defendant were convicted and each of you answered 'no.' Well that day is here.

I have been the State's Attorney now for six years, and I have seen some bad actors come through our courts. I thought I had seen just about every heinous way to take a life, but I must admit that all those other crimes pale at the brutality, the wanton torture of this woman and the sadistic pleasure he took in her pain. Mr. Carlin says we haven't proven special circumstances to qualify for death. He could not be further from reality.

We have a mother, crucified and mutilated in her basement. I have never seen a crime which screams out for death more than this case. You have one last duty. A duty to those who live and a duty to that woman slaughtered in her home. Listen to her silent screams today and finish this Devil's dance on Earth. Do your final duty and render the verdict of death."

The jury deliberated the rest of that day, as a few jurors were not sure of themselves and no clear majority was on either side. The death penalty did not require a unanimous verdict, but a majority. Finally, the next day, the jury voted for death and the Judge concurred.

Chapter 8

"Good morning Mr. Veins," Foreman began. "I have some great news for you and I felt it best if I rushed on down here." Foreman always seemed to sport a Florida tan, perfect hair, a smile which has an annual maintenance cost of more than a blue-collar worker's pay, and suits that cost more than a Ford Taurus.

"Well, then let's begin. I know you have a long drive home and I have a chess game to prepare for," he responded snidely.

"I see. I spoke with Mordeci Habush, *that* Mordeci Habush of the *Sun Times* and the paper will support your Petition for Clemency. BUT there are a few minor requirements. First, he wants a full confession to all of the murders, giving details, dates and supporting evidence you can provide, for verification. They are going to check your confession to prove that you are the real killer and your motive. Now, that confession will be in the form of a 'proffer,' which cannot be used to prosecute you and will be sealed and inaccessible to anyone else. Their attorney and I will meet you for the proffer, which gives an attorney-client privilege." Foreman watched his client for any sign of reaction and got none. Carlin was right, he thought. This sonofabitch is as cold as a hooker's heart.

"Second, Mordeci wants an exclusive interview and an agreement that you will meet with no one else. The reason there is that if the *Sun times* keeps the secret under wraps, then they don't want you to leak the truth to another paper and screw them. I've already agreed to both of these conditions precedent." Foreman watched his client's eyes and saw his own reflection. He wondered, had the victims noticed themselves in these very eyes? He was reminded of a National Geographic story on sharks and the narrator made a comment about their eyes and how cold and black they were. That asshole should see Vein's eyes, he thought to himself, and he'd think a shark's eyes were like "Precious Moments" dolls in comparison.

When Foreman got no response, he went on. "Habush will say that information has recently been discovered which the jury should have heard, is protected by the attorney-client privilege and therefore cannot be printed, but would seriously place your competence at issue. Further, because of the statutory limits on post-conviction relief, you are now precluded from seeking relief in the trial court. Also, between me and the paper's attorney, we will window dress the whole story with some constitutional drivel and hocus-pocus." Still no response. And those fucking eyes.

"Anyhow, Mort will support the Petition and along with Chicago Police Department and Benedict Ori, the Governor is a cinch."

Veins knew the truth. All of these righteous bastards were signing on because none of them wanted the truth exposed. Play along, be a good boy and we will let you live. "Mr. Foreman, you could have sent this information in a letter. I really appreciate you driving down here to see me. I will take what you said under advisement." Veins had heard that quote on "L.A. Law" and knew it would irk Foreman to no end. He had to ask Foreman a question though, and demanded that he answer.

"Why won't Habush publish the truth?" Mort had a reputation as a crime buster, not some Timmy Olson, but a real Clark Kent type.

"Mort lost a family member to suicide and knows how he felt afterwards. Of course, he didn't go on a feeding frenzy like a Great White, but he felt let down by others who could have helped, even prevented it. So, you scored a point there. However, the *Sun Times* does not want to be responsible for a widespread panic among seated and prospective jurors. What you did, the crimes you committed, are unprecedented in history. No criminal has ever gone on such a rampage and had the skill and cunning to avoid apprehension, while offing an entire jury. The bad part is that no one is ever to know about it. You live, you shut up. You want fame; it will be as short lived as you are."

Veins actually smiled at that, stood up and left the room. Jesus, Foreman hated this bastard, but the press would eat this up and he loved the press.

What Foreman didn't tell Veins was that Mordeci sincerely liked Vein's sister. He interviewed her several times, and had become her staunchest supporter. He had garnered thousands of readers who supported her release, without being charged and he condemned the State's Attorney for being callous enough to even charge her after her abduction, rape and when she executed Cavanaugh.

Foreman believed Mordeci had more than business feelings for her. Mordeci was emotionally involved with her and Foreman wasn't sure how or why. But, Mordeci missed that girl. Maybe this was his way of repaying her, by saving her brother? Elizabeth was a charming girl and Foreman had copies of Mordeci's articles, as well as hundreds of others from across the nation, which described the series events which ultimately led to the tragic demise of Elizabeth Conly.

Chapter 9

It all began on a quiet day in middle class America. Betty had just left her friends at that campus rathskeller, where they laughed, had a couple of beers and lamented over final exams, professors, classmates and their lovelorn lives. She had just gotten off the No. 17 bus, two blocks from her home, backpack in hand and was on her way to one of her favorite meals. Her mother was making lasagna, which meant layers of sweet Italian sausage and five different cheeses, with those fat noodles in between her mother's sauce.

A man approached her from behind as she entered a crosswalk and she felt him jam something cold and hard against her right breast, as he looped his left through her right and held it tight as a vice. "I've been looking for you," he said. When Betty looked down, she confirmed her feeling that it was a gun that crushed her breast, as she could see the middle part with its cylinder. People are shot all the time in Chicago and she didn't intend to join those ranks. So, Betty did not resist.

She thought it was just a case of mistaken identity. Once he realized that he has the wrong person, he'll let her go. He told her to get into the car on the passenger side and slide behind the wheel, while he slid into the passenger side himself. The man beside her was about 6'5", 270 pounds, milky white skin from lack of sunshine, large, puffy hands and a Lon Chaney face...friendly features, but somehow the hint of werewolf that made Chaney the "Man of a Thousand Faces."

By comparison, at 5'7", 112 pounds, Betty was no competition for the lumbering giant, even without a gun. Betty had always prided herself on her inner strength, her resolve to accomplish tasks put before her. She always maintained the "glass is half full" optimism. Although scared, she held it within her core, not letting a telltale sign emerge. She knew that panic would get her nowhere.

They drove in silence, for what felt to be about a hundred years, until he finished the last of his instructions, stopping in front of a bungalow in a mediocre neighborhood. It was the "oh-so-typical" house with a white porch out front, garage on the side, small front yard and fenced backyard. Yep, blue collar for sure. He opened the garage door by remote and they drove inside and the door closed behind them.

They exited the same way they had gotten into the car, went out the side door and into the house by the rear door. Once inside, Betty asked if they could talk, as he had made a horrible mistake. All he had to do was to let her go, since nothing had happened, except for her being a little late. The brute slapped her with his right hand and the blow stunned her. While she cleared the stars from her vision, the giant brought his fist down on the top of her head like a sledge hammer and the lights went out for her. No talking permitted.

When Betty came to, she screamed. Now, stark fear took over and the brute ran into the room. His presence quieted her. Betty was completely naked, covered by a sheet and bound to the headboard with silver tape, while her feet were bound with rope. Her body formed a perfect X on the bed and Betty understood, or so she thought.

"If you promise to be quiet, I won't tape your mouth. Do you understand?"

Betty understood perfectly and certainly did not want to be unable to reason with her captor, so she nodded, demurely.

"Susan, why did you run away? We had a nice home in Cleveland. We can be together forever, but you have to stop running away."

Betty tried to reason this out. If she denied being "Susan," it could enrage him. She knew his strength now and how a single blow from those ham-like hands could kill her. "Think, girl," she said to herself. "You scared me, just like you are right now," she said, feeling proud of being so clever.

"Baby, we've been together a long time. I don't like to hurt you, but you have to stop running and breaking up our family." At this, he sat on the edge of the bed and it made Betty nauseous. He ran his fingers through her short, black hair and had that puppy-dog look of innocence on his face.

"Are we under the same names here in Chicago?" she asked.

"No, sweetheart, I am now Christopher Cavanaugh, not William Hess, but you can still call me 'Bo', like always."

The picture became clearer to Betty now. This crazy bastard has done this before and who knows how many times? "If I promise not to run, 'Bo,' will you untie me?"

"Baby, it took me a long time to find you again. I've got to think about that." With that, he got up and left the room.

Being Friday night, her parents would not worry about her until late, as she would often go to friends' houses and hang-out. She had to get him to untie her. "This tape was designed for predators to bind their victims," she'd like to tell the executives at 3M to quit making this shit.

When Bo returned, he had two Pepsi cans, one with a straw as he held the straw to her lips and she drank half of it before he pulled it away. Then, he bent over and kissed her, gently. Chaste. Then, with a smile, he stood up and said he was going to take a shower and left her. She could hear the running water, as the bathroom was just across the hall.

A million scenarios ran through her mind as she lay there. She found herself sweating, even though it was cool in the house. She had to find the psychological key which entered the lunatic's mind. She had to survive.

A few minutes later, Bo returned in a bathrobe and gazed at her. When he opened the robe, he was naked, with a huge erection. His penis was nearly a foot long and thick. Betty was no virgin, but no slut, either. She had never seen a hard-on that big, except in magazines and everyone knew those were re-touched, or latex. But this was real.

Bo lay down next to her, kissed her cheek, then her lips and then her neck. His tongue danced around her ear and pulsing artery. He turned down the sheet to her waist, engulfed her breast in his right hand and began to knead it. She was surprised at his tenderness, caressing her nipple between his thumb and index finger, while he sucked her left breast. She willed her body not to respond, but her nipples rose, hard and leathery. Then Bo suckled her right breast, while his fingers tracked softly, up and down her stomach.

Then the sheet was torn from the bed and she was totally vulnerable. His hands tickled her legs, buttocks, thighs and stomach, finally slipping into the thick pubic hair. He bent down and kissed her mound, then wagged his tongue across her clitoris, before parting her flesh and began circular movements around her opening. She tried not to respond, but she had had lovers who were not this gentle and stimulating. She could feel the juices begin to flow, lubricating her and signaling her readiness for entry.

Bo knelt between her legs now and brought his mammoth cock to her. He parted her and inserted the head of his thick appendage, while bending to kiss her forehead. Then, he thrust inside her and the pain was excruciating. It felt as if he had torn her, like hyenas ripping raw flesh from a freshly fallen beast. Her cry was from the pain, but this monster knew he was pleasing her. "Susan" always cried out like this. She loved his "thing," how it was so big and long.

He began pumping and with each thrust, Betty just knew her internal organs were never going to recover. His rhythm quickened and thankfully ended a couple minutes later, as he must have ejaculated and now lay across her in that after-sex bliss. At least that horse cock was out of her and only dull pain resided.

As the beast beside her dozed off, she began to weep softly, so as not to wake him. But, she resolved herself to live. She MUST live. She will survive this, she told herself.

Some time later, Bo awoke, showered again and returned with a cool washcloth. It felt good on her vagina, and she expected to see it drenched with her blood when he pulled it away, but there was none.

She didn't see him until the next morning when he appeared with toast, orange juice and coffee. Betty had to pee badly and she asked to use the toilet. Instead, he returned with a basin, lifted her bottom off the bed and placed it beneath her. He refused to leave the room or even turn his back and was fascinated, watching her urinate. When she finished, and he had flushed the contents, he returned to feed her the breakfast he'd made. She opted for orange juice, as she needed her strength. She had a plan now.

Saturday was spent in a chain, with him sitting next to her. He told her about their future together, how he would care for her and cherish her forever. He made Banquet microwave dinners for lunch and she ate stroganoff that he spoon-fed to her. After dark, he showered again and returned to her wearing his bathrobe. When he removed it and placed it on the chair, he had that massive thing hard again and dangled it over her face.

"Susan, I want you to suck it like you used to. I'll release your hands and you can sit up, while I kneel on the bed." He produced a knife and deftly cut the tape that bound each wrist. Betty replied that she wasn't feeling well and he wouldn't want her getting sicker. Instead, she tried to sooth him, talk that erection flaccid. "Bo, can I shower?" she mewed. "It would only be a couple minutes and there's no reason for me to run anymore."

He thought about that and undid the ropes that held her legs. He walked her to the bathroom. When she entered she noticed a bottle of Vitalis on the counter-top. Bo opened the shower curtain for her and she stepped in and turned on the hot water. All she needed was to avert his attention for a moment, but the hulk stood guard next to the shower. Betty finished her shower and asked to use the toilet, but Bo would not leave, and watched her every move.

Betty needed to gain Bo's confidence or she was quite certain now that he'd kill her, either with that gun or that freakish dick of his.

When she was done defecating, he led her back to the bedroom. With his manhood throbbing and erect, he sat on the edge of the bed and directed her head to his groin. Jesus, how was she going to do this, she thought. She knelt before him, taking him in both hands, wondering if she could bite the head off and escape. That's when he told her in no uncertain terms to be careful. Did "Susan" try it before?

She took the head of his penis into her mouth, which filled it completely and then some. She had never had her mouth open that far before, not even for her dentist. She began to slide it in and out of her mouth, while she stroked his mighty shaft. Bo started to relax and an occasional moan escaped his throat. She felt his testicles tighten, a sign that he was about to climax, so she tried to prepare, but the flood of hot semen that spurt down her throat was a tsunami and the gag reflex engaged. She spit semen all over the big man's thighs, but he was beyond caring. Sated now, he pulled Betty back on the bed and taped her hands once more. He left her legs untied this time, and she thought that was a good sign.

Sunday morning, he made them eggs and bacon, which he let her eat herself. She cooed about how wonderful the food was and was invited into the shower with Bo. This could be her chance. Upon entering, she spotted the Vitalis bottle on the ledge. When she squatted on the toilet to pee, he stepped past her and into the shower stall, but left the curtain open to watch her. When he bent down to turn the water on, she grabbed the Vitalis bottle by the neck. Just as Bo stood up, she crashed the bottle across the back of his head, sending glass, Vitalis and blood around the room.

The impact did not have the desired impact she'd hoped for. Instead of going down, Bo was somehow energized. Before she could get to the door, he had her hair in his left hand, while his right made a looping punch to her right cheek and eye. He struck her again, this time in the right kidney and she lost all ability to fight and went down. Bo began kicking her, hollering obscenities and she thought all was lost. There was a chunk of glass before her eyes and she instinctively snatched it and put it in her mouth. The Vitalis was oily and fishy, but if she needed it, she had it. Unless Bo saw her, of course.

But Bo didn't notice what she was doing on the floor, just that she was there and not getting away. Besides, his head hurt terribly and the Vitalis stung his eyes. Betty lay curled up in a fetal position, crying and going nowhere.

So, Bo turned to the still running shower, washed his face and hair, and then toweled off. He had been thinking how to teach this cunt a lesson and he had a doozy.

In the closet, Bo had a length of nylon rope, which he retrieved now, pulling Betty along by her hair. He tied her hands in front of her and then tied the rope to the solid oak headboard. He then wound rope around each ankle to be secured to the footboard, but, to Betty's surprise, to opposite sides. She was then turned on her stomach, now forming a Y.

"I don't want to see your face, bitch. All you do is lie, you cunt. You hurt me. Why can't you stop running from me? We're family, Susan and you need to admit you love me. I have to punish you." Betty expected a beating, cigarette burns or whatever shit this psycho saw in some Arnold movie. Bo left the room and then returned about ten minutes later and pushed a sock in her mouth and taped it in.

"Susan," he said, "If you leave me again, I'll kill you, and then kill myself. We can be together in Heaven then. But you were bad today." With that, Betty heard him walk to the foot of the bed, heard him place something on the floor softly, and then climb onto the bed. Suddenly, Betty felt something gooey like paste. No, not paste, more thick, yet slippery. Vaseline. The ramifications of that thought started to register, the carnal images flashed, but before Betty could react, Bo's massive tool was just touching her anus. Try as she might, she could not maneuver away from his aim and the head of that grotesque thing entered her rectum.

Betty had never permitted a man to enter there. Never even considered it, even when the porno movies she and her friends watched sometimes, had that stuff in it. The actors liked it, but they're "actors" and get paid for it. Betty could not fathom how someone could enjoy that.

Bo's dick pushed farther and farther in, tearing Betty's rectal muscles, but this was the only method which permitted Bo to enter Susan to the hilt. When his balls were touching Susan's vagina, he looked down and enjoyed the feeling of his cock buried completely inside this bitch, listening to her muffled screams and seeing her writhing beneath him. He began to pump, driving that penis of his all the way in, then out till just the head remained inside her, then back again.

Bo noticed blood on the shaft of his prick and on the sheet under "Susan," but she always did that when he had her like this. So he continued to fuck her and he came a minute later. He slid out, got off the bed and went to the shower again.

Betty had never felt such searing pain. She almost swallowed the sock, screaming. She lay there recovering, but thinking about that piece of glass which now resided in the palm of her right hand. She was going to live.

Bo left her like that, the rest of the night. She had added pee to the mess of blood and feces on the sheet. The next morning Bo came in, brushed some of her hair away from her eyes, kissed her on the forehead and said he'd see her after work and they would talk. She heard the back door close and she began cutting the rope, or she hoped she was cutting the rope, with the glass.

About an hour later, Betty had managed to cut through two of the three strands. It seemed like another hour went by to cut the third, and she had her hands free at last. A few minutes later and she was off the bed, the tape and sock on the floor, and headed towards the bathroom. She needed a face towel to wash herself a bit, splash some cool water on her face and then find something to wear. She could hardly walk, but the burning pain in her rear told her to move quickly. Her own clothes were gone, but she found a pair of sweatpants, which she tied around her waist with the drawstring, and a shirt of Bo's. She left the house by the rear door and made it two blocks, until she found a taxi.

When the taxi pulled up in front of Betty's house, she told the driver to wait. Betty went in, got money from her room and paid the driver. Her mother was in the kitchen and ran to greet her daughter.

"Where have you been? We were so worried about you. Your brother called your friends and no one had seen you. We called the police last night. Why didn't you call us?"

But Betty had hardly heard any of the diatribe. She was about a million miles away, in pain and her mind rushing along.

"Mom, I'm ok. I'm sorry I didn't call you. I'll explain later. I love you." With that, Betty slowly ascended the stairs to her room and the sanctuary it afforded her, comforted by her stuffed bears and the dreams she wove there. She shed Bo's clothes, got into her robe and headed for the shower, where she remained until the water was too cold, having used all the hot water. Betty scrubbed herself, as if soap and water could wash away the indignities wrought upon her. She gently washed her vagina and her buttocks. She wasn't bleeding, but she hurt like hell.

Betty dressed in jeans and a floppy sweatshirt, then dried her hair with a brush. When she looked at her reflection, she didn't recognize the person who looked back at her. Her eyes were bloodshot, circles under her eyes and a glazed look. Her parents would surely think their daughter was on drugs and had been on some binge for the weekend. She'd have to explain later, if she had the chance.

She went downstairs and went into the kitchen for some orange juice and to tell her mother that she was all right and not to worry. She got the keys to the Camry and went out the front door, promising her mother that she'd be home before dinner after a few errands to run, but not before she had opened the nightstand in her parents' bedroom and removed the Walther PPK and placed it under her sweatshirt in the waistband of her jeans.

Driving back to Bo's place was like traveling to another world, another time. Her energy for this trip came from pure anger and hate. She drove past the house and parked the Camry on the street, by the house next door. She entered his house through the rear door, which was still unlocked. With the Walther in hand, the safety off and the hammer cocked, she went from room to room looking for him, like a soldier doing a sweep of enemy territory. When she didn't find him, she went into the living room and sat down in the softest chair to wait.

Bo had forgotten his lunch, which always consisted of a summer sausage sandwich, "enriched" white bread and some cookies. Bo had eaten this same lunch for as long as he could remember. But today, Bo wanted to celebrate Susan's return and the joy she brought to his life, not to mention the great sex life they shared. So, Bo had ordered carry-out oriental food which he wanted to share with Susan, to show how much he loved her. He rushed home, parked in the garage and entered the rear door as always. Strange, though, he noted he had forgotten to lock the door when he left.

Bo placed the bag on the kitchen counter and headed for the bedroom that held his lover. He stopped when he walked through the living room, surprised to see Susan sitting in his favorite La-Z-Boy, dressed in jeans and a sweatshirt. He went to her, slowly.

"Baby, I brought us lunch. Your favorite, too. Cashew chicken, shrimp-fried rice and beef chow mein." In truth, Betty always hated Oriental food. She said the sprouts and watercress reminded her of worms or lugs.

"Susan, I knew you loved me and would stop running away. Baby, we'll have a wonderful life together." Bo was not sure how she managed to untie herself, but the fact remained that she didn't run away like she always did and to him, that proved that she loved him.

Bo knelt before her, beaming with joy and exuding love for his girl. He gently took her left hand and placed it on his cheek, caressing himself, while closing his eyes. He never noticed or felt Betty remove the Walther 9 mm from her jeans as she sat before him in the chair. She raised the gun and pulled the trigger, inches from Bo's face.

The bullet entered Bo's skull, just beneath the left eye, through the zeugmatic arch. The impact of the slug exploded the occipital lobe, tore through the cerebral cortex and exited the rear of the skull, destroying the ganglia, taking the rectangular piece of bone that forms the posterior portion of the cranium, leaving it folded on Bo's neck. The projectile proceeded to embed itself in the drywall of the wall, amongst a spray of blood, bone and brain matter.

Betty did not flinch at the explosion of the round or the acrid sting of cordite, or even the gore that painted the wall before her. What affected her was the finality of what she had just done and the total release she felt by ending Bo's grip on her psychologically. They say that a rapist always owns the victim. Betty wanted to add to that mantra, "Until the sonofabitch is dead."

Betty sat there in the chair for what seemed an eternity before she recovered her wits enough to call her mother. She gave her mom the address where she was, and asked her to send her father there immediately. Her father arrived twenty minutes later and began to pound on the front door. Betty answered and fell into her father's arms.

Betty's father was a rock upon which the "Veins" family was built. Through the sobs and torrent of tears, all he discerned was "Killed him, Daddy." He stepped into the front hall, saw Bo's body lying in a pool of congealed blood and took his daughter outside. Betty would not let him return to the house, wouldn't let him leave her at all, so together they walked to a neighbor's house and asked them to call the police as there had been a horrible accident and they'd need an ambulance as well.

A few minutes later, uniformed officers arrived, siren blaring, lights flashing, as though responding to the scene of a real accident. Betty's father directed them inside the house and he waited with his baby girl on the porch. A few minutes after that, what seemed like a hundred cops appeared. Cops of all shapes and sizes, uniforms, suits, undercover and surly county and state for good measure.

Betty and her father were ushered towards two detectives by a young uniformed cop. They asked Betty if she was all right, if she needed any medical attention or had any injuries.

"Besides being scared to death and crying her eyes out, my daughter's fine. What's wrong with you?" her father retorted.

"Sir, I have a body inside, his head used for close quarter shooting. I have a bedroom where it appears someone was tied to the bed, and I am willing to bet a month's pay, it's your daughter's blood on the sheets." Obviously, this guy was the lead officer or a supervisor. "I think I have a pretty good idea what happened here, but I need to hear it from her," pointing toward Betty. "So, let's get down to it, huh?"

Betty, who was now venting the hysteria she held in all weekend, was mostly incoherent. What the cop heard was "Raped me" and "Did it in self defense." With that, he summoned a female detective. He'd already summoned a Victim's Unit, after viewing the scene in the bedroom.

They all got into an unmarked car and went to the local hospital, where Betty underwent a pelvic exam, a "Rape Kit" was collected, and she was admitted to the hospital for treatment to her rectum and for observation.

Betty's parents stayed at her side, averting their attention from the I.V. which dripped liquid Cephalexin, a potent antibiotic, into Betty's arm to fight the raging infections from being attacked and raped. Instead, they discussed moving to another city, someplace that would not remind Betty of what had happened.

"Mom, this madman was in several cities. He called me Susan and remarked about the number of times Susan had escaped from him and he had to find her again. There's no telling how many women he's done this to. So, another city doesn't insure either of us is safe. It would mean we'd be even more vulnerable, as we would be newcomers and unfamiliar with that city. Don't you see?"

Despite her parents accepting the logic of what she said, they felt inadequate somehow by their failure to protect Betty from this Cavanaugh guy. They had come so close to losing her!

A female detective arrived and took Betty's detailed statement, pausing frequently to let her recover from the recollections. Betty covered everything, leaving out no detail. There was no reason to omit anything and the detective even shared the sense of relief that Hess/Cavanaugh was dead. She told Betty of the results of their VICAP inquiry, where several jurisdictions indicated that the perp in this case appeared to be the perp in numerous abduction/rape investigations and were requesting Bo's DNA, so they could close their active cases. The detective left her card and the names of Crisis Intervention consultants for the Chicago Police Department before she left. No one ever thought that Betty would need the services of a criminal defense attorney.

Chapter 10

Monday morning brought the news of Betty's abduction and the untimely demise, as if any demise is timely, of one Christopher Cavanaugh, with several aliases. Evidently, the Chicago Police Department had confirmed that he was a serial rapist, who had attacked women in other states throughout his evil career. The investigating detectives were quoted as saying that "Chicago's streets are safer tonight" when interviewed shortly after the shooting. There were pictures of Bo's house, his work and of him, maybe from his driver's license or work I.D. There were statements from "shocked" neighbors and co-workers. Betty's name had not been released by Chicago Police, to protect her privacy in such a time. Public sentiment said good riddance to Mr. Cavanaugh and his predatory ways.

However, Wednesday's news brought a shocking story about the arrest of one Elizabeth Conly for the murder of Christopher Cavanaugh. In a press release from State's Attorney Christian Schroeder, he stated, "The charge of murder results from vigilante-like justice, the taking of life while not under threat of force or use of force, instead of summoning the police." Schroeder went on to justify his actions by saying that, "The intervening circumstances between her abduction and the time of death, did not warrant lethal force."

It was legalese jargon meant to confuse, like the legal world's use of the "red herring" mantra when attorneys wanted to distract the opposition.

When the story reached Mordeci Habush, he decided to follow up on it, the scent of a real story, pungent as ammonia in his reporter's nostrils.

Mort met Betty's parents first, felt their pain at their daughter's ordeal and now her confinement in the Cook County jail, without bond. Mort was given access to Betty's photo album and diary. Mort decided that he would rally the troops in her support and he did just that.

Friday's edition of the *Sun Times* carried the outrage at the State's Attorney, his political aspirations for governor and the thought of Betty being held in some cold prison cell, after having endured the sadistic and vile violations of a serial rapist.

Mort received hundreds of letters supporting Betty to the fullest. The State's Attorney's Office received thousands of letters regarding Betty and the charging decision (decision to charge her with murder). That's when Schroeder knew he had a problem on his hands and called for his "assistant."

Over the weekend, the *Sun Times* received requests from CNN, Oprah Winfrey and "60 Minutes" on CBS for Mordeci to appear on TV segments regarding the Conley case. The

Editor chose CBS for the international exposure, where Mort would appear for a full half-hour with Ed Bradley and his powerful contacts. Both programs would be filmed at the *Sun times* offices, a boon for publication and sales.

Mort admired the talents of Bradley and his support staff. He liked Bradley's approach to reporting so matter-of-factly, leaving viewers to their own thoughts of whether it was right or wrong. So when Bradley appeared for the taping, Mort's spirits soared and he was giddy with excitement. Not only could he meet the acclaimed Ed Bradley, he could do wonders for Betty's cause.

"This is Ed Bradley. I'm with Mr. Mordeci Habush, a veteran reporter of the Chicago *Sun Times*. Good afternoon, Mr. Habush. Thank you for meeting with us."

"You're welcome. It's a pleasure to be here," Mort said.

"Mr. Habush, we're here about the Elizabeth Conly case. You have begun a crusade, have amassed volumes of information and as I understand it, have a pronounced position on this case. Why is that?"

"Ed, I've reported on the human rubbish that walks our streets, the killers and perverts who seem to shock us with each new crime. But, the man who raped and sodomized Miss Conly for three days chills even my spirit. The police admit that he violated this vibrant young girl in the most heinous ways possible."

"Does this give someone the right to take the law into their own hands? I mean, I'm told that she executed this guy," Bradley said.

"Well, sir, I think the state of mind this girl was in, the post-traumatic stress disorder as I'm told she suffered, would legally exonerate her from the premeditation element of the offense of murder."

Mort continued, "Ed, this girl was hospitalized after the attack on her. She is being treated by the Crisis Intervention people. I don't pitch my claim of justification on the rapist's record. What I am saying is that there seems to be a defect in these boilerplate laws which do not account for those acts by victims of certain crimes. Elizabeth was still within the psychological grip of this monster. What she did terminated the continuation of his offensive conduct." Mordeci got this precise wording from the Chief Legal Counsel for the *Sun Times*, who had once practiced criminal law and explained the element of "mens rea" to him. Without that requisite "state of mind," the prosecution had no murder case.

Bradley accepted the elemental theory and left viewers to decide the moral dilemma which faces the justice system and potential jurors. Since Schroeder could not participate in the documentary, except to say he couldn't comment on it, all went very well for Betty's cause.

Sunday night, after the "60 Minutes" program aired, Schroeder phoned his assistant, who was merely his political advisor, for a meeting in his office the next morning at 7:30 a.m. to prepare a Press Release. Schroeder had decided it was time for action.

The subsequent interview with CBS brought a lively exchange, as they interviewed viewers and common people on the street. What was clear, after CBS conducted a telephonic poll, was that the public was overwhelmingly displeased with Betty being prosecuted for murder.

The following morning, Schroeder met with his publicist and gave him his plan. After hearing it, he quickly agreed to it.

"Good morning ladies and gentlemen. Mr. Schroeder has called this conference, as he has an announcement to make regarding the Conly case." At that, the State's Attorney' chooch or gopher or whatever you call him, stepped aside and Schroeder entered the room.

"Good morning everyone. Thank you for coming. The case of People versus Conly presents a difficult equation for any prosecutor. There's a moral side and a legal side. The legal side requires citizens to contact law enforcement officers when they have been victims of crime. As a prosecutor, I would be derelict in my duties if I permitted vigilantism. I would have mobs roaming the streets with rope or hot tar and feathers. As a civilized nation, we set the example for countries throughout the world. We have laws for a reason, and the law is crystal clear that one is not permitted to mete out justice on the streets like in the Wild West.

On the other hand, there is a moral aspect to prosecutorial discretion and a sense of responsibility to victims as well. I have seen the parents of Miss Conly and can empathize with them on the whole, sordid affair. I am not the cold, heartless creature portrayed in the media. I have feelings, too. I have to balance the rights of the People and that of a justice system, which sometimes has a deaf ear.

I in no way condone the actions of Miss Conly, as she had the opportunity to call the police. I am concerned about her state-of-mind when she admittedly committed this offense. So, I have reached a "middle ground," between my position as prosecutor and my moral obligation as a human being." The room was silent now. Everyone there hung on every word.

"At this very moment, at my direction, the charge of murder has been amended to voluntary manslaughter, a probationary offense, and Miss Conly, co-signed by her parents, is being released on her personal recognizance. She will be with her family this evening." Schroeder could hear the approval in the audience and outside in the hallways, cheers started up and smiles were the uniform of the day. He could feel the power of the Governor in his hands. Oh, yes, he was going to enjoy being Governor.

Chapter 11

When Schroeder returned to his office, he had arranged to meet with the lead detectives, two of his assistants from the Felony Division whose general field was homicide. Also present was his publicist, who sat away from the large cherry table which adorned the conference room, behind Schroeder.

"Thanks for coming, everyone. The reason I called this meeting is to prepare for the preliminary hearing in the Conly case. We will be joined by people from our Crime Lab and Cermack Hospital's Psychology Department. But first, as you all know by now, I reduced the charge from murder to voluntary manslaughter. I don't think we'd ever prove the mens rea element for murder at trial and I've decided not to oppose bail. She should be out of custody by now or very shortly. I want you two," pointing at the assistant prosecutors, "to contact her defense counsel to see if we can agree to a 'Stipulation of Facts' and reduce this trial to the real issues. I've had cases with him before and he's not to be taken for granted, but he's civil. Any questions?"

Since nothing he said left room for decision making other than his own, Schroeder was not surprised when no questions came forth, so he continued.

"Ok everyone; this is Mr. Rangus, Chief of our Forensics Unit and Dr. Farmer, Chief of the Psychiatric Unit at Cermack Hospital. Thank you for joining us. Let's get our admissions together, in case the Judge requires an Offer of Proof or a Trial Brief. Our female detective was called upon to sum up the known facts, which the prosecution would either prove or were already admitted by Betty."

With a nod of Schroeder's head, she began. "Yes, sir. First, the Chicago Police Department does not dispute the following:

a) Miss Conly was abducted;

b) She was bound to the perp's bed in numerous fashions, including tape, rope and perhaps both, throughout the weekend;

c) She was raped repeatedly, sodomized and forced to fellate the perp at least once;

d) She attempted to escape once, striking the perp with a glass bottle;

e) She subsequently escaped using a piece of glass from that bottle;

f) She returned to her parents' home, showered, changed clothes and returned to the perp's house.

g) She shot the perp once and killed him."

These were all simple facts, admitted to by Betty and were unimportant baby steps towards a conviction. Schroeder, if nothing else, had a more than adequate working knowledge of the law and knew the twists a case can take. In order to win, he tried to get the defense to tip their hand during discovery, where both sides are required to present all documents and witnesses they intend to introduce at trial. Betty's lawyer was cagey, but in this case there were only two avenues he could choose. Either he argued that Betty was justified, acting in a self-defense mode, or he argued a form of verdict he had read about in law school but had never seen acted out in a court of law, "nullification."

Jury nullification is when a defendant is guilty as hell, but the jury refuses to convict for one reason or another. Schroeder realized the potential for nullification in this case. Hell, if he were sitting on the jury, he wouldn't want to convict Betty, either. She is very cute and every man on that jury will notice that and every woman sympathize with her for her suffering and for having the courage to do what she did.

Edward Rangus is a Criminalist who is highly published in professional journals, and respected by his peers and law enforcement as fair and impartial. He had been known to destroy attorneys in court, both defense and prosecutors. He began, "Mr. Schroeder, let me begin, as I must return to my office shortly." Without waiting, he went on. "The physical evidence in this case is as follows:

1) We have tape, adhesive residue, nylon rope and ligature marks on Miss Conly's hands and ankles;

2) The "rape kit" failed to produce the perp's hair, semen or DNA, but she had showered. However, a pelvic exam presents signs of forced entry, bruising to the labia minora and majora;

3) The swab of Miss Conly's rectum produced semen, which is positively identified as from our perp. Also, an exam presented signs of forced sodomy, with damage to the sphincter and colorectal muscles;

4) DNA from blood on the perp's bed is Miss Conly's;

5) Blood in the bathroom is the perp's, and we found shards of glass from a broken bottle which contained a brand name hair tonic;

6) We matched the bullet removed from the wall behind the perp and ballistics confirms it was fired from the Walther PPK found at the scene and was purchased two years ago by Miss Conly's father, according to ATF records.

7) A GSR test was not performed, as Miss Conly showered. However, the sweater she was wearing when she was admitted to the hospital, which we retrieved, has gun shot residue on the right sleeve and chest area, which is consistent with her shooting the perp at close range, one time.

8) The autopsy presents that death was instantaneous. I won't bore you with medical terms, but the perp died from a single entry/exit wound to the head.

9)   The sweatpants and shirt Miss Conly directed us to at her home, were the perp's. We verified that with hair samples and perspiration.

Does anyone have any questions?"

Schroeder asked, "Was there any physical evidence which tended to negate Miss Conly's statements regarding the events of that weekend or the perp's killing?"

"No sir. Not one iota of evidence indicates that the girl is lying." Finished, he excused himself, shook a couple of hands and left the meeting.

"Dr. Farmer, it appears that this case will come down to your testimony and expert opinion." Schroeder said.

"I realize that, Mr. Schroeder. Her psychological condition before, during and after the shooting, are the nucleus of your case. Elizabeth Conly, prior to the crime, was a well-adjusted adult. She admits to being a social drinker and to trying marijuana, although neither contributed to this conduct. She has an I.Q. of 130, well above normal, has a 3.4 g.p.a. in college courses and participates in academic activities. She is an extrovert who makes friends easily and is popular. She has had paramouric relationships, was not a virgin at the time of the attack, and has had three lovers. She reports losing her virginity during her senior year in high school. Basically, she was a typical college girl.

During her abduction, she was subjected to physical and emotional trauma. She was a substitute lover for the perp, referred to as 'Susan' and raped. Although terrified, she maintained her wits and conned the perp into letting her use the shower, ultimately planning her escape.

This is not consistent with one who has lost reason or cognitive thinking. However, due to the trauma, I will agree that she exhibit's the diagnostic criteria for Post-traumatic Stress Disorder, or PTSD, on Axis III, according to the DSM IV, or Diagnostic and Statistical Manual of Mental Disorders, Fourth Edition, for those of you unfamiliar with our Bible."

Schroeder interrupted at this point. "We all agree that she was psychologically damaged during her abduction. I need to know about afterwards."

Farmer had no tolerance for morons and he considered Schroeder a moron, not only for interrupting him, but for that last statement.

"Let me finish, Mr. Schroeder, and then you can ask all the questions you like. After Miss Conly secured her release, she had the ability to return home, shower, change and operate a car, driving back to the perp's house. She concealed the gun from her mother. She knew what she was doing, without question. When she re-entered that house, she had no doubt that she was going to execute that man, or at least confront him. Maybe even hold him until the police came. Your staff and C.P.D. never asked her what she planned to do when she returned to the house. I think this is your Achilles heel, Mr. Shroeder. She could testify that she returned there to hold him there and call the police." This sounded unlikely to Schroeder, until Farmer continued.

"You see, she could have intended that, but when she sat in the house, waiting, seeing the bed where she had been violated, it could have pushed her over the edge. Here's why. She was non-emotional when she shot him. She admits that she didn't scream, threaten or otherwise respond to his presence. She just shot him, at close range, in the face. Why did she let him get so close? One can easily see that she was almost within his grip again, until she found strength to pull the trigger. Of course, you are free to agree that the lack of emotion is evidence of premeditation or calculation. Was she competent, rational, when she pulled that trigger? It is my opinion, based upon a medical degree of certainty, that she was."

Schroeder hadn't thought of that missing question. What were her intentions when she returned to the house? Well, she's got counsel now and they can't send cops to ask her. Damn! Why hadn't he thought of that?

"I warn you, counselor, there are a number of respected psychiatrists and psychologists who will disagree with me. They could parade several of them before the jury."

Schroeder just realized the answer. Although risky, he had to ask Miss Conly that question on the stand, if she testified at all, and she could say that she only planned to make sure the perp returned and then hold him while she called the police, but lost it when she was back inside. Damn it!

"Thanks, Dr. Farmer. As soon as I learn who the defense intends to call as their experts, I'll get the names for you, along with their reports." Farmer ignored the prosecutor after that and simply left the room. He didn't like or trust politicians whatsoever. Schroeder digested the facts and circumstances of the case he'd heard. His publicist applauded the strategy in the Conly case. Even at trial, the defense could ask for a "lesser included" verdict, so the jury could find her guilty of manslaughter, not murder.

"Boss, that 'middle ground' stuff will play well with the voters. Even the girl's advocates like her out of jail and the right wing groups get a conviction. I think you did well. The *Sun Times* will do another opinion poll and you'll come up in satisfaction points."

Schroeder looked at the whiny little man and detested the weasel, but he knew politics and how to get elected, so he'd put up with him.

Chapter 12

The State Attorney's press conference produced a flurry of writings and reports. Mordeci, who had now arranged to meet and interview Betty exclusively, became the medium for all agencies or reporters who wanted knowledge of the case. Mordeci agreed to a full hour on Oprah and promised to ask Betty if she would appear. Right now, she had to clear that with her attorney and could not commit.

The *Sun Times* headline reads, "Middle Ground in Conly Case," where Mordeci expounded on the political gains Schroeder hoped to win and how he was patronizing both sides of the controversy. "Political maneuvering," Mort called it in a subtitle. He criticized the Chief Prosecutor for using this poor girl's ordeal for political gain. Instead, Mort demanded, on behalf of thousands of readers, why was she even charged, given the whole story? He challenged Schroeder to drop the whole matter and rule it "justifiable use of deadly force."

The local news crews filmed Betty leaving the Criminal Courts building at 26th and California Avenues, then arriving at home and walking into the house, while tearful supporters cheered, clapped their hands and waved. Her attorney made a brief statement asking for privacy for his client and her family.

Mordeci arrived at Betty's home later that night. He and Betty snuck out the back door, through the neighbor's yard and hailed a cab. They went to a quiet Italian restaurant, where Mordeci often ate and knew the owners. They were seated in a room used for special occasions or when the place overflowed with customers. It wasn't too busy tonight, so they dined in complete privacy.

They made small talk for awhile, the getting acquainted sort of thing. Mordeci found Betty charming and quite expressive about her kidnapping. He could feel the anguish in her words, as she described the devastation of her and her parent's lives and their uncertain future. She talked about her life before and how she won't trust anyone now. What broke his heart was that she "knows" that no man "will want to be with her," meaning a normal sexual relationship. She's "soiled" now, has to wait for results from the medical examination, to see if Bo had AIDS, herpes, hepatitis or a sexually transmitted disease, so she can begin treatments.

Mordeci decided right then, to not permit her to become a victim again. This time, at the hands of a political wannabe like Christian Schroeder.

When Mordeci and Betty snuck back into her parents' home, using the same evasive tactics they did to leave it, her parents were waiting nervously in the kitchen. Mort knew that they would always fear for their daughter's safety, when the sun goes down.

"Mr. Habush, is there something that can be done to help her?" Mr. Veins asked.

"With your permission, I would like to accept Oprah's invitation, accompanied by Betty, of course, and get the true grit of this story to the people." Betty's hands clenched as she listened to Mort talk about Oprah, a glassy look in her eyes.

"There are several reasons why I believe it would be good for Betty and her cause. First, once Betty understands that it was not her fault and that she needn't feel ashamed, she will begin to heal more quickly. Oprah will have a psychologist there who routinely deals with women who have been victimized.

Second, Schroeder is a political animal, a man driven by his need to possess power. His current goal is to be Governor of Illinois. I'm sure he pictures himself in the Oval Office one day, which is a scary thought in and of itself. By going to the millions of Oprah viewers, I believe we can ignite a firestorm of public opinion supporting Betty.

Last, is the awareness of victimization. Oprah wants the theme of the show to be a tale of public education, of how it can help people like Betty, not turn them into circus freaks or pariahs. This can help Betty and women like her in the future."

Her parents looked at each other, then at Betty, to see what she wanted to do.

"Mr. Habush, can we talk about this tonight and you call me in the morning?" Betty had never looked at the positive implications of her appearing on Oprah and wanted her parents' blessings before agreeing.

Outside Betty's home, a throng of camera crews were camped out, jockeying for the best spots and drinking coffee. Everyone waited for Betty to emerge and to try to make a statement.

Betty did emerge from her home the next morning, accompanied by her attorney, Richard King, who teaches criminal law in Chicago, lives in Evanston with his family, is Jewish, soft spoken, very opinionated, stands shorter than Betty at 5'6", but his stature as a defense attorney and true advocate, is monumental. He wears "Earth Shoes," the ones that are lower at the heel than at the toe, as a symbolic gesture of his independence.

"Hello," Betty began, "I just want everyone to please respect our privacy, and to know that I intend to go to trial on this case. I'm happy to be home and thank you for all the cards and letters I've received."

Mr. King assumed control of the reporters then. "Ladies and gentlemen, my client and I have discussed her case this morning and feel confident that she'll be vindicated at trial. Because of a 'gag order' from the Judge, we are not to discuss the evidence or witnesses. However, moments ago we had a conversation with Oprah Winfrey and have agreed to appear on her program tomorrow. To you reporters, please report the facts of the case, fairly and evenhandedly. Thank you."

Then, Betty and Richard got into his Volvo and left for their meeting with Mort and Oprah's staff to iron out the details so that Betty did not violate the meaning and spirit of the "gag order." Everyone knew what Betty went through so there was no need to rehash that again. It was agreed that the theme of the show would not jeopardize Betty for non-compliance with the gag order.

They were all set. The taping was to begin at noon, so Betty and her mother made appointments for their hair the next morning and her father took his only suit to the cleaners.

The show with Opra began with a standing ovation as Betty shyly walked onto the set. The women cried for her, the men looked somber as the cameras panned the audience. Even Oprah had to wipe tears from her eyes at the courage and strength it must have taken to survive.

"Welcome to the show, Elizabeth. May I call you Betty?" Oprah asked.

"Of course," Betty said while looking at all the equipment and the audience.

"Before we bring out the others, Betty, I want you to know that everyone admires your courage to survive and wish you a speedy recovery in the healing process." At this, the audience roared to life again, on their feet and raucously clapping their hands. The outpouring of compassion caused Betty to cry and they broke for commercials.

Betty's parents were seated in front and quickly came to her side. Betty's survival galvanized support for women's groups and those that sought stiffer penalties for predators who roamed the streets, even after being apprehended before. She quickly became the poster child for victims of violence and their struggles.

When Oprah continued, Mordeci and Richard accompanied Betty on stage.

The rest of the show was a tremendous success for Betty, the viewers and for garnering support for Betty's cause.

Richard, having first described the areas which the "gag order" prohibited them from discussing, went on to detail the elements of the applicable law, the current bills before the Illinois House and Senate regarding predators and their possible sentencing enhancements and the "Victim/Witness Impact."

Mordeci, who was not constrained by any gag order, was much more vehement on the need to apprehend and warehouse vermin like that which kidnapped Betty.

"I am appalled at the decision to charge this brave girl with anything. The police weren't there to free her. They weren't there when this monster savagely assaulted her. The police didn't stop her abduction. But, they want to be called when you've solved the case for them and captured the culprit. Bah! They weren't around. We don't know Betty's frame of mind that day. All the prosecution's case is that she should have called the police. Well, I ask Mr. Schroeder, where were your police when this girl was screaming?"

The audience applauded this diatribe and Oprah nodded her head.

"I would like to see more cards, letters or whatever form of message, from people all over, giving us their opinion on this case." Mordeci knew what he wanted. He wanted public opinion on Betty's side.

"I want to see State funded programs to help Betty and others just like her, who, unfortunately, fall prey to monsters each day. I also want to see enhanced techniques and methods to capture these monsters. The police need to be more proactive on this and not wait for a call from another hospital that has a victim in their E.R."

After the show, Oprah presented a check to the Defense Fund she began and discussed during the taping. She wished Betty well and hurried to other engagements. Betty was one of Oprah's biggest hits in the Neilson Ratings. Millions watched Betty and felt awful for her.

Just as Mordeci thought, cards and letters began arriving in huge mail sacks. Thousands and thousands of them. All supporting Betty, with only nine that condemned her retributive act. It was beautiful, Mort thought. Schroeder, in his office across town, must be inundated as well. His popularity was sinking. His political cronies urged him to continue the prosecution or funding for his gubernatorial run would dry up. He was stuck. One girl could destroy him. Hell, he may not even win re-election as State's Attorney at this rate.

Chapter 13

Scott Solzenfeld is a 6' 4" tall beanstalk, with a wife and two kids, struggling to make ends meet, working as assistant manager at an office supply company. His wife handed him a "Notice of Jury Duty" from the Clerk's Office. Damn. He'll have to convince the Clerk he cannot afford jury duty. His company just received the Hon line of office furniture and they were planning a large sales event. He had gotten out of it before by having his boss write a letter saying that the business would suffer if he were gone. He'd just do the same thing again.

Meanwhile, Matthew Munschau, an airframe and power plant mechanic maintaining corporate jets for a local company, began sorting through his mail. When he came upon an envelope from the Clerk of Court, he fretted that his ex-wife had filed another demand for more child support. He left it, unopened, on the table in his kitchen. It wasn't until five days later when he mustered the nerve to open the Clerk's envelope and began to laugh aloud with relief. Mathew, known around the shop as "Rocket" because of his constant movement at work, had accepted an offer from a Fortune 500 company in Ohio, somewhere around Mansfield, to maintain their fleet of Gulfstream and Citation jets. However, he had given his current employer a 90 day notice, so that they could locate and train a replacement.

Kelly Rolland, a 5' 6," busty blond who recently graduated from a community college, had applied to John Marshall Law School and was accepted for fall courses. When she received her Notice of Jury Duty, she accepted the responsibility, as she believed in the justice system and hoped to work in juvenile courts after graduating from John Marshall. Perhaps, she could even be a judge. People always have a motive for what they do. Kelly's motive was that, as a child, she was abused by her step-father. Her father, a jet jock in Nam, was MIA from a sortie over Quang Tri, presumed dead, when they found the wreckage of his plane. Kelly looked forward to the prospect of serving on a jury.

Nannette Daley, a retired school teacher from Cicero, was liked by her neighbors, and had maintained the same apartment for 25 years. The downside to her life was the loneliness. A spinster with not one male friend, she served up her opinions in a vinaigrette flavor. Her attire spoke of her antiquated fashion sense, with kaleidoscopic print dresses that resembled curtain material from a Motel 6, those obscenities called "granny heels" which could double as crude weapons in time of need and bright, red lipstick, capable of blinding pilots on sunny days if she stood too close to the airport. At 68, she had served on two juries, both resulting in convictions, and looked forward to jury duty as a break in her lonely existence.

Lt. Colonel Geoffrey McLeon (retired) spent 21 years in the Army. He left when the push came on to downsize our conventional armies and was offered an early pension with reserve status. He currently supervises the maintenance facilities at O'Hare Airport for United Airlines. He trains regularly, is quite muscular and enjoys his life and job. He currently lives with his girlfriend of a year, Fay. He has sent resumes to numerous airlines and has applied for a position with U.A.L. in Sacremento, as Director of Operations of one of its commuter operations. He, too, received a Notice of Jury Duty.

Ronya "Ronnie" Allison is the descendant of a marriage between an Italian mother and a Cherokee Indian. Despite her 5'5", 112 pound build, she possesses the fiery spirit of a hellish demon when provoked. Her husband of eight years is a C.F.D. firefighter, as Battalion Chief. Because of his employment and the inherent dangers, he began drinking with his comrades at a local saloon, almost daily. What began as a way to unwind after a day on the job, has evolved into an ugly habit. He drinks at home now, often becoming rowdy and confrontational. He has slapped Ronnie when she angered him. Then, there were brawls, as Ronnie would stoke the fires within her and things got bad. Their relationship recovers from these domestic wars, usually with mutual apologies. She thought of a stint in the jury box as an escape from the ugly confrontations at home.

Sergeant Rance Daniels, of the Illinois Department of Corrections, is stationed at the Stateville Correctional Center, a maximum security prison, in Joliet. He is 31 years old and gay. He has witnessed gang rapes, murders and bloodshed at work. He has ambitions of becoming a warden some day, as he believes he can have a positive influence on those he serves and confines. He looked at the Notice of Jury Duty and thought it an opportunity to learn more about the system that sent people to prison.

Nancy Krush is a successful architect who resides on North Lakeshore Drive in a prominent high-rise, the kind that sports uniformed doormen and valets to park her Mercedes 500 SL safely. Her office is another high-rise in downtown, has roving security and an officer's desk in the lobby. Violent crime would have a difficult time reaching Nancy Krush. Nancy abhorred the notion that taxes paid for public protection and thought that Betty should have called the police. She had a few friends who were cops, whom she had met at social functions in her community. She figured she could bring a "law and order" outlook to the jury box.

Michelle Dittman is a 39 year old housewife who discovered that day care costs for her twin daughters exceeded the income she made at a part-time job, so she stays home now with her daughters. That pleases her husband, who makes a comfortable salary hauling U.S. mail from Chicago to Cleveland. He is gone two nights a week, but is home every weekend and holidays. It's called a "milk run" and usually goes to drivers with the most seniority or perfect driving records. Michelle and her husband are saving to buy a new Kenworth for his work and earn even more money as an owner/operator. They live in a modest house on the city's Westside. She worries about the economic impact that serving on a jury will have on her family. They had worked hard to save that money and she didn't want to see it go for daycare because of jury duty.

In Winnetka, a mortgage broker with offices in Dallas, Texas and Oakbrook, Illinois, opens an envelope from the Cook County Clerk of Courts. In part it read:

Dear Mr. Enrique Acevedo:

You are hereby summoned for Jury Duty. You have been chosen at random. You are to report to the Clerk's Office, Room ....

"Damn!" The 46 year old Texas A & M graduate said. This would make life rougher for him as he still had work to do. If he sat on a jury during the day, his nights would be gobbled up with work and would deny him quality time with his son and daughter. Generally, while his wife worked at a local florist, he and the kids would make a pizza or go to "McD's" supper club for burgers and fries. However, even with his liberal slant on politics, he realized the need for citizens to participate in the judiciary process. And if the prosecutor proved the State's case, he would vote to convict.

Diane Loswin, a seasoned surgical nurse who is accustomed to blood, does not appreciate the vivid photos of crime on the city's streets. She has no children, due to a hysterectomy, despite being married to a spice salesman. Her husband occasionally travels internationally and brings home cultural practices from around the world, including Islamic punishments and how criminals are treated in other countries. Some of the barbaric sentences meted out make her happy she lives here. As a nurse, she had no idea how vivid would be the photos and medical testimony she would view as a jurist in Betty's case.

BOOK TWO

Chapter 14

"Mr. King, good of you to come," Schroeder said. They were meeting in the law library in the State's Attorney's Office in the Criminal Courts Building.

"What we're trying to do, pursuant to the Scheduling Order and our upcoming Pretrial conference is twofold. First, we have a Plea Agreement to offer you. We'll accept a plea of no contest to the voluntary manslaughter. We'll recommend 5 years probation, with the first 6 months in the county jail. We'll actually hold her at the Cermack Hospital across the street, where she'll be safe. I know you'll discuss it with your client.

Next is to prepare Stipulations for trial. This Judge wants the admitted facts of the case in a Strip, if we can all agree. I have drafted the facts I believe we can all live with."

One of the assistants passed out the two-page document to everyone there. "I believe the factual basis of this Strip is fair to both sides, but I am certain the defense has differing opinions on some, if not all of the admissions."

Schroeder picked up the document before him and began to read.

"The parties agree and stipulate to the following facts in this case:

1)   That the Defendant, Elizabeth Conly, was abducted by Christopher Cavanaugh within the city limits of Chicago, Illinois, Cook County; and

2)   That the Defendant was taken by Christopher Cavanaugh against her will to his   house, also within the city limits of Chicago, Illinois, Cook County, where she was

forcefully restrained by him; and

3)   That the Defendant, Elizabeth Conly, against her will and without her consent, was forced to engage in sexual intercourse with Christopher Cavanaugh; and

4)   That the Defendant, Elizabeth Conly, at some point in time, managed to extricate herself from her restraints and fled Cavanaugh's house and returned to her home; and

5)   That the Defendant, Elizabeth Conly, did return to Cavanaugh's house, where she shot and killed Cavanaugh; and

6)   That if the State called Thomas Dorf, the Cook County Medical Examiner to testify, he would attest that the cause of death of Christopher Cavanaugh resulted from a single gunshot to the head."

Schroeder put the document on the table and sat down. "Is that a fair reading of this case?"

Richard King was shaking his head and smiling, a wry smile one gives when they catch someone with their hand in the cookie jar. "Well, I give you credit for trying. You give me Numbers 1 and 2, which relieves my client from testifying, while agreeing to jurisdiction. However, Number 3 is diluted too much to give an accurate picture of what really happened to her and if I agree to this oversimplification, she could be barred from testifying to what you call 'sexual intercourse.' So, we won't agree to number 3. Number 4 and 5 need a little work. For example," King began as he read his penciled notes on the borders of the proposed stipulation, "in Number 4, let's add 'after three days, the defendant freed herself using a shard of glass she recovered from an earlier escape attempt, where she struck her assailant in the head with a bottle,' which sums up the actual events better." King saw Schroeder making notes, so he was considering the added language.

"In Number 5, I want to see language to the effect that the of cause of death for Christopher Cavanaugh resulted from a 'close contact gunshot wound, entering the face just below the left eye and exiting at the rear of the skull and death was all but instantaneous.'" Everyone anticipated some changes to this document, which was meant to streamline the trial, so Schroeder said that he could live with the changes King proposed but said that they'd need a definition for "close contact," to which King agreed.

"But I'm not finished yet," Richard said. "If we're going to do this, let's get real. We have the physician's testimony about Betty being raped and sodomized. Let's include that and the fact that this 'sexual intercourse' as you call it, required her hospitalization for three days and antibiotics. Let's stipulate that my client gave a statement voluntarily and incorporate that statement." King was on a roll now, as if summing up a case before a jury and he rocked back and forth on his "Earth shoes" as he orated. "Let's include all the events, including Cavanaugh having changed his name from Thomas Hess, and that he is linked forensically to several other similar rapes and abductions in various states."

Schroeder knew King could and would elicit this tidbit of wisdom from the detectives and may call officers from other jurisdictions to substantiate this claim. He wished to downplay the sordid history of Cavanaugh and his sexual fantasies, so he would acknowledge this "link."

"What you propose, Richard, renders the whole trial to expert witnesses and their opinions on *mens rea.*"

"Isn't that what this is all about, Chris?" Richard had used his first name by design. He wanted to remove him from the pedestal that he placed himself on and this was a simple way to begin that process.

"I'll grant you that this will come down to that, but if I agree to all this, I would be tacitly agreeing to this Cavanaugh guy being a monster and even remotely condemning his extermination." Schroeder didn't give a shit about whether the jury thought Cavanaugh, or whatever his name was last week, was a monster. He needed to maneuver Betty to the stand. If he agreed to everything, there'd be no need for her to testify and that was unacceptable.

"O.K., let's do this," Schroeder took command once again. "We'll add Number 6, that Cavanaugh was linked by DNA, but that he was not charged or convicted of those cases.

"Chris, he couldn't be linked because he was still alive, and we had no DNA sample for comparison. If he were alive right now, he'd have those states yapping at his heels."

"Agreed," Schroeder said and with that, Richard won the concession that Cavanaugh was a serial rapist and Schroeder downplayed his crimes elsewhere.

"Everything else is viable Richard, except for the incorporation of her statement. That, constructively, is her testimony and she was not cross-examined when she gave the statement. So, we'll agree that she gave a statement and let her tell her story." Richard couldn't force the prosecution to agree. He'd tried to relieve Betty of having to recall all those horrible things, but lost.

"We'll want an agreement on the weapon as being registered to her father by ATF records and that ballistics proves it was the gun that fired the shot that killed this guy, so our lab guys can forget about appearing. Any problems?"

With a shake of the head, it was finished, or as much as it could be, and Richard gathered the document, now almost unreadable with pencil notes all over its face, placing it on top of the legal pad he used, inside his briefcase. The final draft would be sent to Richard for his signature and returned to Schroeder, who would have it delivered to the Judge. Both sides had gained a little and had given a little. That's how the justice system works in America. Bullshit! That is how Schroeder wanted it to appear.

Chapter 15   Trial

"Good morning everyone," Judge Robert Smart said as he seated himself. "Are we ready to begin the Conly case?"

"State appears by Christian Schroeder and is ready for trial."

"The Defendant appears in person and is represented by counsel, Richard King. We're ready for trial."

"Have both sides submitted *voir dire* questions for the venire?" the Judge asked.

"We have submitted our 'consolidated' questions to your clerk," the State's Attorney responded.

The trial process was thus begun. The clerk would call out 14 numbers and the prospective jurors whose names corresponded to those numbers would be called. Each would then be questioned, using the questions submitted to the Judge. Afterwards, each side would be given the right to accept or challenge that person, either peremptorily, or "for cause." A peremptory challenge means that there doesn't need to be a specific reason, but for some reason, they're undesirable for that jury. Some lawyers live by a maxim that you never let a schoolteacher sit on a jury, as they're too bossy and believe they are smarter than everyone else. "For Cause" means that there is a specific reason, like a prior criminal record, a preconception on the case or some other disability which renders them inappropriate to sit on the jury. Each side is given a certain number of peremptory challenges, usually three each. There are no such restrictions on "for cause" challenges, however.

It was not until later that afternoon when the jurors were selected, including two alternates. Instead of hearing Opening Statements that late in the day, Judge Smart adjourned until the following morning.

"Good morning, ladies and gentlemen. My name is Christian Schroeder. I am the State's Attorney for Cook County. Mr. King, the Defendant's attorney, and myself, are given this opportunity to tell you what we believe we can prove in this case. You will hear an agreement called a Stipulation of Facts, from Judge Smart. These are facts of the case that are not disputed by either side, and shorten the trial by not requiring witnesses and other evidence to substantiate those facts. You are going to hear that the deceased in this case did some horrible things to the Defendant, things that are untenable and shocking. The State admits that the Defendant was kidnapped and raped. However, none of those offenses were capital offenses which carry a legal penalty of death. The State will prove that this Defendant, after escaping her captor, returned to his home and without lawful authority, killed him with her father's gun. That is voluntary manslaughter and the State is going to ask you to return a verdict of guilty. Thank you."

Schroeder, standing an imposing 6'6", 220 pounds, clean shaven, with meticulous hair, looked Romanesque in his Armani suit of blue pinstripes, with 1" shirt cuffs exposed. The summer wool suit, silk shirt and Allen Edmonds wingtips transformed him into a model. Schroeder graduated from Georgetown Law School. it is his father's alma mater as well. He originally worked for his father's firm doing corporate law, but Chris's heart was always yearning to do criminal work instead. He applied with the Republican State's Attorney, Richard Delay, who was planning to retire soon and wanted to groom a successor. Chris seemed perfect for that task and he rose rapidly through ranks, and was appointed Chief of the Felony Division after only 2 years. Some of his coworkers were miffed at his rapid ascent, but there was nothing they could do about it.

"Good morning ladies and gentlemen of the jury, Your Honor, and Mr. Schroeder. The State is correct when it states that you will hear about horrible things done to that young lady seated at the table next to me. Horrible, vile things that were perpetrated by a sexual rapist, a man who had done such horrendous acts on numerous prior occasions to other victims.

Both sides have agreed to shorten this trial and get to the crux of the case. However, I want you to keep in mind one thing when you listen to the evidence. As a matter of law, the distinction between murder and manslaughter is the lack of premeditation. Premeditation is a state of mind in which someone methodically plans to do an act. When one does not plan to kill someone, it's called manslaughter. At the close of the State's case against Miss Conly, the Judge will instruct you on several elements of law. One of those, and the most crucial, is 'reasonable doubt.' The definition of that is what a reasonable person, given the same set of facts, would find prudent. The Judge will instruct you that if you have a reasonable doubt, you must find Miss Conly not guilty. As I look around you, I feel confident that you are all capable of comprehending that instruction and you will, in fact, find Elizabeth not guilty. Thank you."

With that done, the trial began before the Chief Judge, Robert Smart, who had headed up the Cook County Public Defender's Office, where he cut his reputation as a fierce defender, subjecting prosecutors' cases to the true meaning of the adversarial process. King liked Judge Smart, liked his fairness and the continuing control he exuded over a trial. No one pulled shenanigans in his court without facing summary contempt and a night in the klink.

Chapter 16

"The parties have agreed to numerous facts about this case, called a stipulation. This is nothing other than a measure to expedite trial and to avoid a parade of witnesses and evidence. It is not to be construed by you as an admission of guilt," the Judge began and with that he read into the record all of the facts and circumstances King and Schroeder discussed and agreed upon.

The State began its "Case in Chief," calling the lead detective to the stand, introducing the photos of the crime scene and the condition of the body and defendant upon their arrival.

Last to be introduced was Betty's confession to shooting Bo, the introduction of her father's gun and the Ballistics Report confirming that the fatal round came from that gun. With that, the State rested. It's not the State's burden to introduce expert witness testimony, like psychiatrists or psychologists, in its Case in Chief. Instead, it reserves that testimony in rebuttal, after a defendant raises a "diminished capacity" defense. Schroeder had his witness waiting.

"Your Honor, I move for a directed verdict at this time. The State has failed to prove beyond a reasonable doubt that the defendant possessed the requisite state of mind to support a finding of guilt, as a matter of law. The State has failed to prove that the defendant acted in other than self-defense or was otherwise justified in the use of force, or, has only proven the offense of involuntary manslaughter, a lesser included offense."

"That motion is denied," Smart ruled and they broke for the day.

"Your Honor," King said, "the defense calls Dr. Jeffrey Franks." And so, King introduced the extent of Betty's injuries from the prurient fantasies of her assailant. The sometimes graphic depiction of Betty's genitalia made the male jurors blush with discomfort. When the sodomy was discussed, the women flushed with rage. Schroeder saw both emotional responses.

King called the Crisis Intervention workers who met with Betty immediately after, at the house and while awaiting trial.

He called two clinical psychologists, both respected in their field. Both agreed, "beyond a reasonable degree of medical certainty," that Elizabeth Conly suffered "Post-traumatic Stress Disorder," P.T.S.D., as a direct result of the assault by Christopher Cavanaugh. Further, Betty was in psychological shock, her cognitive abilities reeling at the time of the shooting.

"In your expert, medical opinion, did Elizabeth possess a sufficient state of mind to plan the calculated execution of Christopher Cavanaugh?"

"No, sir, she did not," they mirrored each other.

At last, King called his client. Through tears and Kleenex shredding, Betty went through the events of that weekend. Nothing varied from her written statement, all the way to shooting Bo. King took her to the after-care she required, including hospitalization and psycho-therapy. When King finally says, "I have no further questions of this witness," not a dry eye existed in the room, not one heart failed to reach out to her and share her pain in the hopes of erasing it from this wonderful girl.

"We'll recess for the night. The State will cross-examine beginning tomorrow at 8:30."

Schroeder and his minions met for most of the evening, planning their strategy, researching the precedent on "hostile witnesses."

"Good morning, Miss Conly," Schroeder said, and began his calculated approach to a question that could stun the momentum of the prosecution. Like a shark, to whom lawyers are often compared to, Schroeder must find a wound and strike swiftly, while not making Betty a martyr.

"Miss Conly, when you were about to leave your parents' home, you retrieved your father's gun, didn't you?"

"Yes, sir," Betty said softly.

"Mr. Cavanaugh hurt you, didn't he?"

Betty's voice was resonant, clear. "Yes, he did!"

"And you were pretty upset with him for doing so, is that correct?"

"Of course. Anyone would be," Betty said.

"Were you mad enough to want him dead?"

"I'm not sure, Mr. Schroeder," was her reply.

"You aren't sure. Well, when you got your father's gun, what were your intentions?"

"I'm not sure. I just wanted it when I went back to his house to confront him."

"You've learned how to handle guns, haven't you?"

"My father taught me."

"Before you use a handgun like your dad's, do you check to see if there's a live round in the chamber?"

"Yes sir."

"Did you look in the chamber of your father's gun to see if there was a live round in it?"

"Yes, sir, I did." Betty sounded like she had surprised herself with this revelation.

"So, you made certain the Walther your father owned, the one you shot Cavanaugh with, was loaded and ready to use. Is that correct?"

"Objection. Asked and answered," King interjected.

"Overruled," Smart replied.

"Yes, sir, I guess I did."

"Miss Conly, it's safe to say then that before you returned to that house, you intended to use that gun?" After a pause, Schroeder said, "Miss Conly?"

"I suppose in retrospect, I guess I did."

"No further questions."

The damage had been done, but King needed to try to rehabilitate her testimony.

"One question on re-direct, Your Honor. Miss Conly, did you specifically recall that you intended to shoot Mr. Cavanaugh, or was the reason you took your father's gun to detain him?"

Normally, this is objectionable and routinely sustained as "leading the witness," but Schroeder had prepared for this question and actually wanted it.

"I guess I could've held him, unless he attacked me again, that is."

"So," King had a niche now, "you may have considered holding him for the police?"

"That was a possibility."

King sat down and said, "Nothing further."

Without waiting, Schroeder rose and asked her, "Miss Conley, you gave a statement to the detectives. Why is it you fail to mention your intent to hold Cavanaugh until police arrived?"

"I had a terrible time then. Maybe I wasn't thinking straight."

King used the same maneuver, rising from his seat and merely asked his question. "Miss Conly, you were interviewed by a large number of police officers and detectives. Did any of them ask you if you returned to that house, intending to shoot Mr. Cavanaugh?"

"No sir, none of them."

"Defense rests, Your Honor."

"If it please the Court, the State will call one rebuttal witness. The State calls Dr. Jack Farmer." Farmer entered from the hallway, strode to the witness box and waited to be sworn. He had been in courtrooms hundreds of times. Having been sworn, Schroeder stated that like the defense psychologists, there was a stipulation as to Dr. Farmer being qualified as an expert.

"Dr. Farmer, are you personally acquainted with Elizabeth Conly, this defendant?"

"Yes, I am."

Schroder continued, "Did you have occasion to examine her, in relation to this case?"

"Yes, I did. Several occasions, actually," Jack admitted.

"And as a result of these examinations, have you reached any diagnosis?"

"Well, I've written a Report, if that answers your question." Jack did not like Schroeder and was going to make him work for every inch.

"I see. Well, in your Report, did you determine if Miss Conly suffers from any mental disease or defect which would deny her the ability to make a conscious decision between right and wrong, the night she shot Christopher Cavanaugh?"

"It is my clinical opinion that she did not."

"Your witness, counsel," Schroeder said.

"Dr. Farmer, would you agree that Betty suffers from Post-traumatic Stress Disorder as a result of the vile assault on her at the hands of Cavanaugh?"

"Yes, sir, she presents the symptoms of P.T.S.D. as I would expect of anyone who experienced what she did."

King had to be careful now, as he would be walking on objectionable grounds. "Dr. Farmer, is it possible, in your clinical opinion, that Betty could have left her parents' home planning one course of action, and once inside the Cavanaugh house at the scene where she was brutally assaulted, her mind lost control and cognition was no longer an option?"

"Mr. King, I would conclude that anyone who survived what we know happened to her and then returned to that very scene, would be capable of losing control." Jack had considered this line of questioning, ever since his meeting with Schroder.

"Dr. Farmer, can you testify today, beyond a reasonable degree of medical certainty, that Miss Conly did not return to that house with any other reason than to kill Cavanaugh?"

"No, sir, I cannot," Jack said. He warned the pompous prosecutor that this could come up!

"Nothing further," Richard said, proudly.

The closing arguments were predictable, about the same as the opening. Except, when the prosecution bolted to their feet, all three of them in harmony and Schroeder shouted his objection and Judge Smart immediately dismissed the jury and ordered counsel into his chambers. Once there, Smart began a tirade on Richard.

"Damn you. How dare you come into my court and try for a jury nullifcation. You know damn well I would respond just the way I am right now. Explain yourself, counselor."

Richard tried to explain. "Your Honor, there have been a few instances of nullification in our jurisprudence. A jury is the ultimate trier of fact. If it believes that Cavanaugh deserved what he got, that is their prerogative. I simply advised the jury that it had that power." Richard was mad himself now. "Judge, the Illinois Pattern Jury Instructions relate that those people are the triers, what they decide is the law. You know that this case is emotionally charged and that we're dealing with a serial rapist, not a Boy Scout."

"Your Honor, I am not moving for a mistrial, but I would like a limiting instruction, admonishing the jury to disregard his statements," Schroeder said.

"I will direct Mr. King's statements stricken from the record and disregarded."

With the trial phase done, the Judge gave the jury their Instructions and sent them to deliberate. At 4:30, the Judge adjourned until the following day at 8:30 in the morning. This routine went on for three full days and it appeared that the jury was hopelessly deadlocked, according to juror Number 6, Geoffery McLoed, the foreman.

There is an instruction, called the "dynamite jury instruction," where the Judge gets to vent his anger and frustration on jurors for not doing their duty and reaching a verdict. On the fourth day, Judge Smart did his venting and two hours later, the jury returned a guilty verdict.

Betty was continued on bail and directed to submit to a probation officer to prepare a presentence investigation report.

Chapter 17

The *Sun Times* called the verdict outrageous, on the front page. Mordeci was livid with the jury's decision, ignoring the horrendous acts Betty suffered. Thousands of letters poured into the *Sun Times* offices, after C.N.N. and Associated Press disclosed the verdict, all supporting Betty and demanding leniency. Even Oprah lamented over the finding and said that her staff would deliver any correspondence from viewers to Betty and her attorney. King was not prepared for the boxes of mail he received from Harpo Productions.

In the interim, Betty met with a probation officer, where they discussed her education, family, health, finances and even how she felt about her celebrity status.

Betty actually had no position on the "celebrity" stuff. Yes, she was recognized frequently, but it embarrassed her more than anything else.

The report was finished a few days later and Betty's probation officer, for the first time in Richard's practice, offered no sentence recommendation. This was unheard of, but there it was written, in the space for a "Sentence Recommendation," it said, "None."

On the morning of sentencing, Betty went to church and made her confession. She attended morning mass and returned home, spiritually nourished.

Betty consoled her parents. With the volumes of supportive letters and public opinion, it was a given that she would receive probation. But Betty, having confessed the killing to God, had no fear of what the mortal Judge would do to her, as long as God forgave her.

At sentencing, a packed gallery of onlookers and Betty's family watched the State's Attorney made no recommendation regarding a sentence. He was not going to become a pariah in the media for requesting jail time. It was bad enough that his popularity and confidence polls had fallen dramatically. His hope was that this time, the wounds would heal and voters would return him to his present office. Then, in just two more years, he would seek the Office of Governor of Illinois.

Richard King, after relating the heinousness of Cavanaugh's acts and the confused mental state Betty was in immediately following the shooting and her total cooperation with authorities, clearly demonstrated her character. Furthermore, while free on bond, she had never missed a court date or become involved in any criminal conduct. She was an excellent candidate for probation as a first time offender.

"I submit, Judge, that we have a unique set of circumstances here and there is virtually no chance of Miss

Conly re-offending. Therefore, I request that a period of probation, which is permissible under the statute, be imposed."

The Judge asked Betty if she had anything to say and she declined.

"Miss Conly, I believe you returned to that house with your father's gun, for one reason. I think you demanded vengeance. I think you executed that man, but since the State has not charged you with murder, your premeditation is not an element now. However, I am permitted to consider a wide range of factors at sentencing and I cannot overlook the fact that a man lost his life. Therefore, it is the sentence of the Court that you serve a term of 1 to 3 years in the Illinois Department of Corrections, at Dwight. Your bail is revoked and you are remanded to the Sheriff, where I direct that you be transported forthwith."

Betty was handcuffed, removed from the courtroom and taken to the lockup. There, she was chained at the waist and ankles, placed in a van with two deputies, and taken an hour and a half south, to Dwight Correctional. She was stripped naked, searched, both visually and her vagina and rectum examined by a nurse, for contraband. She was then sprayed with a "delouse" solvent and directed to a filthy shower. After toweling off, she was handed a jumpsuit and taken to segregation, placed in a cell by herself and left alone.

Whether or not the Judge intended the swift change in circumstances to upset her frail mind, it did. About four hours after her arrival at Dwight, while making routine rounds, a guard found Elizabeth Conly, hanging from a rope of braided bed sheets, dead.

When this news reached Mordeci, he got drunk. Even drunk, he managed to cry for Betty.

Chapter 18

Veins was sitting in his cluttered office, blueprints of designs rolled into cardboard tubes or spread out on tables. He was looking over one such design, when the music he was listening to, was interrupted by "breaking news."

"Elizabeth Conly, whom this City has come to know affectionately as Betty, has been found dead in her cell at Dwight. Department of Corrections officials have reported it as a suicide. Betty has been the center of attention recently, after being kidnapped and raped."

Veins dropped his coffee on the floor, which just moments before, he savored. He felt as if he were jacked in the solar plexis with a hammer. He found it difficult to breathe. He walked out of his office, leaving his jacket behind, pushed the little magnet next to his name to "out" from "in" and left the building. He walked to the beach, where he found an empty bench and sat. It did not take long for the tears to flow freely. His little sister had gone through so much. She survived and became a real hero. Women looked up to her for her strength and courage. She became a national monument to rape victims. Oh, my god! He remembered the dreams they shared, her with the 2.5 children the Census Bureau says is the usual

American family.   The husband she had only dreamed of in her life some day. All of that was gone now.

Veins sat there long after the sun disappeared. He had nothing important in his life now. Nothing seemed important except one thing. He would find out how the justice system had failed her. He had stayed in the background during her trial and all. Betty knew his temper when it came to her. She had seen him whip bullies who had harmed or scared her. She didn't want him involved in the mess around her.   Veins left with the resolution to investigate this travesty and whoever was responsible would answer to him.

Veins, a graduate of DeVry Institute in Electrical engineering, stands 6'2", weighs in at around 210-220 pounds with a   sturdy build and   light brown hair.   But the most remarkable feature is his Coke bottle glasses. The lenses are so thick they resemble the bottoms of those green Coke bottles. He has never had a problem with the law, not even a traffic ticket. He makes an excellent salary, lives comfortably and is never in a hurry to get someplace. He's been dating the same girl for three years now and they're quite comfortable with the way things are.

So, when he decided to begin an investigation, he really didn't know where to start.   He knew of only one place to start, and that was the court file. Maybe a clue resides in Betty's file, he thought. He is shuffled around from clerk to clerk, and then informed that he could look at the file in the office only, but he would need a case number to get the file. When he said he didn't have it, the clerk quickly charged him five bucks to look it up in 30 seconds.

When he received the file and walked the few steps to the table provided for such research, Veins really didn't know what he was looking for. He began with the complaint, then the Indictment and the Motions.

He could not understand how the prosecutors even charged Betty with exterminating that vermin. The complaint gave him no clues, with its "without lawful justification did cause the death of Christopher Cavanaugh." The Indictment was even vaguer, but restated the same crap as the Complaint. The Motions were worthless legal jargon to him. However, Betty had immediately appealed her conviction and sentence, so transcripts had been typed and were in the file. Hundreds of pages of transcripts.

Veins bought coffee from the machine in the hallway, its flavor like acid reflux, but soothing nevertheless, and settled down to read. He read every word. He made fastidious notes on events and the players of the drama that took his sister from him. One could actually see the emotions flow through him. He reddened with rage while reading what the State's stipulated facts, as having happened to Betty. He wept when he read the physician's testimony about his examinations of her afterward. He clenched his fists when he read about

Cavanaugh's history as a serial rapist and how no one had stopped him.

As the Clerk's office was preparing to close for the day, they asked him to return the file. When Veins closed up the last folder, he heard a slight tearing noise and two sheets of computer paper flittered to the floor. He was embarrassed at first for damaging the file, but when he retrieved them off the floor, he looked at them closely. There were no other pages like that in the file and he was curious. What he read was the list of jurors, their addresses, along with "age, sex, race" in neat columns. Perhaps these were the people to ask? Then again, the way this document fell out and nothing else could be a sign from Betty. They used to remark about how they knew how the other felt or what the other was thinking. Betty must want him to have this list. Veins placed it into his open briefcase, closed the lid, returned the file and left with his booty. He could hardly wait to study this list. He even opened his briefcase in the cab, just to make sure it was in there. It was!

When Veins got back to his Madison Avenue apartment, he changed into his sweats, got a Mountain Dew from the frig and sat down in his living room to study this list that Betty wanted him to have.

Betty was more than family, she was his best friend. Ever since she had arrived at their house, she had filled their home and lives with young girl charm and zest for life. She was always worried about what people thought of her. She dressed neatly, never a tomboy type. She had tried hard to make a good impression on everyone she met. Naturally, she had people she had disliked. Everyone does. Like the snooty bitch next door to his folks, whom he didn't like, either. She would complain to their parents every time one of them parked in front of her house. She felt that the space was earmarked for her use only. But, Betty didn't hate. She didn't have the psychological constitution for it. To get her to do what she had done, took a lot. She really must have been in pain. Now, he was in pain.

Chapter 19

Foreman was apprehensive about today's meeting with Veins. He wasn't sure how Veins would react to being confronted with these revelations. He sat in the "glasshouse," as he called it, because the room had no concrete or block walls, just thick glass on all sides. It felt like an aquarium. He knew that it was for security reasons and that cameras outside the room permitted constant surveillance.

When the two guards escorting Veins, who was always wrapped in chains and manacles, opened the door, Veins noticed the stack of file folders on the table. They were in bright colors of blue, orange, red, yellow and even some fluorescent ones. There were a dozen of them and the show was about to begin.

"Good Morning," Veins said as he seated himself and waited for the guards to leave.

Foreman placed a Mountain Dew in front of Veins, with a straw in it for him, as his hands were chained at his waist.

"Good Morning. I suppose you're wondering why I'm here. I have a problem when my clients lie to me, Mr. Veins."

Foreman watched for some reaction, but there seldom was any. Veins seemed to be void of emotion, but Foreman was determined to change that today. He opened the top folder, removed a color photo and placed it in front of Veins. It was a picture of a body, or what was left of one.

"Admire your work, Eddie?" Foreman said with obvious venom. "It seems this guy fell off a fucking bridge in Ohio."

He opened the next folder, removed another photo and placed it before him. "Recognize this poor bastard? He seemed to have hooked himself up to a deep-cell battery and forgot about the burning sensation in his ass."

Foreman scattered a few more in front of Eddie, bodies in various death poses, but he got no reaction. Eddie was as stoic as a slab of granite.

"Listen to me you maniac fuck!" foreman shouted, attracting attention from the guards. "They pieced it together, Eddie. It took some time and a lot of luck, but they did it. Mordeci Habush of the *Sun Times* did it, Eddie. People are scared that the story will leak out and they have an offer for you." Eddie, Foreman assumed, was somewhere else, perhaps in a park with Betty or returning to wherever it was to be with her. He wondered what ritual he went through when he did these things.

"Do you hear me? They KNOW you killed that jury. You have made the record books, you asshole. How you managed to avoid being caught or why there's no physical evidence, is a mystery, but they have an offer to save your life. I have met with Mr. Habush, who has all the evidence, the link to these cases. He has only printed in the paper, that one of

Illinois' convicted murderers has been linked to other murders. He has not identified you or your motive. He's scared, Eddie. He knows the panic it would cause and the embarrassment to law enforcement across the whole country. His Editor doesn't know what to do with the greatest news story of his career."

Foreman began to calm down, but made it clear that he was genuinely pissed.

"I've met with Benedict Ori, both as the arresting officer and on behalf of C.P.D. and they are scared, too."

Foreman removed a folder from his briefcase, a manila one this time and placed it before Eddie. "This is your cab fare to live, Eddie." Foreman saw Eddie begin to read the document inside.

"I have been in practice a long time and I never thought I'd see or be part of anything like this. Before you is the 'Petition for Executive Clemency,' which the Governor is willing to endorse, with certain restrictions, as follows:

1) You will meet with the law enforcement people from every jurisdiction where those murders occurred and explain how and why you committed those murders;

2) You will agree to those statements being placed under a seal with the U.S. Attorney, as part of a grand jury investigation, as some of these murders crossed state lines;

3) You will never be indicted there or in any other jurisdiction as you'll be given transactional immunity by all jurisdictions and the U.S. Attorney;

4) You will meet with the Governor's counsel on clemency and explain this to him or her, in the form of a 'proffer,' once again, under the terms and conditions of immunity;

5) In return for the above, after these agencies verify to their respective satisfaction that you are the murderer in those cases, the Governor will commute your sentence to "Life," which means, Life in prison without parole;

6) You will be moved to a federal prison in Marion, Illinois, where you will live out your days.

7) You will not be permitted to meet with anyone other than your parents, who are aware of none of this. However, be warned that if you disclose any of this to them and they leak the story, they will have problems and you don't want that. That's why you've never told them thus far."

Foreman had seen the look in Eddie's eyes before, kind of like a wolf glaring at prey - trapped, but not humbled, with nowhere to run. There it was, in Eddie's eyes, right then. Foreman could see the inhumanity this man was capable of when he looked like this. The people in these pictures must have seen this look before they died.

Foreman had never talked to his client like this, but then again, his client had never told him he was a mass murderer, either. Had Foreman known this, he could have paraded a dozen psychologists before that jury, which would have cast a dark cloud over the trial and sentencing. Eddie would have been found insane, never to see the inside of a prison, much less death row.

After what seemed an eternity, Veins spoke.

"I will think about this and let you know." That's all the bastard had to say, before he got up and walked to the doors for his trip back to the land of the living dead. Foreman remembered the saying, "Dead Man Walking," and he felt sorry for this guy, Eddie, in a peculiar sort of way, as he felt that Eddie was already dead. The man once known as Eddie Veins died the same day his sister did. The State was only going to stop his heartbeat! Imagine the irony of killing a dead man, Foreman said to himself.

Chapter 20

Willis Houston, a veteran over-the-road driver, called his rig "Proud Lady." She was a real beauty. A Kenworth, T-600, with a 90" Aerodyne sleeper with all the amenities of a home, pulled a Great Dane, Dry Van, 50' long, all aluminum built. It was polished to a mirror-like finish and was chrome plated. In contrast, Proud Lady was gloss black, the epoxy paint looked like black glass. It was definitely an owner/operator rig, as companies did not waste money on aluminum wheels, polished fuel tanks and chromed stacks.

It was about 2:00 A.M. on a stretch of highway somewhere in Ohio and he was narrowly within D.O.T. restrictions on the hours a driver could operate without resting. He didn't have much further to go though, and he could drop the load of gadgets from Texas Instruments and get some sleep. On the radio, Garth Brooks was moaning about friends in low places, as he approached an overpass which had a sign reading 13'6" clearance. He was looking forward to getting home. That was the last moment of sanity he had for several hours. He was going to be late getting home. Days late, as it turned out.

As the Proud Lady roared along at 75 mph on cruise control, something smashed into the Lady's hood, tearing off the KW emblem and crashing through the passenger's side of the windshield. In a nanosecond, Will was splattered with blood, glass, and warm, wet tissue of some sort. He saw what he believed was a face, a ruptured eyeball and torn cheek. Whatever it was, it now rested on the queenside bunk behind him and he dared not look. Instead, he fought to control both his rig and his bowels. Trying to stop abruptly from 75 mph, hauling sixty-thousand pounds in a 50 foot shoebox that had a tendency to try to pass the truck which pulled it, calls for total concentration. Even veterans ended up jackknifed in ditches and he was determined to retain his immaculate driving record and not let that happen to him.

He had seen fellow truckers die from such accidents and he could not panic now, but he had already stabbed the brakes on his tractor when the apparition flew past him. He cursed his amateurish response, now reaching for his trailer brakes instead, to recover control of the rig. The sudden jerk on the trailer righted it, directly behind the Kenworth, as it should be, and he began easing his rig towards the right shoulder of the highway.

Once stopped, he focused on his heart rate and breathing. He had no immediate desire to look behind him. Instead, he opened his door, shut down the Lady's engine, turned on his emergency flashers and slowly climbed down. He was thankful for the crisp air awaiting him and breathed deeply. Then Will removed the bandana from his back pocket and started to wipe the gore from his face. He noticed wet, snail like globs on his western shirt and jeans. He'd have to change, but first, he dialed 911 on his cell phone and told the dispatcher he was on the Interstate and parked directly in front of Mile Marker 173.

Will pulled his duffle bag from the roadside compartment, removing a sweatshirt and fresh jeans. He knew it wouldn't take long for the State Patrol guys to get there. He walked to the blind side of the rig and quickly changed his jeans in the dark, when cars weren't around. By the time he pulled the sweatshirt over his head and dropped the bloody clothes in a heap at the rear of the trailer, he heard the wail of the first squad car heading his way.

The accident investigator for the Ohio Highway Patrol that night was a 17 year veteran named Demetrius Bradley, "Meech" to everyone around him, who arrived about 20 minutes later. He was met by Corporal Marty Hinson, six years on the job, who started to fill him in on what they had.

"Meech, we've got a flyer. He's white, mid-30's, was about 5'10" or so the M.E. claims, but right now he's road pizza in the sleeper of this rig. No tattoos that we can see, black hair, a scruffy beard like they wear today and used to weigh 160-175 pounds. No identification, wallet or money. The driver of this rig, a Willis Houston from Fort Worth, Texas, was driving along when he crashed through the windshield. Wham!"

"Anyone check out the overpass and several miles on each side?" Meech asked.

"Already done. No abandoned vehicles on any access roads or feeders to this area. I've got guys going from house to house now, seeing if anyone is missing who matches the description. So far, nada."

Meech walked toward the Medical Examiner and Forensics vans, parked beside the Kenworth. Camera flashes were going off and then the steady lights for a video cam as the M.E. documented the condition of the "body," which resembled raw hamburger more than human life. When he reached the open door on the passenger's side, one of the Forensic guys was climbing out of the rig.

"Jesus, Meech, the guy's in fuckin' pieces." Meech waited for the Medical Examiner to finish up and climb outside.

"Whatta we got, Doc?"

"Meech, how are you? God, it's been a long time. What's it been, 6 hours? You're on overtime with this one."

"Great, I can use the money to rent that Mercedes you drive."

"Huh, my truck is so old the junk man follows me around." The M.E. had always dreamed of having a Benz. "Well, our guy comes through the windshield, where his head was all but severed, spilling brain parts all over the place, one eyeball and a cloud of blood and spinal fluid. Most of that ended up all over that poor bastard standing over there. The torso continued past him, impacting the rear of the sleeper, where he deposits organs, urine and feces. It's too early to confirm foul play, but I suggest you notify Homicide."

Meech would like nothing more than to get rid of this case, but before he called Homicide, who are too busy as it is, he had a protocol to follow. Since the M.E. couldn't confirm it, he had to find out how this guy ended up where he was.

"Marty, I want that overpass blocked and taped off. Until further notice, it's crime scene. Also, I want this stretch closed off. Divert traffic to the frontage road from that interchange a mile back and block the entrances here. Spectators will remain no closer than the frontage roads. Tape it off from 100 feet before the overpass, all the way to here. Until further notice, this rig is mine! Inform the driver he'll have the option of waiting for Forensics to clean it or he can go home and we'll call him. We can release the trailer after Forensics 'walks it' for evidence. Make arrangements to tow this thing to our secure shop. Keep a chain of custody on it and the clothes the trucker dude was wearing. OK?"

Marty Hinson now accepted that this was not an accident investigation, but being treated as a crime scene. "You got it, Meech." Marty got on his portable radio giving orders to his guys as Meech wanted, walked to his own squad and removed rolls of "Crime Scene" tape from its trunk. "Shit, I hope we have enough of this tape to surround the mile he was told to secure," he mumbled to himself.

Meech looked at the mess inside the Kenworth and decided to look at the overpass, instead. Either the flyer jumped in front of this rig or he had help. "At Daybreak, Marty, I want your guys to search the ditches and grassy areas around that overpass and on the highway from there to here," Meech said into his radio.

"10-4," Marty replied.

"Meech, what's your 20?" Marty called on the radio.

"On the overpass."

When Marty arrived, he showed Meech a copy of a note left at a "weigh station" heading towards Indiana. The original of the note was now resting in an evidence envelope, after learning of the scene here. Meech looked at it.

"MUNDSCHAU COULDN'T LIVE WITH HIMSELF FOR WHAT HE DID TO MY SISTER."

"Guy walked into the weigh station and handed it to one of the contract guys we have there. Said he found it on the road where an accident took place. Meaning here. No description. The guys said he looked like any other trucker, including the calfskin gloves. Just handed it to 'em and left."

"I don't suppose they bothered with a license number or description of what he was driving?"

The look on Marty's face gave Meech the answer to that question. "Call Homicide and shag their asses out there."

"Marty, get Forensics up here, dust the rails on both sides, set up emergency flood lights up here and see if VICAP or

NCIC has anything on that name, "Moonchow" or whatever it is, OK?"

"10-4."

Meech wondered what kind of pervert this "Moonchow" was and what he could have done to some little girl that would get him tossed off an overpass into a 100,000 pound semi. "World's turnin' into shit," he said to himself out loud.

Chapter 21

Ori, the Chief of Homicide at 11th and State, is seldom called to an active crime scene, but the Captain called him personally on this one. There must be something unusual or intriguing.

When Ori arrived at the address on North Lake Drive, there were a dozen squads, blue lights flashing like a disco light show. It was a quaint bungalow styled house on a quiet street and he wondered what type of evil visited, that he would be called in on this. As Ben ducked under the yellow ribbon, he was greeted by an old friend and current Homicide cop from his old district.

"This one is making a statement, Ben. I thought you needed to be a part of it, so I called my Captain, who called yours." Together, they walked to the front door, where an evidence technician finished rolling out white paper on the floor so it could be walked on.

"It's clear to the body, guys, but don't touch it. We're still not done down there."

Ben walked into the kitchen and to the basement door. He noticed the bright lights for the video cam and proceeded downstairs. He was met by a half-dozen grim faces, who looked more at the floor than at him, as if they were ashamed.

When Ben arrived at the epicenter of the officers and techies, he saw what shocked them all. Hanging before him was the most ghastly sight he'd ever seen. A woman's body hung and nailed. She was skinned for God's sake. Her breasts remained but the genitalia were missing. So was her skin! Her face remained, but there was some rag or towel over her eyes. The techies were kneeling on the floor, taking samples of blood on long Q-tips and placing them in clear, plastic tubes. One of the detectives handed him a clear evidence bag. Inside was a note, which read, "HOW DO YOU LIKE LADY JUSTICE NOW?"

"What the hell was that supposed to mean?" Ben thought. Then he saw Tommy Dorf, the M.E. "Tommy, how are you?" Ben said, extending his hand.

"Ben, I heard you were coming here. I'm glad of that. We've got a mean one, who makes a statement in killing. Our guy knows his way around the human anatomy. He skinned her from the neck down, as you can see, leaving the breasts, but brutally removing her vagina. He bled her out, Ben. And, he hung her. The nails through the hands are at post-mortem, so she was too far gone to realize it. I'll do the autopsy myself."

Tommy went outside for a smoke and to wait for Ben, now the ranking officer at the scene, to release the corpse. A hearse stood quietly by, waiting to take it downtown.

"Ben, we've got the victim's daughter over at District. She's pretty shook up. We have the Crisis people with her now. She found her mother like this, Ben."

"Jesus H. Christ," Ben responded. He often wondered what the "H" stood for when he and others used that phrase. "When the techies are done, release the body to Tommy."

When Ben arrived at the District where the daughter was meeting with the Crisis Intervention people, he saw this young girl, Melissa Kilponen, wrapped in a blanket, rocking in a non-rocking chair. Ben asked if he could join them and the rocking girl nodded emphatically.

"Hi, my name's Benedict Ori. I'm Chief of Homicide downtown. I know you've been through hell tonight, but I need to ask you some questions. Can you help us?"

With tears running down her pretty face, she nodded again, only more guarded this time, as though she had to think about it.

"Melissa, is it?" Ben watched and she nodded again. "Melissa, do you have any idea why someone would do this to your Mother?"

"No, she was a good person. It must have been him."

"Who is *him*, Melissa?" Ben inquired.

"That sonofabitch that grabbed me two months ago. I filed a report but haven't heard anything. I gave all the information to one of your people out there," as she pointed to the Detective Bureau deputies.

"Besides, Mom liked everyone and everyone liked her," Melissa responded.

"Did someone get your statement, Melissa?" Ben asked while rising.

"Yes, the same guy out there," Melissa said before returning to rocking.

To the Crisis worker, he asked, "Is she OK or should we get her to the hospital?" The Crisis woman advised Ben that she had already called for an ambulance because she was afraid Melissa would go into shock.

Ben found the detective who had Melissa's statement and the prior incident information. "What's with this other case she tells me about?"

The detective responded, "Sir, I found the report in District 5. The detective there tells me that Melissa was abducted two months ago and released unharmed, except for some inhalants used on her. They have a lead they're trying to work, but they're swamped with cases right now and doing their best."

"What kind of lead?"

"It appears that they have a cleaning form used by car rental companies. They're trying to find the company office, but they're shorthanded." Ben walked to the nearest desk, picked up the phone and dialed District 5. "Give me the Captain, please. This is Benedict Ori, Homicide."

When their Captain came on the line, Ben told him that he was authorizing him to expend whatever man hours were necessary to find the office that the cleaning form originated from. "Captain, as Chief of Homicide, I can authorize these things. I can also send you help. That form has just become the primary lead in a particularly gruesome murder. I want that office name and address as soon as possible." That said, Ben next called his own boss and was assured that he would receive all the support he needed.

By the time Ben had finished, Melissa was on her way to the hospital and he had copies of all the preliminary reports thus far in this case and even some photographs. He went home to his family and told them he loved them.

The next day brought Ben some excitement. He got into a shouting match with the District 5 Administrative Captain, actually coming nose-to-nose with him. It started when the Captain called Ben into his office and asked him when he took over command of District 5.

"This is my command, Ori. You don't give orders to my men. You ask me for help on a case, not walk into 5, like you're George Fuckin' Patton. Do you understand that or are you deaf as well as stupid?"

Ori seldom lost his temper, but when he did, it was nothing nice and would shock truckers getting drunk at the "Titty Twister Saloon."

"Listen, you dago cocksucker! The next time you get into my face and disrespect me like I hear you do to these men, I'll tear your fucking heart out and eat it while it still beats. I am NOT one of your soldiers. I wouldn't stay around a piece of shit like you. But, hear this, asshole; the Chief of Police has personally authorized me to use whatever means I deem appropriate to solve a murder. If you have the balls, call him and tell him you run the show. Do you hear me, prick?"

Yup, nothing' nice. Ben grew up in this city. He has a mild demeanor, until pushed.

The extra men Ben had ordered punished the streets for solid leads on the rental company. It took two days before they got a break. Not only did the overworked detectives find the office that issued the form, but the exact author, who was standing before them at the desk.

In forty minutes Ben strode into the office, where he was introduced to a pimple-faced kid with about a pound of metal protruding from his body parts. He had orange and blue hair, for Christsake, which formed colorful spikes. He was in his 20's and was certainly a drug user. Just his luck, Ben thought.

"Young man, my name is Benedict Ori, Chief of Homicide," he said while he opened his badge case, which held a gold star and his ID card, with his picture. "I'd like to ask you a few questions about this form you use for cleaning inspections. But, first I have to ask you if you're on anything right now."

"Well, let's see. I'm on this chair, which is on the floor, which is on this fucking Earth. How's that?"

"Are you on drugs right now?" Ben asked in a perturbed manner.

"Yeah, I'm floating right now on the high I got when your daughter gave me a blojob! I'm tired of assholes like you who take one look at me and assume I must use something."

Ben was seething with anger over the comment about his daughter, but willed his hands to stay put and not throttle this punk kid.

"What's your name? Let me see some ID." The kid produced his Illinois Drivers license.

"Jonathon McCormack, age 21. This address still current?"

"Yeah, if you want to send me a ticket, it'll reach me," McCormack said with a spirited gleam in his eye.

"Listen, freak, we can discuss this here or downtown at my office. I ask the questions and you answer. Anything other than that and your ass goes into a wagon downtown. OK?"

McCormack looked at Ori, a wry smile crossed his face and he responded, "You listen. In **Terry versus Ohio**, it says you can ask me to identify myself and pat search me for weapons. That's called a 'police/citizen encounter.' Now, as I understand it, I'm not a suspect or under arrest, so don't threaten me. You have three choices now, you big sonofabitch. You can talk to me like a citizen who pays your salary, you can leave to get a <u>deuces tecum</u> subpoena, or you can arrest me and my father, who is a senior partner at a prominent law firm and will sue you and your employer."

Ben knew the kid was right. He had no legal right to take this kid anywhere. He couldn't force him to talk to him. And, the little bastard was accurate about the law. Damn kid's smart. Ben had to take another approach, as the other officers waited for Ben to snatch him from behind that counter and drag him off. But that was the old way, Ben knew. Now, the Chicago Police Department wanted a softer public image.

"Listen, killer, I am trying to find out who butchered a woman and crucified her. I am in no mood to joust with you. Either cooperate with me, or step outside, as I am seizing this place as a crime scene. And when your boss gets here, I'll tell him that because of your smart mouth, I'm getting a search warrant and will take all of his files. I don't think he'd like that. Your call."

Jonathan didn't want to lose this gig. "What do you want? I told those two morons that it's our form and it's my handwriting. Now what?"

Ben was calmer now. "Is there a way to match this form with any particular car, genius?"

"Yeah," was all Jonathan said, and then waited.

"Listen, dickhead, while we're here playing this little game, some guy is killing women. Perhaps he's with your mother right now and is slicing her up in your basement. Now, are you done?"

"The bar code, Columbo. I need to scan the bar code for the file number."

With a simple swipe of a red-eyed gadget, a file came out of the "active" file cabinet. This meant that the rental was still out. It was a corporate rental and with the file in hand, Ben left for their company headquarters. In the car, he radioed for uniform patrols to drive through the company's lot to see if the blue Crown Victoria was there and gave the license number, so all units could locate this vehicle. And so it began, the chase to find the man who abducted Melissa Kilponen. They now had the list of names of employees who had access to that car, their photos from drivers' records and spread them out on the table for Melissa. She identified Mr. Edward Veins as her abductor, but that was not murder. He had to link Mr. Veins to Melissa's mother. Ben was not Chief of Homicide because he looked cute. He got there because he was smart. He knew that by using a search warrant which he could easily obtain now in Melissa's case, searching for evidence of another crime at the same time is called "pretextual" and is unconstitutional. He needed advice.

Due to the nature of the crime, Ben was ushered into Christian Schroeder's office, a steaming mug of coffee in hand. When Schroeder got off a phone call, Ben explained the situation.

"Ben, I'll draft the Arrest and Search warrants myself. You can pick them up in two hours. Now listen closely, Ben. At no time are you to tell your guys doing the search, that we really want this guy for murder. If Veins' attorney ever learns of our discussion or that you used this search as a pretext to look for evidence of another crime, we're in deep shit. The Warrant will include the statement 'and other evidence related to this offense,' which means your guys should keep their eyes open. Use your best men, ones who know evidence when they see it."

Ben understood what Schroeder meant. They were going in, looking for evidence of a murder on a search warrant for another offense, because they had no probable cause to get a warrant on a murder case. That is a classical, textbook example of a pretextual search.

All Ben could say was, "I'll tell them to be careful."

The tactical briefing took place at 4:30 p.m. at the downtown building. Ben decided he wanted twenty men on the assault on Veins' house. This is far more than customary, but he couldn't tell his men that the man they sought was probably a murderer.

"Listen up everyone. All of you have been briefed on where and how this house will be breached. No one goes in until I say. We have no 'intel' on weapons he may have, so we assume he's armed. This is a felony arrest. Use of lethal force is authorized to prevent escape." The SWAT team leader then read off groups of names that were teams and had specific assignments to perform. Ben sat in back and listened. He had briefed the leader on the arrest and search. He told him that he wanted his most experienced people on the takedown and that Veins was a suspect in a murder. The team leader embellished the assignment during the briefing when he said, "Also, you are to keep your eyes open for evidence that this guy was a perp in a murder. Ben spit coffee all over his slacks and the floor at that comment. Christ, he hoped no one ever repeated that statement to anyone.

After they watched Veins enter his kitchen, stirring something in a saucepan, SWAT hit the front and rear doors simultaneously, and breached two bedrooms through their windows, to prevent Veins from reaching any weapons. Veins made no attempt to resist whatsoever and was tackled by three men wearing the typical SWAT garb and designed to menace the opponent. Eddie was not scared. He almost expected this, after releasing the only eyewitness alive, but he had no cause to harm that girl. He did wonder how they got onto him, though.

"Mr. Veins, you are under arrest. You have the right to remain silent…blah, blah, blah…"

"I want an attorney," was all Eddie said and was whisked away to the District.

The rest of the team removed their helmets and put away their rifles and heavy vests, when the house was cleared. Now came the tedious part of locating, handling, tagging and bagging in the "Evidence" bags with their initials on the seals, along with an itemized inventory of every item seized.

They fanned out in pairs now, each wearing latex gloves, looking into drawers, closets, cabinets, wherever items could be easily stashed. Then, the Crime Scene guys arrived with blue flashlights, bottles of spray and more gizmos than an episode of Star Trek.

Someone found a chrome straight razor, which seemed odd, since there was an electric razor and no shave cream. It was bagged and tagged.

There were leather driving gloves, a box of latex gloves, nylon rope in the garage, that infamous gray cloth tape called "duct tape" because HVAC people used it to patch holes or to cover seams. And, they found an array of kitchen knives and other household items customarily present in the average American family's home, or that of a serial killer. Boxes of items were carted to a waiting cube van, all properly inventoried and tagged. As it turned out, it was this excessiveness in grabbing anything that might link their suspect to another crime that got them into constitutional hot water, before trial.

Once the boxes were transported, evidence techs sifted through each item to ferret out the non-evidentiary items. For instance, some moron even took the suspect's toothpaste and a box of Trojan Ultra Thin condoms. Ben wasn't interested in anything other than the chrome razor, and met with the Forensic Chief, Ed Rangus.

"Ed, tell me good news about that razor we found at the Veins place, will ya?"

The Chief pulled a freshly typed report from his desk drawer and handed it to Ben.

"Can you reduce all this to English for me, Ed? I'm a little short on time here. My suspect has a bail hearing in the morning and could walk."

"Ben," Rangus began, "I disassembled that razor. I took the blade apart from its support spine, even. I think the removable blade is new. No traces or anything else. Peculiar about the razor's body, though. Not only was it wiped clean, like it was polished, we found trace elements of bleach. He must have cleaned it with it.

"Why would he use bleach?" Ben asked.

"Come on, Ben, we've been doing this shit a long time. If a perp has blood he wants to clean up and leave no DNA behind, he uses bleach."

Ben remembered in an instant now. He had a perp once who cleaned up his kitchen floor with bleach, after he wacked his 'ol lady over a burnt pot roast. Odd way to clean a razor. Most people would use alcohol. Someone was extra careful with this razor and that fascinated Ben. Ben's next step was the M.E.'S office and Tommy Dorf.

"Mornin' Tom. I came by to see if you've looked at the razor Ed Rangus sent over?"

"Yeah, Ben, I was looking at it this morning. I presume you want to know if it's consistent with the cuts and such on that poor woman. Well, the answer is yes, but I can't say this is *the* weapon, but it's got the length of blade and rigidity to produce the flat slices of flesh and muscle inflicted on her. Whatever was used, it's very much like this, if not it."

"Thanks, Tommy." Ben had hoped for a positive match on DNA or blood, but he realized that Veins was no ordinary killer. Ben had been reading his resume, which was among the papers seized from Veins' desk. Very impressive. The guy worked hard. He graduated from DeVry in the top 5% and was immediately snatched up by a prestigious architectural firm that designed fancy homes and skyscrapers. Veins made at least three times Ben's salary and lived modestly in a Madison Avenue apartment which was Ben's monthly salary for rent. This was no ordinary killer and Ben doubted if they'd ever have solid evidence on this guy.

Ben contemplated Eddie's style, his intelligence, and asked himself if he were Eddie, how would he do this? As smart as Eddie is, he planned carefully. He would be extremely cautious, after making a mistake the first time. So, what was his plan? He must have watched the house. By car, maybe? Ben made a mental note to have the patrol logs checked around the Kilponen house for the last two months. Maybe there was a suspicious man, car or parking citation which could link Eddie to the murder?

Ben picked up the phone on his desk and called the forensics lab, and asked for Ed Rangus. "Ed, I want Veins clothes gone over closely. I don't think you'll find blood, but look for anything unusual, OK?" Ed agreed and hung up.

"People, listen up," Ben shouted over the din in his squad room. "I want any receipt or other documentation we have which places Veins near the scene of the murder. This guy is smart and won't miss much. Any questions?"

"Chief," a junior grade detective responded. "I checked that Crown Vic we impounded. Veins did not have it the entire week of this murder. Anything else?"

"Of course not. Veins would not keep driving the same car to these things," Ben thought but didn't say. Instead, he said, "Check the company records where he works. See if he had another one of their rental cars. I want the license number, color, make and present location of that car. I want someone to check out when Veins was or was not at work, where he should have been and where he was. If he was supposed to be on a job site and wasn't, I want to know about it." Circumstantial evidence has been used to convict many murderers. Ben wanted to add Veins to that list.

Ben's people obtained the list of rented vehicles from Eddie's company and checked the schedule of car assignments. They had a rotation which corresponded to projects under construction, where their employees would be on the job site to assure quality of the project, work and compliances with design and building codes.

It is not uncommon for the city dwellers not to buy personal cars, as they have parking fees, higher insurance and the purchase cost. They found taxis, buses or trains to commute to work. Besides, they could always rent a car for the occasional weekend trip. Therefore, the company Eddie worked for would provide periodic transportation so that the engineers could travel to and from the projects.

Ben now had the list of the company vehicles, and when Veins had possession of what car. "I want a volunteer to go downstairs to Records and do some hi-tech police work." The young, junior-grade, or "greenie," quickly raised his hand to please his Chief.

"Good. I want you to take this list of vehicles and search the parole logs, reports and citations books and see if they come up for the past two months." With that, the youngster hurried to the task.

Ben had some homework for himself, so he left the squad room and headed for the library. Ben needed some information on the victim. He already had the usual, mundane stuff. What he wanted now was the magnet that attracted

Veins to her. He would check the newspaper articles to see if the reporters had ideas.

Ben spent four hours looking at microfiche at the library researching the victim. Page after page. Not one reporter had a clue as to why she was murdered. That was unusual. Reporters worth their weight in rock salt always developed an angle. But not this time. No vices, church-going, cake sales, benefits and she participated in groups. Not one negative thing in her biography.

Next, Ben did a search by name, to see if the library had any other articles about her, besides of her death. There were two articles, actually. One, that she was involved in some rally outside the Criminal Court Building and the other regarding her being active in a group called WAVE, or Women Against Violence,. "That didn't help her much," Ben mumbled to himself.

When Ben returned to headquarters, he met with Ed Rangus again and received more grim news. "Ben, we've been over every inch of clothing. We've brushed them onto linen paper, looking for hair or foreign fibers, where we found common lint, some pet hairs, mostly dog, some tobacco, concrete dust, sawdust and dandruff. No long strands of hair, like a woman's. No blood or unusual chemicals. Sorry. We're doing shoes now. We'll scrape the soles, edges, tongues and laces. We'll match soil samples and the vegetation around the Kilponen residence with what we recover. They all make mistakes, Ben, we just need to find Veins'."

Ben returned to his office where he checked in on the "greenie" to see if he found any useful information on the cars. Damn it. He needed to put Veins there at the Kilponen's home or close by. The new detective had nothing for him. Ben went home for the night, but not before trying to reach an acquaintance of his at the *Tribune*. He left a message.

The next morning, Ben was in an unusually good mood. He and his wife made love and while he showered, she had made him a Denver omelet and wheat toast. He felt optimistic that something significant would come his way soon. It did that morning.

The "greenie," haggard and disheveled, sat at his desk waiting for him, with two file folders and some cold coffee. Ben noticed that the kid was wearing the same clothes from yesterday, which means he pulled an all-nighter.

"Chief, you need to see this. A week before the lady was killed, Veins was using a company car. This time, a silver Crown Vic, like our squad cars. I've matched an accident report to the car, which you should read."

Ben took the folder and sat back in his chair. The report was filed by a teenaged girl who was driving her dad's car when she bumped into this car at a stop light. At first she thought he was a cop because of the car, but when he got out, she was relieved when he failed to ID himself as a cop. The man looked at the damage to his car and told her it was too minor to report and to forget about it. Besides, she'd get into trouble with her folks for the accident and got back in his car and left.

The girl had been taught by her parents to leave the car where it was and always report an accident. The insurance company required one before it would pay the claim.

So, the girl remained and a uniform car appeared on routine patrol, took her statement, which included a description of the car and the driver, along with the license number. It was not uncommon for people to believe the damages to these slight fender-benders were too insignificant to bother with and just leave. So the report was filed, more for the girl's benefit than anything else.

The scene of the accident was one block away from the Kilponen home. When Ben read this, he jumped up and gathered everyone together. Silence fell over the squad room.

"It appears that our youngest member of this squad has just connected Veins to the home, one week before. Here's what I want. I need two of you to find out where Veins was signed out to be at that time. Locate any company documents which reflect where he was supposed to be then. Confiscate them. I want this car impounded immediately and towed here for the techies.

I want two of you to go to the jobsite where he was supposed to be and get their Visitor Log. I want to see if he was there and when. I want someone at the car rental company to see if a claim was filed with their insurance company on the damage. If the damage was reported, I want every form related to it. Then, I want two of you to interview this girl and show her the photo spread of the employees again, like we did this woman's daughter. If she picks Veins' picture, I want her down here immediately for a line-up. This bastard goes to court for bail today and I want some solid evidence that this guy is our perp."

Everyone began grabbing their jackets, notebooks and file folders, running for the doors. Ben turned to the "greenie" and told him, "Thank You," and to go home and rest for a while. "Good job, kid," was all Ben said, but he made a mental note that this kid was going to be a good detective and a dedicated member of their team. Ben would put a letter to that effect in his Personnel File, too. Later.

Ben called his friend at the *Tribune* again and got through this time. He asked her if she would do some homework on the victim and Veins, to see if there was anything newsworthy, other than her getting killed and him arrested, respectfully. She said she'd do it, if she got "the story" if something useful came of it and Ben promised that if she broke the case for him, she'd get exclusive.

Ben called the State's Attorney, Christian Schroeder, advised him of the situation and asked him for more time before Veins' bond hearing. "Mr. Ori, he has been in custody now for over two days. The statute says he must have an initial appearance within 72 hours. He is on the Court call for 1:30 this afternoon. I'll talk to the assistant handling bond court and have them ask for a high, cash bail. However, if he has no prior record like you say, with what we have on him, it'll be tough. He'll probably walk today." Ben was not pleased to hear that, but the law is what it is. He had just over three hours.

Ben needed to be on the streets with his people, doing something besides sitting in his office. He decided to join his team at Veins' employer. He arrived there 20 minutes later and was brought up to speed.

"Chief, we have the records. Veins had that car for almost a month, including the night of the murder. The car was in the lot this morning, so it is enroute to our shop as we speak. When one of the other employees noticed the damage to the rear end of the car, Veins filed a report here that it must have been done in a parking lot or garage. We have the original that he signed. No mention of an accident at a traffic light. Two guys are getting the report from the rental agency and their insurer now. He lied, Chief."

Ben could feel his good fortune. He had Veins lying and close to the victim's home. Now, he needed to know where Veins was supposed to be. He entered the building and asked for Veins' supervisor, which was the Director of

Operations. He was shown to his office, given hot coffee and seated in a huge, wingback chair.

"Mr. Ori, what can I do for you?" The Director asked.

"I need to know if one of your employees signed out of here for a particular job site. Do you keep a Log?"

"Yes sir, we do. Give me the employee's name and the date. I can print out his or her entire activity for the day." Ben gave him the date and Veins' name. It took a minute and Ben had the printout, which he had the Director sign and date.

When Ben returned to his squad car, he radioed a pair of detectives to the job site on the printout. He wanted their Visitor's Log and a statement from the General Contractor as to Veins' visit, the policy on the Visitor's Log and the Log's placement at the security post and the requirement that all visitors must sign in before entry. He wanted the name of the security guard that day, as well. He directed them to gather everything and meet him downtown as soon as possible.

Ben headed back to headquarters. There was a phone message waiting for him from the *Tribune* reporter. "Ben, we have a file on your victim. She was a founder of Women Against Violence, WAVE, and advocated harsher penalties for domestic violence offenders and became an ersatz expert on "female domestic violence." She gave a speech one night and pointed out the cases of female offenders, citing law enforcement statistics showing a trend in violence by women and called the "Battered Woman Syndrome" a crock. She infuriated a number of people and advocacy groups that did not agree with her perceptions.

"Ben, this girl pissed off some people with her attitude and ranting. She gave a talk once to a mob of protestors arguing on behalf of women and the cops were needed to get her out of there."

Ben asked if reporters covered that story and if photographers were there.

"Yes, everybody was there, Ben. It was on the news. Why?"

"When and where was this protest?" Ben asked.

"I'll look for the exact date, but it was in front of a women's shelter on the North Side. It was an angry crowd, Ben. She even pissed off men with crap about how men think with their penises and are subservient to the vagina. Pretty controversial stuff, Ben. Do you think her opinions got her killed?"

"Can you find out if WAVE and the women's shelter had mailing lists for that night?" was all Ben responded.

"I suppose they did. Do you want me to try and find out if I can get copies? Do you think our killer is among them?"

"I don't know. I have to look everywhere, though. Would you try for me?"

"Sure, Ben. I like playing cop," the news hawk lamented. "Am I getting anything for doing all your legwork?"

"You'll have the Department's gratitude and mine as well. An exclusive, if I can."

Ben's next call was to Forensics. He wanted to know about the car towed in and a question about the boxes of documents from Veins' home. "Ed, have you got a silver Crown Vic in your workshop?"

"Got two people on it. What am I looking for, exactly," Rangus said.

"I'm not sure, Ed. Anything that would give me where it's been, if there's blood and DNA from our victim. I'd like that, but I doubt it. I'm not much help, am I?"

"We'll look in the bumpers, fender wells and the brake calipers. I'll send someone to get some soil samples around the home. Anything else, Ben?"

"Yeah, I want someone to look through the documents from Veins' house. I'm looking for a flyer or invitation to women's rights groups or Crisis Intervention groups. Anything along those lines."

"Any particular reason? Is Veins gay or like women's apparel or something?" Rangus said with a raucous laugh.

"Ed, I wish we'd found some spike heels, a bra, panties and a gown at his house. I'm having a bitch of a time trying to figure out why he killed her. I need motive, Ed. Any ideas, call me." Ben hung up. One hour to Veins' bail hearing.

As Ben looked up, the two guys he sent to the construction site walked in. One of them carried some green, cloth bound ledger books. One was marked "Visitors." Ben opened the Log to the day of the auto accident. Veins was not at the site all day. Gotcha, asshole!

Ben now had Veins doing recon on the Kilponen house. Little by little, things were falling into place. The third element to a circumstantial case still eluded him. Motive.

"Chief, how'd you guess about the documents? Veins had some women's rights shit, some crap about us men being extensions of our dicks, some stuff about rape victims and crazy shit from an outfit called WAVE, whatever that is. Why does he have all this stuff, Ben?"

"Listen, Ed, the WAVE stuff. Who is the author?"

"Let me look, Ben." There was a pause on the line and Ben could hear paper rustling.

"Shit, I'm sorry, Ben. I missed it. We're tired down here, buddy, and we missed it. Our victim wrote it!"

Ben nearly dropped the phone. It was an unlikely connection, but a connection nonetheless.

"Ben," State's Attorney said, "Veins' bond is $10,000 dollars. He has to post a grand and he walks. Any luck on this other thing?"

"Sir, I'm close. I need some more time. I know Veins is our killer. If you let him go, he'll flee or go on some killing spree and then shoot himself. You gotta buy us time."

"Mr. Ori, I have no control over how long it takes to process someone out of the county jail. Do I make myself clear?"

"Yes sir, perfectly," and Ben hung up. The State's Attorney had no control, but Ben knew someone who did.

"Sergeant Pollard, please. This is detective Benedict Ori from Homicide."

"Ben, how the hell are ya? I haven't seen you since the Policeman's thing at the Shriners Club. So, to what do I owe this call?"

"Polly, you're going to process a guy named Edward V-E-I-N-S on a 10K bond. I need you to stall as long as possible. Can you do that?"

"Ben, you know how things work around here. I am not responsible for delays of up to 12-14 hours, due to the 12,000 inmates. You tell that to my boss, will ya?"

"Polly, call me before he walks, OK? And thanks. I'll explain later, but it's important." Knowing people is what it's all about.

On his way to Forensics again, Ben was run down by one of his guys. The girl from the accident picked out Veins as the driver of the car she hit. He was handed a copy of the insurance claim which Veins had to sign. Veins claimed "under penalty of perjury" that the damage was done in some parking lot or garage.

"This is Benedict Ori, Homicide. May I talk to Mr. Schroeder, please?" he waited for the receptionist to transfer him.

"Mr. Ori, how can I help you?"

"Sir, I have a felony charge on Edward Veins for fraud and perjury. I need one of your people to do the complaint so I can arrest him."

"Detective," Schroeder responded, "this had better not be bullshit. If you've concocted some cock 'n bull charge, I will have you in front of a Judge. Do you read me? I will have an assistant wait for you to review what you have. If we issue, I expect every piece of what you tell my people, will fit. Also, tomorrow morning, I want you in my office at 8 a.m. sharp. I suggest that you be early, because if you're late, I'll call the Chief of Police." At that, Schroeder hung up the phone and called the Felony Division.

Veins sat in a holding cell, expecting to be released any time, when the staff called him to approach the bars.

"Good morning, Mr. Veins. You are Edward Veins, are you not?" Eddie nodded that he was. "I have a warrant for your arrest here, charging you with fraud, perjury and theft by deception. I'd ask you if you'd like to talk to me, but I think I'd be wasting my time." Ben sauntered away, a smile on his face and the knowledge that Eddie was trying his best to figure out who the hell he was. For Ben, he had bought more time for his people to nail the monster who was only inches from where he had just stood.

The next morning, Ben had a message waiting for him from Ed Rangus. "Call me, urgent."

"Ori here. What's up, Ed?"

"Ben," the Forensic Chief began, "I have a pair of Rockport shoes from Veins' place, with trace residue from a yucca plant. Interested, Ben?"

Ben was wondering where this was leading to. "What's it mean, Ed?"

"People don't generally walk on yucca plants, Ben. They're usually a house plant. So, I got to wondering how this jerk walked on one. I have the photos from the victim's house. Ben, there's a yucca plant under the bedroom window on the north side. I have someone enroute as we speak, to dig it up, bag it and bring it here. Ben, the bastard was there."

Ben was ecstatic. The pieces were falling into place nicely. He had the connection to this WAVE literature. Now, he needed to figure out what pushed Eddie's buttons.

Ben decided to try a long shot and talk to Veins' coworkers. He arrived at the company offices, was given a "visitor's" badge and went upstairs to the area where Eddie's office was located. He began by looking around Veins' office and failed to see anything unusual. That's when the revelation hit him between the eyes. He was looking in the wrong place.

As Ben exited the building, intuition told him that in one of two places, he'd find some tangential point for Veins and the victim's worlds. Once in the car, his dispatcher put him through to the *Tribune* again. He was transferred to an extension and she answered, "Amanda."

"It's Ben. Can you get me addresses for this WAVE outfit and where Mrs. Kilponen gave that little speech of hers?"

"Give me two minutes. Oh, I got mailing lists for both events and your guy Veins wasn't on either list. There were only a few men on the lists, so no surprise. OK, I have the addresses, are you ready?" Ben almost sideswiped a woman in a Chevy Suburban and got the finger as a reward, but both addresses now resided in his notebook. He thanked Amanda, gave her the update that Veins now had a fraud case as well and promised her he'd call her first, if he arrested Veins in the murder.

Ben had four people report to the shelter where the speech took place while he met two more at the WAVE offices on the Northwest side. It was a grungy building, built in the 1930's, given the design and materials. Inside, it was clean and freshly painted in cheerful colors. Posters adorned the walls, calling for reform in women's rights, pro-choice and finally, "Wrap that Rascal" to prevent STD's.

Ben was met by the Director, who explained their mantra, funding resources and how much clout they'd built up over the years.

Ben asked the Director abut C. Melissa Kilponen, as her views were so unusually slanted and often pissed off men.

"Mrs. Kilponen was extremely intelligent. I will admit that her views were 'colorful.' She wrote a small thesis on male roles in violence, which we sent to publications and reporters. One of her flyers, called 'A Penis With Legs' was rather amusing. She believed that men are incapable of using their brains. She told me a story once, where god was talking to man and said, 'I have good news and bad news for you. The good news is that I've given you a brain *and* a penis. The bad news is that I've only given you enough blood to use one at a time.' She had her moments."

"Did you ever receive any 'hate mail' letters from upset men?" Ben watched her smile.

"Which box would you like to start with?"

That's why Ben brought help. He figured they'd received such mail and that they were smart enough to save it. He and his associates settled down to begin sifting through the hordes of mail. He had already told the other team at the shelter, what to look for.

"Chief, there're some nasty letters here. Do you think Veins will just sign his name to one of these?"

Ben thought for a moment. No, Eddie would do nothing of the sort. "I want you to look for an envelope with no return address, with an Oakbrook postmark. Call the others and tell them the same."

They spent two hours sifting through stack after stack of letters. Some of them were real hateful and probably fodder for various federal prosecutions. It always amazed Ben how stupid people would be, to threaten others in writing. Ben was in the last pile before him when he came across a Hallmark card and envelope. No return address, but an Oakbrook postmark and he just stared at it. It was as if there were some ephemeral bond with Veins now. Ben knew that the manifestation of pure evil had set his hand on this card.

Ben pulled on latex gloves and slid the card from its sheath. It was a Smiley Face on the cover. There was no printed message inside, just a written one.

"Lady Justice, we'll meet soon."

Ben bagged and tagged it and told the Director his associates would need her statement on how the cards and letters were received and then stored. Ben even had her initial the "Evidence" seal, so that the defense couldn't argue the chain of custody or the authenticity of the card. Ben shuffled out the door thinking that people watch too many "Dirty Harry" movies and believe cops manufactured the evidence to get convictions. He did not.

Ben radioed headquarters and asked Ed Rangus to stay and to have his handwriting expert there. While enroute, Ben received a call from his team at the shelter. They came across three pieces of mail from Oakbrook. Two had Post Office boxes as a return address, so they grabbed them anyhow.

One was a card with a bright, yellow Happy Face inside the envelope. Inside the card read:

"Kilponen does not understand the law."

No threat, so the shelter people never considered forwarding it to WAVE or the victim. Ben decided to "Code 3" to headquarters and activated his siren and emergency beacon. He had to know if Eddie wrote these cards.

When Ben arrived at the forensics lab, Rangus met him at the door. They dropped the card in front of a woman who has worked handwriting examples for over 15 years. She already had samples of Veins' writing from the documents taken from his home. She removed the card and envelope from the Evidence bag, wearing latex gloves in case there may be fingerprints and took out her magnifying glass.

Meanwhile, Rangus took Ben to another portion of the lab, filled with books on plants and narcotics identification charts. The technician who worked there had left for the day, but had left a report for Ben. The yucca plant which had been brought to him, reportedly from the Kilponen home, emitted the identical isomer in its sap as that from Veins' shoe. In other words, the residue on that shoe came from the exact species of yucca before him.

Also, the techie had documented and photographed where there was a curved indentation into one of the yucca's leaves, which broke the surface of the plant and caused sap to leak. The technician had used the shoe like a French curve from drafting and the outside arc where the residue was on the shoe, matched the indentation perfectly. "This shoe caused this yucca damage and the sap on this shoe came from this plant, ergo, wherever this plant was, the wearer of this shoe had been," Ben reasoned to himself. Veins had been outside the victim's bedroom window.

By the time Ben and Rangus returned to the woman comparing the handwriting, she had already begun her report.

"Using a comparative method, anonymous exemplars were submitted for testing. Sample A is a three page document in cursive. Sample B is a printed card from Hallmark, with one line of cursive, but sufficient for comparative testing. It is my opinion, in my expert capacity, using standard technique and micro-photography for intrinsic and extrinsic evidence of consistencies, that the author of Sample A is also the author of Sample B."

Ben finished reading the report as he rushed from the lab, thanking Rangus and his team for everything.

"Mr. Schroeder, please. This is Benedict Ori again and he's expecting this call. I hope."

"Detective, what have we got Veins for this time? Parking tickets? Adultery? Or maybe public drinking?"

"No sir. Not yet. But we'll forward those suggestions to the respective departments for you. In case you've forgotten, I work in Homicide. I'd like to meet with you right now, as we have solid evidence now. Veins killed Mrs. Kilponen."

Ben ran downstairs to his squad and hit his lights and siren again. It was getting late and Veins could walk out of the county jail at any time. Schroeder had told Ben that Veins was released on his own recognizance in the fraud charge and would be processed out of the jail. What Schroeder didn't know was that a certain sergeant there would remember Veins and be in no rush to release him. Mentally, he thanked Polly for being overworked.

"Go right in, Mr. Ori," the receptionist said as Ben strode into the state attorney's office.

"Mr. Ori, this had better be good. I hope you're not wasting my time."

For the next hour, Ben showed Schroeder and his Felony Division Chief the reports, photos and lab reports. They both made copious notes, some of which related to the evidence, while others were on holes in their case, which needed filling.

"Mr. Ori. I'm a little vague on the motive side of our case." Ben noticed that he used the possessive "our case" now. "Run that by me again."

"Veins," Ben began, "somehow obtained a copy of a speech Mrs. Kilponen wrote, which attacks men as being penile robots. Veins wrote two cards, anonymously. One to WAVE, the other to the women's shelter where Mrs. Kilponen appeared. In the card to WAVE he says 'Lady Justice, we'll meet soon,' which is innocuous in and of itself. However, the note found at the Kilponen home the night she was murdered read, 'How do you like Lady Justice now?' if you will recall."

The two prosecutors scratched busily at their yellow legal pads. "My theory is that Veins was mad at Mrs. Kilponen because of her views and how she approached reforms in the law."

"Ben," Schroeder started, "we have enough for a warrant, but we have lots of work ahead of us. I'll get the warrant ready and we'll get the emergency motions Judge to sign it."

Ben needed a phone now and the state's attorney offered his. "Polly, is Veins still there?"

"He's getting into his street clothes right now. Everything is signed and I was getting ready to call you. What's up?"

"I've got a warrant to serve, but I don't want you saying anything until I get there. I'll be there in about twenty minutes. I'm with the State's attorney now."

"Hey, bring me an Orange Crush from the machine and some Fritos. You owe me that much."

"Polly, I'll buy you dinner and bring the soda and chips. You're a saint. Too bad you haven't got enough staff to cover the work." Ben hung up the phone, laughing out loud.

Ben waited by the receptionist. Schroeder entered and handed Ben the warrant for "Homicide in the First Degree."

"Ben, you guys did well. You let your team know that, huh? I'm sorry if I was a little gruff with you. I'll be writing a letter to your Captain. Thanks." Schroeder extended his hand to Ben and Ben took it reluctantly.

"Mr. Schroeder, I want the death penalty on this case. Is that going to be a problem?" Ben would not let his hand go, until he got an answer.

"If I have an evidentiary problem, Ben, I'll have to plea bargain. I'll file our 'notice,' but you'll have to make sure the case sticks. If there's a problem, he gets life in prison. Understand?"

Ben let go of his hand and said, "There won't be."

"Mr. Veins, we meet again," Ben said.

"Have I got some unpaid tickets or something?" Eddie responded.

"Mr. Veins, I am Chief of Homicide. My name is Benedict Ori. Do you know why I'm here?"

Ben watched Eddie closely, for any sign of a physical response. Nothing. Not even a tick in the corner of his eye, a smile or balled fist. This bastard is cold.

"Should I, de-tec-tive?"

"Does the name Catherine M. Kilponen sound familiar, Eddie?"

"You assume that it does or you wouldn't be here. If that's the case, I guess I need my attorney. Right?"

Ben slid a folded sheet of paper from inside his suit coat and unfolded it ceremoniously. "Mr. Veins, you are under arrest for the murder of Catherine M. Kilponen. Will you talk to me without counsel?" Eddie just shook his head and sat down on the metal bench in the holding cell, holding the warrant in his folded hands. It was almost as if Veins expected it. He seemed at peace somehow.

"Sergeant Pollard, I suggest you process this prisoner and place him in a secure area where he cannot harm himself or others."

The sergeant said, "Yes, sir," in a theatrical manner and even saluted, with a smile.

Eddie was processed back into the jail, dressed in a red jumpsuit, which designates him as a maximum security prisoner and placed in Division One, ABO, where prisoners are confined in solitary cells, under constant watch.

"Amanda," Ben said into the phone in the lobby of the jail, "I just arrested Veins for the murder of Catherine Kilponen and the State's Attorney has indicated to me that he will personally seek the death penalty." He believed in keeping his promises. That night, Ben took his family to dinner and watched the evening news.

Chapter 22

No matter how many times he came to Thames and the "Death Row," Foreman could not overcome the eerie feeling of the place every time. This is where men and women wait years to die. Unlike a nursing home or hospital, these were healthy human beings that had forfeited their right to live. He could not imagine the stress on someone on "the Row" for years, waiting for their walk to die only a few yards away.

Eddie was escorted into the room in chains, as always, where Foreman had an A & W Root Beer waiting for him.

"Eddie, law enforcement from Ohio, Indiana, California and several departments in Illinois are here, along with the FBI, all waiting to hear your decision. Are you going ahead with this deal or not?"

"I will agree to all this, but there are a few conditions. First, I want the deal memorialized in writing, with me holding the original. Two, a federal grand jury subpoena for this agreement. Three, you will be at any meeting with any law enforcement, with a properly executed Proffer Letter with immunity. Four, I want a certified court reporter at these meetings, for transcripts. Last, I want Warden Barnhill at the meetings. He's the agent for the Department of Corrections, so I know I'll get transferred to federal marshals afterward."

Foreman jotted down Eddie's demands furiously and when he finished he thought about the implications of each. Eddie, I don't see a real problem with any of them, except the last. What purpose is served by having the Warden present?"

"Since I've been here, J.D. has treated me like a human being. He's never understood why I'm here. I want him to hear the truth, the reason why I did what I did."

"I'll ask," Foreman said, "but I'm not sure if the Governor wants any witnesses to this. Barnhill is not an attorney, not party to the Proffer Letter and the immunity, so therefore, could run his mouth if he chose to. But, I'll try."

"And after I clear the books on these crimes, these agencies are all going to co-sign this clemency petition to spare my life?"

"That's the deal, Eddie. As long as you agree to never talk about them to anyone."

Eddie knew that once he was transferred to federal custody, he'd be moved to a place called Marion, right there in Illinois. It's a United States Penitentiary, maximum security and has what's called a "Control Unit," where prisoners are confined to their cells 24 hours per day, seven days a week. He would never have a chance to leak the truth, so that part of the bargain was ironclad. Everyone would make certain he kept his end of this agreement.

Chapter 23

Mordeci made an appointment to visit Eddie's parents and arrived promptly, carrying a box, salvaged from copy paper at work. This time, the box held the chronicles of those mortal moments in a dozen people's lives.

"Mr. And Mrs. Veins, thank you for meeting with me. I realize the emotions right now must be reaching a critical point. What I have to tell you is extremely serious or I would not impose upon you at this time. You won't want to hear some of what I have to say, but we may be able to save your son's life. May I sit down?"

"Of course, Mr. Habush," Eddie's father said.

"Mort. Please. It's really Mordeci, but that's too formal. Just Mort is fine."

"Would you like some coffee, tea, a soda?"

"Coffee, please, Mrs. Veins." While Florence was in the kitchen, Mordeci asked Clay if his wife is strong enough to endure the truth about Eddie.

"Mort, my wife and I have been through hell these past years, after his arrest, the trial and sentencing, and now the news that the state intends to kill our only child. You could not possibly have anything more that could harm her."

They waited for Florence to return and Mordeci continued.

"Mr. and Mrs. Veins, in this box I have eleven files on murders. I cannot express my sympathy enough for what you're about to learn. When your daughter Betty committed suicide, we were not the only people who grieved. Over the last six months, I have been working on the greatest news story I've ever had and I pray that it is never written." Mordeci removed the file folders from the box and set them on the table.

"Mrs. Veins, your son was very close to Betty." Mordeci took Florence's weathered hand in his, while Clay watched intently.

"It's a terrible thing to lose a child. Your son, without any doubt whatsoever, cherished Betty. You see these folders? Each of them represents a murder."

"What has this got to do with us?" Florence said.

"Mrs. Veins," Mordeci said as he looked directly into Florence's big brown eyes. "Your son killed every one of them." A thunderbolt coursed through her body like a jolt of high amperage. "Your son loved Betty and since her death, has hunted down each of the jurors and killed them. I'm sorry."

Clay wrapped his arms around his wife and pulled her to him gently. The tear ducts were dry, but the wounded animal sounds that came from his poor woman would have brought a flood of tears if any were there. Mordeci felt really bad for these people.

"Mr. and Mrs. Veins, that was the bad part. Now, let me bring you up to date on the better part. The Governor has agreed to grant clemency and commute your son's sentence to life. Patrick Foreman advises me that your son has agreed to the conditions. My editor endorses the plan and has committed the *Sun Times* to support the commutation. The Chicago Police Department does not object. The state's attorney agrees to clemency. All we needed was your son to approve the agreement and the sentence is changed."

The crying ceased, but it was followed by silence. Mordeci had to wait for some kind of response from these folks, before continuing.

"Everyone understands the loss your brother felt when his sister died. Eddie must meet with all of the law enforcement agents on these cases and tell the truth. He will not be prosecuted in any case. He will be moved to the Federal Bureau of Prisons, to a facility they designate. He will live, folks, but I think he's waiting to discuss all this with you."

Clay looked at Mordeci. "Are you telling us that our son is a serial killer and the state is going to forgive him and let him live?"

"I'll tell you the truth here. The reason for doing this is so the truth never comes out. They don't want anyone to know that they cannot protect jurors and that Eddie did this." Mordeci did not sugarcoat the truth for these people.

"Mr. Habush, for years we believed in our son, that the evidence was circumstantial and that he was innocent. We prayed that one day he would be cleared of this and come home to us. Now you tell us that he is some monster who killed a dozen people. I think you should leave now. And please, don't bother us again." Without ceremony, Clay rose and headed for the front door. "We do not care to see your files, Mr. Habush, or the photographs they probably contain. Take them and go. Your story has brought more pain to our home, when we thought that impossible."

"Mr. Veins, I urge you to talk to your son and advise him to live. If you wish to talk to me, please call me at any time. My home phone number is on the back of this card. Once again, I'm sorry." Mordeci carried his box back to his car and departed. He felt bad for this family and he had done his best to save their son.

Chapter 24

Sergeant Rance Daniels nonchalantly exited the main guardhouse at Stateville Correctional, a maximum security prison in Joliet, where he has worked for over 6 years. The guardhouse is out in front of the forty foot concrete walls, with fixed, turret-like gun towers strategically placed at the corners and at median points along the sides. In all, the walls surround 60 acres, making it one of the largest walled prisons in the country. Stateville has housed some of the most famous criminals in history, including Richard Speck, who murdered eight nurses because of "vaginal envy."

Daniels has seen the worst of the worst. Violence is a way of life at Stateville. Either you hold your own, or you're someone's bitch, getting banged in the ass every day. People in the community could not believe what Daniels saw every day even if he told them, which he didn't do. If asked, he'd say, "I work for the State" and leave it at that. He would change out of his green uniform every day before he left work, as he did not want people to know his employment. He wasn't embarrassed about it. He didn't want the risk. Some punk could think him a cop and shoot at him or some gang member could try to persuade him to bring contraband into the prison.

It was an autumn afternoon. His shift ends at 3:30, but after he changed and got to the front gate, closer to 4 p.m. He said his "good nights" and "stay safes" as he left. He stopped at the Arco gas station on Route 53, heading for Joliet Junior College, where he's working on his Associates Degree in Criminal Justice. While in the Men's Room, on the East side of the station adjoining the parking area, there's a tap at the door.

"Coming. Just washin' my hands." He noticed the doorknob turn and did not protest as it opened. There was a man there who raised his hand with what appeared to be a gun at first. When Daniels realized what it was, two little darts sprung towards him. He felt them bite into his flesh like those scarabs from *Indiana Jones Tomb Raider* flicks, and then everything went bright-white and his legs folded under him. He went down, striking the ceramic tile floor like road kill.

When Daniels came to, he was handcuffed to an overhead metal pipe, which is part of the sprinkler system in the building. He was completely nude. On a chair in front of him sat the man from the Arco station. He was reading Daniels' text book from Criminal Justice.

"I see that you believe in justice, Mr. Daniels. So do I. Criminal justice is mere retribution, don't you think?"

"Who are you?" was all Daniels said.

"My name is unimportant. Call me 'Justice'," Eddie said, as he hugged the textbook to his chest. Daniels could see the thoughts scrolling behind those shark-like eyes and none of them pleasant. "Do you recall Elizabeth Conly? You were on the jury!"

"Yes, I remember. Why?" The cuffs were digging into his flesh from his own bodyweight.

"Did she deserve justice, Mr. Daniels?"

"You a relative of hers?" Daniels asked.

"Her brother, Mr. Daniels, and I must admit that the justice you gave her seems misplaced when you look at what that bastard did to her."

"Listen, whoever the fuck you are. I fought for that girl during deliberations. I argued that she was justified for what he did to her."

Eddie smiled behind that one. "Then why did you vote to convict her?"

"You don't understand. We were tired and the Judge screamed at us for not doing our jobs. There were two of us holding out. When I saw her agree to convict, I gave up, too."

"Where you work, they have the electric chair, don't they?"

"They don't use it any more. Since they said it was cruel and unusual, they went to the needle."

"When Elizabeth died, you were still using the chair, though. Right? That's how justice was carried out?"

Daniels, blood now trickling down his arms from the handcuffs, feared where this was going with his captor. "I don't think justice is ever served by killing."

But Eddie had already decided what to do and began looking around him. They were in the basement of an empty store that once tried to complete with the big three, Wal-Mart, K-Mart and Shop-Ko, and failed. The store had been vacant for some time and the owners would probably celebrate if it was set afire and razed. Not yet, Eddie thought. I have use for it just a little longer.

Foraging around, Eddie found the crude, but effective implements he needed. He was quite familiar with electricity, after all, so he knew what he was after. He found an extension cord, like those used in workshops, with thick, orange insulation. He opened a pocket knife, removed the female end and stripped the wires back one foot on each, then cut the insulation about three feet, separating the wires.

Eddie looked at Daniels and Daniels looked at what rested in Eddie's hand. "Fuck you, man!" Daniels shouted. An animal fear appeared in his expression, as when a feral creature is cornered by a true predator, like a cat. Eddie wrapped one wire several times around Daniels' left ankle, twisting the end around one loop. Then, he wrapped the other around the captive's right wrist.

Eddie realized that he was about to make a human resistor out of this character, using 120 volts and 30 amps. It would take a while for the current to overtake him. It would be a slow and quite painful way to die, but since there were no lights or other electric devices being used, the circuit breakers would not blow out. He took one of Daniels' socks, balled it up and stuffed it into Daniels' mouth, while using the other sock as a gag.

"Mr. Daniels, I've enjoyed your company about as much as I do your concept of justice. Now you can witness mine." At that, Eddie walked to the other side of the basement, about 30 feet, and plugged the cord into the receptacle. Immediately, Daniels started screaming and thrashing, his eyes wide, giving them globe-like dimensions.

Eddie sat back down and watched as the condemned man continued his death throes. He began to print a note. "'JUSTICE IS SERVED."

When Daniels hung limp, urine running on his legs and the acrid smell of burning flesh convinced Eddie that Daniels was with his God, he walked upstairs, pulled the fire alarm box and left. "They're all going to pay, Betty. I promise," Eddie said as he got into his rented car and left. He just knew his sister was proud of him.

Chapter 25

Mordeci was in his office, the Veins trial and sentencing six months past, working a new case of a young man named Robin Gecht. The press had dubbed him "Rockin' Robin" because of his rock-n-roll lifestyle. The State's Attorney was positioning for camera time, while C.P.D. made an "official announcement" that the slasher/mutilator of prostitutes had been arrested and charged.

Someone will write a book about Rockin' Robin someday, Mordeci thought, but not him. He was just gathering the news, although losing his zeal after the Veins case. The vivid photos of that woman, or her remains actually, still haunted him. And the audacity of Veins to write a note about "Lady Justice." The method of execution for such a monster should not be peaceful and painless, but the Constitution protects these creatures even in their last minutes on Earth.

Mordeci had fielded calls about Veins, had given reporters from other media companies outside Chicago and the State, inside information on how the people felt, the cops, the surviving relatives and the persona of Edward Veins. There's always a "share network" or co-operative between professionals, as long as they were not competitors of the *Sun Times*. In rural Illinois, there are farmer oriented dailies, sometimes called "gazettes" or "reporters." These small publications had a niche market and had no incentive to expand.

Rockford, for example, is far enough from "the City," for Mordeci to share information with them. He frequently talked shop with a reporter there by the name of Alfonso Witt, who represented the entire news department of his publication. He relied mainly on the Associated Press, Reuters and CNN for his sources. However, he'd also talk to cops, firemen, prosecutors and even defense attorneys. He would attend functions for various reasons and mingle with guests, always alert for some morsel of newsworthy information.

And so it was one night at a Will County promotion for State Police Awareness Programs, like DARE and Child Abuse Prevention. Witt was talking to a detective named Petty, who had voiced his opinion on what the courts should do to the sonofabitch that slowly cooked an Illinois Department of Corrections sergeant and calling it "Justice." It was the message that got Witt's attention, so he asked the detective if they had figured out what the meaning of the note was or if they had arrested anyone so far.

"Al, we can only speculate that the guy, Rance Daniels, must have done something on his job which motivated it. But he never did anything serious enough to warrant execution. We're looking at violent offenders who were recently released, to see if one of them may be responsible. The guy was fried.

He must have been hooked up to the electricity for an hour before firemen found him. I heard that he was so well done, the Coroner said he was like a piece of chicken, where the meat comes off the bone easily."

Witt had not heard about this case and was wondering why? "Because it's strictly a State Police matter, since he was a State employee."

Witt made a few notes and wrote the contents of the note verbatim, "Justice has been served." He made a mental note to nose around a bit and to see if this meant anything to anyone else.

Mordeci answered his phone. "Habush."

"Mort, Al Witt. How's the news business by you?"

"Fine. Has John Deere changed colors or are your readers racing combines yet?" Mordeci always enjoyed the banter with Witt.

"Naw, Shucks, we're entertained by you city dwellers and your thirst for blood. We slaughter pigs and cattle, while your readers slice and dice each other."

"That's true, unfortunately. So what brings you to my line?"

"Mort, have you ever come across some kook who metes out his brand of justice and leaves a note?"

"Good Christ," Mordeci thought, "I can't get away from this Veins case. Now this hick reporter wants to talk about Lady Justice." Instead, Mordeci said, "Why?"

"I was at this party last night and a State cop mentioned an old file of theirs about some DOC sergeant who was found fried like a piece of KFC and a note, 'Justice is Served,' and I wondered if you've encountered some freak using this same MO?"

Mordeci was stunned for a moment of silence. "Mort?" Witt said.

"Al, give me some specifics and let me check it out. I'll get back to you if anything pans out. OK?" Mordeci made notes of the date, victim and circumstances. He wondered if there was a copycat killer or worse, was Veins innocent? Shit.

Mordeci summoned a couple interns to his lair and gave them their assignments, to research the archives downstairs. Mordeci logged onto the Internet website Lexis/Nexis to see if anyone had reported the Daniels story. The State Police kept a tight lid on it, for sure. On a hunch, he went to the "topic search" and tried "Crime Scene Notes" and hit enter. His screen was full of references and indicated that 167 pages followed. Holy Shit! Mordeci had no idea that notes were so popular. There was no way he could go through all these and wrote a note to his interns. "Log onto L/N, search Crime Scene Notes, review those for references to Lady Justice, Justice Served, or Justice Anything. I want to know if some copycat killer is or was leaving notes at crime scenes. I expect some real reporting here."

Mordeci had a meeting to go to about this Rockin' Robin character, with detectives and the victim's mother. It's always the same routine.

Mordeci was preparing his latest expose' on Rockin' Robin, when the interns magically appeared like Hansel and Gretel at his office. He was handed a sheaf of papers, which somewhat surprised him. "Someone here care to do the Cliff's Notes on this for me?"

"Our search located numerous cases where the word 'Justice' was used in notes at crime scenes. Most of those notes were left at suicides, which we assumed you weren't interested in, but printed out anyhow. Then, we narrowed our search in time, once again assuming you weren't interested in cases from ancient history. Based on the new search parameters, we located about 20 cases. Those are cases on top, with the spring clip on the left corner. Is there anything else you need?"

"Naw, you guys stick around in case I need you or I find screw ups in this homework of yours." Mordeci realized and accepted the ritual of hazing interns, which in this case, would send these two plebes to archives for material that never existed. They'd be hollered at by all the reporters, but in the end, would be welcomed into their flock like lambs. They had spent most of their day sitting in front of a computer, reading 168 entries to find these articles for Mordeci, just like days he spent as a green reporter trying to learn the business.

Of all the 20 cases, Mordeci noticed that most had occurred in Illinois, in various jurisdictions, with one in Sacramento, California, involving a Geoffrey McCloud, who was found, anchored to a "blast wall" behind the business end of a jet engine that was being static tested on a stand. A note was taped to the central panel which read:

"Behold, the Long Arm of Justice."

There was another case of a guy named Stolzenfeld, in Clawson, Michigan, an office worker, who was found in a salt water aquarium, with miniature sharks swimming around him. Someone had put a nail gun to his temple and pulled the trigger, driving a 10 penny nail into his brain. A note taped to the aquarium in his living room said:

"Justice is for Real Sharks."

There was an obscure file from C.P.D. which reflected the discovery of a female architect at a building site. She was suspended upside down, her feet bound to an exposed girder. She was fully clothed in designer jeans and some fancy label on her silk blouse, under a cardigan sweater. She had died from multiple aneurisms in the brain. The vessels, due to the overflow of blood to the brain from being suspended upside down, had ruptured. Although dying instantly once the vessels burst, it took a considerable time being hung like that, for the fatal reaction to occur. It was not a pleasant way to die. A note was suspended from a miniature hangman's noose which read: "Justice is Sometimes Upside Down."

Another file regarded a firefighter's wife who was found in her home, charred. Her name was Ronya Allison, a promiscuous housewife, married to an abusive Battalion Chief, who was the primary suspect, as she was found in their bedroom, taped to the headboard of their marital bed, with dildos protruding from her mouth, vagina and anus. An accelerant was used around and underneath the bed, not on her, sending her to the Valhalla for cheating wives, in a funeral pyre. A note taped to the front door read: "Justice Cannot Be Cheated."

C.P.D. detectives were sure it related to her promiscuity. Either a jilted lover or jealous husband. Her husband had an alibi for that night, founded on the statement of a fellow firefighter who claimed they were getting drunk at his home. C.P.D. always suspected that loyalty, a sort of "espirit de corps" was more probable than truth here.

The files captivated Mordeci so much so that he called his Editor and requested that someone else cover Rockin' Robin and give him two weeks of open schedule. He briefly explained that he had some leads he needed to check out and that if his hunch was remotely accurate, the Sun Times would have the scoop on a serial killer. With Mordeci's tenure and reputation, the Editor had no quarrel in approving his request, with the sole proviso that Mordeci keep him informed.

Mordeci gathered the articles and took them to a scheduled conference room where he wouldn't be bothered.

He began by making notes of the different law enforcement jurisdictions, the lead detectives that were mentioned, made a time-line and pasted those sheets to an unused chalk board which stood in the corner. Thus far, he had McLeod, Stolzenfeld, Krush, Allison, from the notes before him. Then, with a Sharpie he wrote "Kilponen?" on another sheet and taped it with the rest.

He shrugged out of his suit coat, tossed it on a chair, pulled the phone close to him and called the interns for fresh coffee, a stack of legal pads and colored pens. By the time these complimentary items arrived, Mordeci had rolled up his shirt sleeves and immersed himself in the remaining files.

One file was quickly ferreted out when Mordeci read the part about the lengthy letter which mentioned "justice is a venerable opponent" and two pages of pscyho-babble, before some nitwit murdered his neighbor suing him because he had built on the man's property and had lost. "Weirdo," Mordeci said.

Michelle Dittman, age 37, a housewife; husband drives over-the-road. She was found in a lakefront park, bound to a tree in the seated position. The teen lovers that found her thought she was asleep, until they noticed blood had coagulated on the lapels of her Helly Hanson windbreaker. Mordeci could picture this poor soul, the hapless expression on her face, as these kids approached her from the west, towards Lake Michigan. As he finished the article, he could almost feel their shock when the east side of the woman's head contained a carpenter's hammer, claw buried in her brain. There was a note tacked to the tree: "Justice Never Sleeps."

The Evanston P.D. was handling the investigation, but so far, came up empty. Mrs. Dittman was active in a movement to "hammer sex offenders with life sentences," as her letter to the Editor advised, so E.P.D. was concentrating their efforts on locating registered sex offenders and confirming their whereabouts that night. So far, they had a number of suspects who could not provide an alibi for that night. A few were brought in for questioning. One, his probation officer revoked for a curfew violation, because he admitted he was at a "friend's place" all night. So, to extricate himself from being a suspect, he gave himself up on a technical violation of his parole. "Dumb Criminals II."

Mordeci's next file was on a mortgage broker who lived in Winnetka in a two million dollar home with his two children, one boy, and one girl. His wife worked part-time as a florist. Enrique Acevedo, born in Texas to Mexican parents, became an icon in the mortgage business, cultivating investors to finance homes in the "secondary market," where the interest rates were ten points off prime, generating a billion dollars in transactions per year. Creating his financial empire, he had ruined competitors along the golden path. When Winnetka Police discovered Acevedo in his $3,000 wingback chair of burgundy leather, his throat slashed almost to the cervical vertebrae, his eyes gouged out and replaced with $100 bills, they began to search the vast number of civil actions in which he was a party. The note found on his desk read: "Money Cannot Stop Justice."

Mordeci recognized the undeniable fact that these cases were the work of some evil hand. He needed to talk to his Editor, quickly. His first impression is that they have a copycat killer on their hands, but once all the names and dates were posted on the chalkboard, one fact leaped out at him. All of these cases occurred prior to the arrest of Edward Veins. Is it possible that Veins butchered these people or was Veins innocent of the Kilponen murder?

"Here's what I have thus far. I have about 20 files of articles about murders where notes were found with the word 'justice' in them. I have already deleted some because they don't fit the pattern. I'm convinced there's a serial killer, but law enforcement in the cases, do not have the info I do, or at least I don't think so, or we would have seen an 'alert' come our way. Every note left was a one-liner with justice somewhere and related to the style or method of killing. If I go to the different jurisdictions to ask questions, they'll ask me why or what I have. Lexis/Nexis is not considered a confidential source; ergo I would be obliged to disclose everything. That would be the death knell of the scoop.

The Editor decided to allocate two interns to work with Mordeci, full time. He also said that Mordeci was not to breathe a solitary word of this story to anyone other than him. Mordeci was directed to the paper's attorneys, who would file official Freedom of Information/Privacy Act Requests, with every law enforcement agency involved. Mordeci was not to approach any agent or officer about these cases. The files and records would be produced and the interns would pick them up. Mordeci could not discuss, much less print, the most vicious crimes imaginable.

Over the next two weeks, volumes of records, photos and statements began to consume the conference room. Each file now became a box or more often than not, a number of boxes. Word spread between the various departments that the *Sun Times* was collecting files on murders, but the administrators believed it would be no more than a compendium of active cases to showcase evidence.

Before Mordeci could compare, he needed something to compare with. To determine if Veins did or did not commit these offenses required Veins' complete itinerary, bank records, employment records and anything that could reflect the whereabouts of Edwards Veins when these offenses happened. There was only one man who had the materials he sought.

"Good morning. My name is Mordeci Habush with the *Sun Times*. I have an appointment with Benedict Ori."

"One moment, Mr. Habush. The Chief says he'll be right out to get you. Can I get you some coffee or soft drink?" the receptionist beamed.

"Yes, ma'am, coffee, black, please."

A few minutes later, Ben appeared through a side door, handed Mordeci a steaming mug of cowboy-blend coffee and led the way to his office.

"What brings you here, Mort?"

"Ben, I need some materials from one of your investigations. I need documents from the Veins case."

"Mort," Ben stated, "your paper can obtain the court file and file an FOIA Request to our department for the balance."

"Ben, what I'm looking for is probably not in your file. Your case's epicenter was the day and time of the Kilponen murder. I need documents relating to almost five years before that. I need to know where he was at all times during that period of time."

Ben looked deeply into Mordeci's eyes, trying to read the reporter's heart. "Mort, why would you need that much information? Where are you going with this?"

"Ben, I have reason to believe that Veins may not be guilty of Mrs. Kilponen's murder, or he is a serial killer. I need you to trust me that the minute I know which, I will bring you the evidence. I am under direct orders not to divulge any more. I need this stuff to compare to the other cases. Will you trust me?"

"Mort, what you ask of me is highly unusual, if not unprofessional. Before I can agree to give you that information, if we have it, I will need to clear it upstairs. Can you make this request of yours in writing, so I can show my Captain?"

Mort removed an envelope from his inside pocket and handed it to Ben. "Our attorneys anticipated such a request, Ben. I trust that will suffice."

Ben began reading the document, which read much like a FOIA Request, when Mordeci got up and said, "I have taken up too much of your time already. Please call me when you have a decision," and left.

Ben phoned upstairs and ran out of his office to meet with his Captain. If Mordeci Habush says he has something, he is not to be taken lightly. The Captain was going to be rocked by this and the consequences.

When Ben returned from upstairs, he now understood why they made the decisions. Ben had been authorized, no, directed, to cooperate with Mordeci in his Request, with the proviso that he would notify Ben and provide him with the reciprocal disclosure of everything Mordeci possessed, prior to any publication. The Captain explained that it's better to work with Habush and have him as an ally, than to send him off in a disgruntled state and then he kills you in the press.

"Mort, I have a decision, but you may not be happy. I am authorized to comply with your request, but with conditions."

Ben went on to explain the Captain's demands and Mordeci agreed instantly.

"I will have the documents sorted, copied, Bates numbered sequentially and delivered to your office at 8 a.m. You will have to sign a receipt and guarantee that no copies will be made while in your custody," he replied as Ben said good-bye and cradled the phone. He could not stop from wondering what he had said and what his people missed, and how it could blow up in his face. He didn't dare summon his unit together and ask them if Veins could be either a serial killer or innocent. All he could do was to wait for Mordeci and hope that he kept his word.

Mordeci and his interns were waiting for the documents to arrive. They had moved two more chalkboards into their now cramped work area. One board would be used for a "victim," listing the date, time of death, location. The other board would be strictly for Eddie. As a victim's information was posted on the other board, Mordeci would read out information on Veins, such as date, work at office, job site, travel time to/from job site, travel time to victim from home/work and "rental car available?" For example, using Mrs. Kilponen's case the board on Veins would reflect that Eddie had a vehicle, was discovered in the area surveilling, evening kill, travel time from home 40 minutes, no alibi.

Mordeci and his two man crew began to pour over the fresh materials. The crucial item they needed was a copy of

Eddie's itinerary, which the employer had printed out for C.P.D., since Eddie was hired years before the Kilponen case. They had Eddie's phone records for 3 years, bank statements and credit cards for 5 years and his monthly planners for 6 years.

Mordeci and his crew were not cops. All they were doing was to chronologically support a finding that Eddie could have committed these murders. He did not have to prove beyond a reasonable doubt that he did kill them. However, as Veins' "opportunity" on each case grows, one by one, the probability that Veins did the crime and that probability grows at an exponential rate. In layman's terms, if Veins could have killed all twenty people on Mordeci's list, the probability that he did, is in the millions to one. On the reverse, if Eddie was someplace else and the alibi was airtight on just one of the "Justice" killer's spree, the game was over and Eddie was not their man.

Either way, though, Mordeci was a hero. If he shows Veins to be a serial killer, he wins. If he fails to show Veins did these murders, he turns over his findings about the "Justice" killer and the notes to Ben and he's a hero for putting C.P.D. onto a serial killer. Mordeci was in the catbird seat on this one and the Editor realized the potential in either scenario.

Each case file consumed hours and hours of piecemealing historical events back together, into a single layer. Mordeci and his aides worked 10 hour days, six days a week. They drank lakes of coffee, ate stale sandwiches from the deli where Mordeci would buy them on his way in and they'd sit for hours and little by little he had painted a picture of Eddie's whereabouts during eleven "Justice" killer cases. Mordeci had excluded 11 of the 20 original cases, as not fitting the killer's M.O. of one-line notes. One by one, the first chalkboard was filled with the faces of the Justice Killer's victims and in the end, Mordeci was convinced that Veins could have done each and every one of them. Not one case permitted Eddie an alibi, not even the McLeon in Sacremento, California, whose body resembled a Sunsweet prune or raisin, after being given a makeover from a Westinghouse jet engine on a test stand. At that time, Eddie was on vacation, his credit cards showing him at Lake Tahoe, which coincidentally, is only a couple of hours away from Sacremento, by car. Mathematically speaking, Edward Veins is most likely a serial killer and it was time to call Benedict Ori.

"Ben, I think you need to see this. Could you come here, so it's easier to explain?"

"How about is 20 minutes, good enough?" Ben had been waiting for this moment for three tortuous weeks. He was anxious to learn if he and the department would be made to look like fools.

When Ben arrived at the *Sun Times* Building, Mordeci was waiting for him in the lobby and they went directly to the conference room that had become their world for weeks. Upon entering, Ben realized that they would not be alone. Joining Ben and Mordeci was the paper's lead counsel, Mr. William Pitts, the Editor and two young men dressed in grunge.

For the next four hours, totally uninterrupted, except for the interns coming in and out for coffee, soda and food, Ben learned the graphics of Veins' evil. Mordeci was right. The coincidence factor that Veins was available for each of these crimes was nil. For reasons unknown, Eddie had apparently hunted for almost 6 years and no one had even noticed.

"Ben, the *Sun Times* has decided not to print the whole story at this time," Mr. Pitts said in a guarded manner. "We are a public oriented business, true, but we also have a duty to the Chicago Police Department to give them the opportunity to capture the killer, if it isn't Veins."

"Ben, what we plan to do," Mordeci began, "is to print that there appears to be a link between a man on death row and several other murders. We are still missing a vital piece of the puzzle. Why were these people chosen by Mr. Veins?"

"Mort, we will get onto this immediately. Only a few people will know in our department. Because of your exemplary cooperation thus far, when we have the mystery solved, you will be notified."

The meeting broke up and the ride back to headquarters was the longest in Ben's life. The ramifications of Mordeci's revelations were far reaching and ominous.

When Ben arrived back at his office, a message was waiting for him; "See Me!" The Captain's handwriting was quite familiar to him.

"Come in, Ben. Is it as bad as we projected?"

"Yes sir. It appears we have a serial killer and I believe Mr. Habush is correct in his conclusion that it's Veins."

"Shit, Ben!" the Captain shouted, "We are going to be eaten alive in the press. How the hell did we not know about this?"

"Well, sir, that is a question I cannot answer just yet, but I assure you, I will very soon."

Without disclosing the true nature of the investigation, he dispatched his entire squad in different directions to gather evidence in the eleven cases. Ben explained to them that they had been asked for help by other districts and they were to make contact with the head detectives and advise them you are there to help. "Your reports will come to me first and I will forward them. You will not discuss these cases amongst each other. Do I make myself clear on all this, people?" Everyone could see that the Chief was serious and understood that any screw up and they'd be patrolling the city's streets in a Big Wheel with a flashlight.

Ben devised his own board system, only issuing cork and push-pins, but it resembled Mordeci's in substance. As the reports began to flow through him, Ben fleshed out the facts from conjecture. Unlike Mordeci and his team, Ben's people had access to far more data and databases. The holes Mordeci could not fill in were substantially filled by Ben and his squad. In just one week, it was abundantly clear that Veins is their Justice Killer. The killings stopped with Veins' arrest. "Son-of-a-bitch," Ben shouted as he slammed his fist into the desktop. "Why did you kill these people, you bastard?" That attracted the attention of everyone in the squad room. The Chief seldom cursed or raised his voice. When both happened in concert, the Chief was better left alone.

Once again, the "greenie" in Ben's squad, worked overtime on his own. He volunteered for every detail Ben needed. Exhausted, Ben figured a pair of fresh eyes on the documents which filled 8 boxes now, would not hurt. So, the "greenie" loaded up all of them in his SUV and took them home, which was a loft apartment on the Chicago River. He shared the place with his brother, who was a uniform cop on the West Side.

Sunday afternoon, he called Ben at home and asked if Ben could come to his place. It was important. Ben arrived after taking his family to brunch, a ritual in Ben's home, where he found the "greenie" looking like death warmed over. At first Ben had thought it was a hangover, but the "greenie" told him he'd been up for 60 hours now.

"Chief, I found something in several of the reports from our guys and I think we've got something. The reports mention that the victim, a Michelle Dittman, believed sex offenders were treated too leniently. She said that she had served on a jury once and a serial rapist got away with it for years. She believed the streets were not safe from these animals.

Another victim, Kilponen, was upset about being summoned to jury duty and fulfilled her obligation, while watching others avoid it.

One more, a Diane Joswin, mentioned to her husband, the outrage she felt while serving on a jury with a sex offender." Ben saw the pattern now and was thankful that the "greenie" had called him on his day off. He told the kid he did great work, grabbed the list of victims and once again, told him to get some sleep. It seemed like this had become a habit with this kid. A good habit.

Monday morning Ben met with the Clerk of the Circuit Court and asked her if there was a way she could look up names for juries.

"If you give me the names, I can put them into the data bank to cross reference when or if they were called to jury duty. If they served on a single jury together, they'll all come up at one time." Ben gave her the list of names and it took her only a few minutes before the results appeared.

Detective Ori, you were right. They all received Summonses at the same time, but I'll have to go into hard files to see if they served on a particular jury. What number can I reach you at later?"

Ben left his number and asked her to have the operator patch her through to him if he was out, thanked her and left. He decided to take a trip to the State's Attorney's Office and see if he could talk to Shroeder before the news broke. Shroeder was in court or somewhere, so Ben left.

When he reached his car, the dispatcher was calling him. It was the Clerk.

"Ori here."

"Detective, we looked at our log for juries, for the month these people were summoned. We got lucky on the first try. It was a publicized case, which you may recall. It was **People versus Elizabeth Conley.**"

Ben slammed his foot on the brake, skidding into a flower planter. "Oh shit, shit, shit!" Ben had read a report once that Elizabeth was taken in by the Veins family when her parents were killed. "God-damn-it!" Ben screamed as he pounded his fists onto the steering wheel. The number 11 stuck in his head. There were only 11 names on the list. Where was the twelfth name? "This is impossible. Veins killed the whole fucking jury from Betty's case and no one knew?" He asked himself. The Captain did not want to hear this. Ben thought about having a stiff drink to settle his nerves. Someone was going to pay for this. He'll need barbeque sauce on him for the roasting he'll take in the media. Ben pictured himself back in uniform.

Chapter 26

Captain Chance gathered his officers who would carry out the execution. They had enlisted another staff member to stand in for Eddie. They all met at the Warden's office at "o-dark-thirty" for practice. Chance started by asking his team random questions concerning the official protocol. He was proud of these men, as not one failed to answer quickly and correctly.

"Mr. Veins, step forward, turn around, kneel down and place your hands behind your back." The stand-in for Veins did as directed. He was handcuffed and shackled at the ankles.

The cell door was racked open and he was walked on the other side of the "green door." Everyone on "the Row" knew what was on the other side, and that those who make that walk never return. It was the execution wing.

Once on the other side, Veins was taken to the "48 hour cell," where he'd be under constant observation by a staff member. Veins would be stripped naked and a nurse would perform a digital, rectal exam to make certain Veins had not hidden contraband in his rectum. For this run, the stand-in was happy to hear that they would forego that part of the practice session. However, he was changed into a fire truck red jumpsuit and house slippers, as the real Veins would be.

The team then jumped in their practice schedule, to the night of the execution where the four guards approach, cuff, shackle and waist chain the condemned, while a nurse cuts off the right pantleg about 8" above the knee. They followed the protocol, except for the cutting of the pant leg.

In order to make the execution rehearsal as surreal as possible, even the clocks were turned to 11:40. The team moved "Veins" to the room where the crucifix table awaited. Even the actual physician who would end Veins' life awaited them and participated in the exercise. Once "Veins" was strapped and secured, the Captain read the Death Warrant, nodded and pumps began an eery rhythm. This is how death would sound and the last voice Veins would hear.

Chapter 27

Nannette Daly returned home from the grocery store, where she purchased some of her favorite items and looked forward to a dinner of lamb with mint jelly. She was greeted by her two obese cats, who had been her only family for over a decade now. She set the paper bags on the kitchen counter and proceeded to the closet in the front hallway. When she innocently opened the closet door, she froze in terror. Eddie, wild-eyed and exuding evil, gripped her in an iron fist. Eddie viciously grabbed her by the hair, almost lifting her off the floor. There was a resident evil in those eyes, so mesmerizing that Nannette was no more than a stuffed rag dog in his grip. Eddie half walked, half carried her to the sofa, where he produced large electrical wire ties and bound her hands and feet.

Nan sensed that was in the presence of a superior force or being and did not even whimper. She was a proud woman. She had helped mold the attitudes and lives of thousands of children. She would see what this thug wanted and then let him take whatever valuables he desired. She did not consider him some rapist, so she was "safe" there, although she may welcome some sexual fantasy with a stranger, but not this one! She couldn't remember the last sexual encounter she'd had. But, this guy didn't want sex, he just wanted to rob her, she figured. She had been robbed five years ago, on the street. Since then she had always been careful and made a mental note to call a locksmith to get more locks on her doors and windows.

Eddie stood behind her, and now a color picture suddenly floated before Nan's eyes. It was one of those photos students have taken for yearbooks. The photo showed a vibrant girl, with a future in her smile and eyes. Nan had the strange feeling she had seen or met this girl before. Perhaps one of her prior students? Maybe.

"Do you remember her?"

"She looks familiar. Was she a student of mine?"

Eddie inhaled deeply, and then said. "My sister."

"She's pretty. What has she got to do with me?"

"You don't remember, do you, bitch?" Eddie hissed.

"Don't talk to me like that. This is my house."

"Does the name Conly, Elizabeth Conley sound familiar? You killed her. You and your friends on the jury. Remember her now? Do you recall what that man did to her?"

"But she killed that man. She should have let the law deal with him. She was wrong. What do you want from me?"

"I want you to see her now." With that, Eddie lowered a picture of Betty as she had lain on the stainless autopsy table, pale, utterly void of life and the future she once had.

Nan began to whimper now, her head shaking from side to side, denying the reality of what hung before her.

Eddie walked around from behind the sofa to sit in the chair across from her. In his hands was a nylon rope. Eddie sat down and reveled in Nan's pain, a smile on his pursed lips. Eddie tied a knot in the rope about two feet from the end. Then another, four inches below the first. Nan had no idea what he was doing, but was sure it was not good.

"You strangled my sister." Then he added "Bitch" as an afterthought.

Nan did not recognize the classic garrote, how those simple granny knots crush the fragile cartilage of the larynx, sealing oxygen from the lungs, unless surgical intervention provides a new passageway.

Eddie stood, walked around the room, looking at the memories this woman displayed for guests. There were photos of classes of students, awards from schools and civic groups, diplomas, certificates and awards of appreciation. Eddie had hoped to see his sister's home some day, decorated with photos of innocent smiles on his nephews and nieces. All those dreams destroyed. In one moment of injustice, it was all obliterated. He sauntered around the room, caressing the memories of Nan and his sister. An almost dream-like state overcame him, as he walked behind Nan. He looked down on the gray hair that lay on her head like steel wool. He took the rope in both hands, wrapping it around his fists, then lowered it over her head, until it rested about eight inches below her chin.

"Go to hell, bitch," said Eddie as he placed his left knee behind Nan's back and savagely yanked on the rope while crossing his hands. The knots performed as expected, crushing Nan's larynx in an instant. The rope now restrained Nan, while she thrashed about, her eyes bulging, tongue protruding and her entire head colored bright red in a fatal blush.

Nan struggled like that for three minutes and Eddie wondered if his sister suffered that same fate or whether a merciful God broke her neck so that death was swift.

Eddie removed a note from his pocket and placed it on the coffee table.

"One Can Choke on Justice."

He closed the front door when he left, but not before he turned the thermostat up to 85 degrees and then blended into the night from whence he had come. His company car was parked two blocks away, so he began a leisurely walk, enjoying the clean night air. For a brief moment, Eddie could hear Betty thank him. He knew that she loved him, even from the other side. Eddie awakes sometimes at night, the sheets and blankets strewn around the room, sweat coating his body with a patina of gloss. The killing had become mechanical, the memories have mounted, becoming a monster that tramples his dreams and turns them into hellish vacations to the macabre. He used to dream of Betty, the things they shared and hoped for, but lately, she only came to him for the briefest of time, to thank him for avenging her death.

Chapter 28

Foreman noticed that ground fog surrounded Thames every morning he came to see his client. He wondered if it was only on the days he visited, like some sign from weather gods, or if it was every day? He'd leave Chicago early in the morning to avoid traffic and return early in the afternoon for the same reason.

Foreman's mission today was to present his client with another option besides asking the Governor to spare his life like some Christian, moments before being given to lions. It is called the Illinois Post Conviction Relief Act, codified in the Illinois Revised Statutes, under Chapter 38. Basically, it permit's a defendant relief from conviction or sentence, if an egregious error occurred of a constitutional magnitude. Foreman was convinced that Eddie had a viable chance of winning something from the veritable grocery list of challenges he proposed. However, his client had expressly forbidden him to file any further appeals on his behalf. This had become a contemporary thought among those who languish for years on death row. They just want it over with. Today, Foreman hoped to change his client's mind.

Foreman waited for Eddie to be seated. He bought him a Pepsi today and Eddie drank thirstily.

"Eddie, I came here because we've prepared a Petition for Post Conviction Relief for you to sign. We've alleged several grounds for relief, including a) ineffective assistance of counsel under **Strickland**, b) that you were denied due process under the Fourth Amendment, c) equal protection under the Fourteenth Amendment, and d) subjected to cruel and unusual punishment under the Eighth Amendment."

Eddie was familiar with **Strickland v. Washington**, where the Supreme Court had defined the arbitrary term, "ineffective." A defendant wasn't guaranteed a perfect trial, but a "fair" one, represented by an attorney who met a reasonable standard of competence and who subjected the prosecution's case to a true adversarial attack. Eddie had an idea where Foreman was going with this. It was buttressed by the challenges that accompanied it, as his trial counsel should have been better prepared. Had he done his homework or persuaded Eddie to tell him his motive for the Kilponen murder, then he could have argued it to the jury in mitigation. Smart.

"Eddie, your trial counsel erred in not pinning you down on a few things. 'Intense Provocation' ameliorates the charge from murder to manslaughter, based on your state-of-mind at the time of the commission of the offense. Arguably, based on what we've pieced together recently, we can put together a viable attack on your mens rea. I've got a number of reputable psychologists who, after learning the truth, would support our case of mental disease or defect."

It all sounded so smooth rolling off Foreman's lips. In front of a jury, he must be hypnotic. Eddie had been the appellate route before and on the journey down the street of broken dreams. His faith in appeals was not well rooted. He had little interest in this contrived assault on his conviction. Even if it were successful, he would remain in that prison within him. He'd never be free of that one. He had built it brick by brick by brick and was reinforced with the souls he took to get there.

"I'm not interested," was all Eddie said.

"Listen, asshole, I'm trying to save your miserable life, one way or the other. I came all the way here, spent hours researching and having paralegals prepare this and all you can say is you're not interested?" The latter portions of Foreman's diatribe got loud. Really loud. And Foreman was red with anger. He was trying to save this prick and with a smug attitude he says, "Not interested." Damn it!

"I told you before, no more appeals and this petition of yours smacks of just another appeal."

"Do you want to die, Eddie?" Foreman yelled. Eddie did not answer that question, but the look on his face sent a clear message that he was tired of life on "the Row." If you compared the booking pictures from his arrest with his appearance today, he had aged a hundred years. Crows feet were significant at the corners of his eyes, an iguana style sag under his chin and lines in his forehead appeared carved by Ice Age waters like the Grand Canyon. This was normal on "the Row," where life hung on a decision by a judge, hundreds of miles away. Eddie had the Death Warrant read to him four different times, when his direct appeal was denied, when his habeas corpus in the federal court was denied, when the appeal from that was denied by the U.S. Court of Appeals for the Seventh Circuit, and then when the Supreme Court denied certiorari on that. To run that gauntlet again would be more stress. There was a morsel of sanity now. He knew he was going to die and the unknowing part of all this was over.

"Mr. Foreman, leave your Petition and Brief in Support with me. I will review it. If I can agree to this, I'll call you immediately. I'm sorry if I seem ungrateful, but you do not understand how I feel about this." And just like that, Eddie was out of the chair and gone.

Foreman remained at the table a few minutes and then left. In the parking lot, he passed Eddie's parents arriving. He decided not to impose on them and drove away.

Chapter 29

There is a misconception that prisoners live in the lap of luxury, that they reside in air conditioned comfort while eating better than the average family with working parents. Truly, that is not the case. Thames is a contemporarily designed prison designated for maximum security prisoners who are condemned to die. Although it is equipped with a "chilled air" system to reduce the inside temperature, that measure of comfort is attributable more to federal court intervention than the whim of prison administrators. The interior colors are designed to psychologically induce tranquility, to relieve stress and promote cooperation between the keepers and the kept.

The hallways are a pastel blue with cell doors a gentle shade of green. There are no harsh colors here, except on emergency equipment and the one door that is never opened where they could see. The unit has a hospital smell, with all the cleaning solvents used daily. The lighting is harsh, florescent, with each cell having a four foot light which is controlled by staff from the outside. A 30 watt bulb remains on in the cell at all times. A prisoner is never in the dark and learns to sleep in the light.

The cells themselves are 10' by 16', with 10' ceilings, and contain a single bunk with a security mattress which cannot burn and is filled with useless cotton batting. There is a combination sink/toilet made of stainless steel and is bolted to the wall. Each cell has a small steel desk with a fixed seat, all bolted to the wall. A prisoner's personal property is kept in a cardboard box. The prisoner is issued two clean sheets, one blanket and a small pillow. Certainly, these Spartan conditions, although humane, do not constitute luxurious accommodations.

The most ominous sight is the solid steel door which has a window made of safety glass, along with two small doors, called "bean slots," where meals are passed through, or through which the prisoner is cuffed and shackled. Showers are permitted twice a week, last ten minutes, and require three staff members to move each prisoner from his cell and back again. Showers are in a separate cell, one prisoner at a time, and always under staff observation.

The Hollywood depictions of Death Row, with the raucous inmates banging metal cups on the bars or the lights dimming when the switch is thrown on the electric chair, are not the case at Thames. It's deathly quiet at night and only mechanical hums are heard during the day. It's the sound of security machinery at work, slowly extinguishing the lives of those who gave theirs up while taking another's life. It is nothing like the old movies. Society has learned how to kill in the name of justice, in hospital-like surroundings and with precision.

Veins sits in his cell on "the Row," along with 156 others. Lately, he has been unable to avoid the mental slideshow of those upon whom he invoked his firebrand form of justice. In brilliant color, he sees each and every one of them. He has asked his sister to stop the constant flow of morbid images, but they keep rolling. Eddie realizes that he is slowly going mad, and soon he will be a blithering fool. He concedes these cognitive movies quite well. The Warden believes that he gets "slightly distracted" because of the impending execution. But even that cannot overshadow these wakeful nightmares.

Eddie has come to realize the horrible truth that preys on the most prolific killer's experience. For each and every human killed, for whatever reason, justified or not, a part of them enters the killer. You may call it what you will. The religious will label it a "soul." Others call it a "spirit." What non-killers don't fathom is that you can kill once and let it go. But, as the bodies pile up, so do those spirit-souls that enter the killer. Over time, they become demonic and torture their host, driving him or her insane. In military jargon, they call it PTSD or the Viet Nam syndrome, the mental aftershock of combat and mass killing.

Eddie had no such claim as a combatant, only the cries of his sister as she rests on the other side. There is no respite for Eddie. Not awake and certainly not in his sleep. The pictures of people in their death poses just keep flashing before him. Recently, he has begun to ache or feel sharp pains in limbs and torso, without explanation. His skin has felt like fire on more than one occasion. His throat has felt as if acid had been poured in his mouth. Sometimes he experiences migraine headaches, with shooting pain at the back of his skull. He wonders if his victims are transposing their pains into him, as well. He can recall their screams and pleas for mercy, too. How that sow mewed when he started slicing her with his razor. Oh, she paid dearly. Her sobs were exquisite on the pallet of colorful moments. He kept that razor to remember her by, but immersed it in bleach to destroy any traces of her, then changed the blade with a new one. The old one was dull from the slicing of her flesh, like they do at restaurants that serve gyros. She bled and bled. Eddie burned all his clothes at a job site where they kept an incinerator to dispose of leftover materials and old pieces removed from the building being remodeled.

He had memories of each of them. Perhaps, once he met with these cops and agents, purging this pent-up knowledge, he could gain some escape from the horrible images. Maybe their spirits would leave him alone then, somehow moving on to wherever it is they go.

Whatever may happen to him, Eddie had made the decision to cooperate, to debrief on the most vicious attack ever on American jurisprudence, for he knew that a simple death would not deliver him from the devil within.

Chapter 30

Eddie's parents had arranged to meet with Mordeci and Foreman at their home. Foreman welcomed an alliance with his client's parents. Mordeci was more a broker of media influence than legal authoritarian, but critical to pressuring the Governor to act.

"Gentlemen, my wife and I asked you here because we need to know what to do to save our son's life. We cannot stand idle while the State murders our son."

Forman, forever the showman, assumed the lead. "Mr. And Mrs. Veins, has your son admitted anything to you lately?"

"Mr. Foreman, if you are referring to those lunatic allegations that our son is some kind of monster, no, he has not," Clay answered.

"Folks, there is an offer on the table from the Governor's Office. We have good reason to believe that your son has personal knowledge of these crimes." Foreman noticed the protestations cross their faces and held up his hand, like he was directing traffic. "Please hear me out." He waited for them to settle down. "Mr. Habush, C.P.D. and myself, have expended countless hours going over what they have. Believe me, the evidence is pretty substantial. The jury that sat on your daughter's case is dead. That has never happened before in this country. It's scary, folks. I've been doing this for a long time and I've never encountered anything remotely close to this."

Mordeci interrupted. "Mr. And Mrs. Veins, what we are trying to say is that he is the primary suspect in these cases. Circumstantially, Eddie is the only person we can locate with not only a motive, but the opportunity to do these things. If he did do them, the Governor will commute his sentence to life. No one, and I repeat, no one, will ever know."

Foreman picked up the cadence then. "I suggested to Eddie to let me file a petition in court, which would stay the execution and we'd have a hearing on this newly discovered evidence, which could mitigate your son's circumstances. He told me he'd think about it. I want to save his life, but he has to give me permission."

"Mr. Foreman," Florence said, "Our son loved Betty, as we all did. Are you certain he did these other things?"

"Yes ma'am. I believe he did or he knows who did. If he had an accomplice to these, then we have no clue who it may be."

Clay sat up now; his interest in this topic was intense. "Has he indicated if someone else may be responsible?"

"No, sir, he has not, but as I said before, we have no other suspect."

"What would happen if he said he was not alone? Would the information still be under this seal thing you mentioned?" Clay asked pointedly.

"Mr. Veins," Foreman said solemnly, "that is a question we have not contemplated. Until that situation arises, I think it best to abstain from conjecture or muddy the waters around this deal."

"Mr. Habush," Florence started, "what is your position on this? If my son is guilty of all of this, how is it possible that they'll just let him go?"

"Mrs. Veins, in all honesty, the reason the Governor will commute the sentence, is to buy his silence. Your son, by a simple letter, which he can either mail out directly or smuggle out with a guard or an attorney, would have a devastating impact on elections and future jury trials. If Eddie agrees to the terms, he lives."

Florence continued with, "What will you and your paper do, if the Governor does this?"

"Our official position is that a Petition for Executive Clemency was filed, setting forth numerous problems with sentencing and the trial itself, that cast a pall of speculation as to his guilt or innocence. Therefore, to err on the side of caution and spare his life would be a prudent measure. If anyone snoops around, the entire file of the Governor will be under seal for investigation."

"So, the Governor won't look too bad. How about that pompous ass Schroeder, the prosecutor?" Clay asked.

"The state's attorney," Foreman responded in his best courtroom baritone, "will become the Governor's whipping boy, I'm afraid. But they are opponents in the upcoming election anyway. I think this sort of case could become a hotly contested issue. In any event, Mr. Schroeder will not look good. The lesser of two evils is to look slightly bad in having your son's sentence commuted, versus the murders of twelve jurors on his watch as prosecutor."

"Mr. Foreman, we all know that time is running short. Eddie told us that you discussed something, a plan of some sort, that you hoped would help him. What you tell us now is that it would be a sure thing. I assure you both that my wife and I will do our best to convince our son to live. However he decides, my wife and I will support him completely. We are not the ones who must survive in those terrible conditions. It must be his choice."

When Mordeci left the Veins home, he suffered from mixed emotions. His heart went out to a family so devastated by tragic events, beginning with a wonderful girl and ending with unimaginable brutality.

Foreman on the other hand, was trying to figure out how he could use Eddie's execution to his advantage. How, if Eddie nixed the deal and opted to die, he could glean some favorable press. Practicing law, Foreman believed, was more marketing oneself, than the actual skill. F. Lee Bailey was only famous because, as a public defender, he was appointed to represent "The Boston Strangler" who raped and killed. And he lost his case then. Now, some people like Bailey inspire him to market himself better and then get the same sort of respect.

Chapter 31

The room is lit only by Moonlight, which only highlights her lithe body lying peacefully asleep. Her two children are asleep in their rooms; her husband has gone away on business. Diane slept on top of the blankets, naked, the warm summer breeze caressing her. She was drop-dead gorgeous, with her short, black hair, long, silken legs attached to a tight little ass, perky breasts with nipples the size of a shirt button. She is six feet tall, weighing about 130 pounds, with a smooth stomach and the hairiest pubic mound Eddie has ever seen. It is a black bush, an inch high and a perfect equilateral triangle.

Just looking at her gave him an erection. He would like to slide himself between those long legs and ride her for an hour or two, but that's not his reason for being here.

Diane Joswin is a surgical nurse who happened to be sitting on Betty's jury. McLoed, the foreman, before he died, told Eddie the ferocity with which this woman had fought for acquittal, and then gave in to the chauvinistic persuasion. Eddie stood over her for a while, watching the rise and fall of her small breasts and that inviting mound of hers, with the swollen lips of her vagina. In his homework, Eddie knew that Diane was not faithful to her husband. Actually, he is number three in the husband department. Diane fooled around with

Number Two, while married to Number One. Now she played around on Number three, whom she kept around because he was stupid enough to trust her and believe she'd never do that. Dolt. Diane loved sex, enjoyed riding her lovers until she shook from pleasure, then lay on the bed for the man to serve himself. She has two children, but a hysterectomy ended her worries of becoming pregnant from her promiscuity. Eddie felt like waking her, pushing her legs apart and slamming his now rigid cock into her, but she'd enjoy that and tonight his mission was to collect, not to give.

He withdrew a cigar tube, with Cohiba on a rich, gold label and unscrewed the end. The aroma of Cuban tobacco wafted around him, but it was not one of his cigars that awaited him inside, but a syringe. Eddie looked at the small breasts floating on Diane's chest. He held the syringe in his right hand and deftly cupped the left one, reaching across her, while pushing the needle in to the hilt and pressing the plunger. Diane emitted a cry of "ouch," but then her mouth was covered with Eddie's hand.

"Diane, you could have saved my sister. McLoed told me about your arguing to let her go. You should not have changed your mind."

In a modest gesture, Diane tried to cover herself with the spread, but Eddie told her it wasn't necessary, pulling the spread back.

"What did you do to me?" Diane prayed.

"Insulin, Diane. In a minute you'll go into insulin shock and your heart will stop." He could feel her feeble attempt to get up, but Eddie was way too strong and had the leverage. "Be quiet, or I'll hurt your kids."

Eddie lifted her slightly and slid behind her at the headboard, while cradling her head and shoulders in his lap. Diane was tense and felt like a cat, looking for an opportunity to sprint off. Eddie rested his arm across her and fondled her breasts and nipples. This beautiful woman, with the morals of a dog, would soon be dead. He would not defile her, for her cheating heart. He owed her that for defending his sister, but she would die for her ultimate vote.

Diane began to shake, her head rolling from side to side, her eyes white orbs, devoid of any pupils. Eddie consoled her, cooed her with visions of the heavenly place she was going. Finally, she lost consciousness and Eddie knew it would not be much longer. He returned her head to the pillow and got up. He could not resist the urge to run his fingers through that luxurious pubic hair, soft and supple. He slid his fingers over the cleft of her mons and stroked her clitoris and then slid two fingers inside her. Somehow he had thought her opening would be tighter. He now has four fingers inside her, with room for more. The number of lovers that pounded this flesh and had this woman so many times had rendered this delicate girl to a common whore. On second thought, Eddie would not have enjoyed being with her after all. He would have realized her slutty ways, by the obvious overuse of this cavern between her legs. What a shame that she lacked respect for herself, he thought. Eddie removed his hand from her crotch and placed it over her heart. A faint pulse was all that remained.

It only took two more minutes for her to expire. Eddie watched as urine and feces stained the spread beneath her. He removed a note from his pocket and placed it on her stomach.

"Justice Can Be Beautiful."

Eddie went to the children's rooms, to make sure they were asleep. He had to pull the blankets back up on the little girl, who resembled a Barbie doll, only with brunette hair.

He lifted the phone and placed it on the kitchen counter and used a knuckle to dial 911. When the operator came on, he walked out the front door, making sure it wasn't locked. The police would be there soon and he didn't want them to scare the kids.

Chapter 32

Breakfast was Eddie's favorite meal. Besides being the only meal where he got a cup of fresh brewed coffee, it brought him some of his favorite foods. Today, it was scrambled eggs, two strips of bacon, two pieces of dry toast, an apple, and, of course, that cherished cup of coffee. Eddie ate real slowly, as if dining at a five star bistro and tasting every morsel. People have often used the phrase, "I ate like it was my last meal." Well, here on "the Row," such colloquialisms were never said. "The Row" is where such things come true.

Eddie had finished his food and sat on his bunk, plastic cup in hand, like a king on his throne, when two officers came to his door. "Hook up, Eddie," which meant he was to submit to being chained up. "You have somewhere to go." Eddie quickly gulped his coffee, which he did not like to do and was cuffed and shackled.

He was taken to the recreation yard, where the Warden sat at the table, chess pieces already set up, two mugs of steaming coffee and a silver carafe-like thermos next to him. "Good morning Edward. Care for some real coffee?"

"Thank you, J.D." as Eddie sipped his coffee. This was real coffee, French Roast with a hint of vanilla. Eddie decided he'd stick around for the coffee, no matter what drivel the Warden spouted. This was good stuff!

"Edward, you've become most interesting to a vast number of people, well beyond those usual hounds that smell headlines. We have received hundreds of requests to witness this fiasco, but I'm getting calls from the Governor's personal aide de camp, federal agents and prosecutors, the Attorney General, the Cook County State's Attorney, the Director of the Department of Corrections, the Pardon Board and notable counsels for all of them. I've never had attention like this. It's like they're looking for something from you. Would you care to explain any of this to me?"

"J.D., I've come to respect you, your ethic of right and wrong. I admire a principled man. When the time is ripe, I assure you that you will be informed and I count on you to do the principled thing, no matter the pain it may cause the political players."

"I guess I can live with all that nonsense, but how will I know what the right thing to do is? I mean, if I don't understand, how do you expect me to figure out what to do? I hope what you're referring to has nothing to do with my duty as Warden here?"

"J.D., you have a job to do, if it comes down to that, which it may not. What you'll face is a moral issue, not a question of duty."

They played a game of chess which Eddie won, having a queen and king only, after marching a pawn down the board one move ahead of the Warden. Their games were always an exercise in concentration, with no room for idle chatter.

"By the genesis of the calls, it's safe for me to assume they are looking at an appeal or clemency. If you are applying for a stay, I would appreciate our attorney being in the loop. If there's going to be an execution, I'd like to know. I don't want to put you through all that or my staff. Will you do that for me, Edward?"

"Of course," Eddie said, watching Barnhill rise and prepare to leave.

"Edward, it is a wonderful morning and I'd hate to see this coffee go to waste. Take your time out here and enjoy it, but you can't take it inside. I don't want others to whine about it. I'll wait for word from you."

Eddie watched him as the guard let him out and he disappeared inside "the Row" where he would make his daily rounds. Eddie filled his mug with a fresh brew, sat down on the park bench and looked up at the clouds. Somehow, even those ever-changing whisps of moisture reminded him of the faces of those souls that torture him. Oddly, though, no matter how long he stared, Betty never looked down on him.

Chapter 33

The chamber of the Chief Judge for the Circuit Court of Cook County is a lavish affair of exotic hardwoods meeting domestic oak. The triple crown molding, sconces, six inch trim around doors and floor, coupled with the solid oak paneling, is an artist's creation in woodwork. Some artisan spent many hours routing and scrolling these one-of-a-kind designs, then the countless hours of staining. By comparison, Foreman liked the chambers more than the courtroom.

Foreman was on a mission today. He wanted the Judge's input on whether or not he would entertain the Petition for Post-conviction Relief, if his client did not agree.

"Judge, I have ethical and moral motives for the Petition. First, as an officer of the court, I'm obligated to advocate all viable issues before the Court. Ethically, I don't believe that I am constrained to ask my client's blessing in strategic decisions. If I ignored issues, I would be ineffective and contravening the Sixth Amendment." The Judge listened stoically, hands folded on his massive desk.

"On the moral side, I oppose capital punishment entirely. I'm Catholic. So, when the opportunity arises, my religious beliefs beckon my best effort." Foreman paused a moment to gather his thoughts. "I believe, even if this Court would require me to first obtain my client's blessing, that I could file as *amicus*.

"Patrick," the Judge said, "we've known each other for years now. I expect complete candor from you. So, let me ask you, did you obtain this newly discovered evidence as Mr. Veins' counsel?"

"I learned it from an independent source, not from my client."

"Did this independent source contact you because you represent Mr. Veins?"

"Yes, sir, I believe that's the case, but it was from a newspaper reporter and definitely not within the attorney-client relationship."

"Did you talk to anyone else about this new evidence, on behalf of Mr. Veins?"

Foreman had not anticipated this question and he realized how it would change the complexion of his argument. If he argued this new evidence with any court or the Governor, he had become an advocate and had constructively built that attorney-client relationship.

"Would discussing the case with counsel for the Governor qualify?"

"You know the answer to that question already, counselor. I'm afraid the *amicus* angle is done. Let's consider the requirement that you gain your client's consent."

Foreman had done some work on this approach. "The Illinois Revised Statutes are silent on whether or not an attorney must file only what his client agrees with. If layman knew the mechanics of the law, they wouldn't need us. It is well settled law that strategy is the province of the attorney when it comes to motions and trials. Since Veins has not terminated me or requested substitution of counsel, I remain the attorney of record. Based on these premises, I believe I am justified in filing with or without Mr. Veins' assent."

"Very eloquent, counselor, but flawed. The statutes provide that a defendant in a capital case controls appeals decisions. He or she can decide not to seek any appeal beyond the automatic appeal directly to the Illinois Supreme Court, after the death sentence is passed down. A petition like this is considered quasi-appellate in nature. Therefore, Patrick, you will need his consent."

"Your Honor, what if another attorney wished to file as amicus? What if counsel for the newspaper that developed the evidence, filed?"

"Patrick, did you discuss the evidence with this attorney?"

Foreman knew he had to admit discussing the case and this evidence with the paper's attorney, the end result being the same. "Yes, sir," Foreman mumbled.

"Then there's a conflict of interest, as some of the information or evidence arguably is derived from that discussion. You would need a neutral and detached attorney,

Patrick, but I wouldn't put much faith in that. Standing will be the primary obstacle there. Anything else?"

"No. Thank you for your time. I appreciate that." Foreman left the courthouse, determined to convince his client to consent. What a coup it would be for him if he could get a new trial for Eddie! He'd be on TV and all the ABA releases. Marketing!

Chapter 34

Three days and counting down, the nation poised for Illinois' execution as if NASA were launching men to Pluto. Veins' case became a media darling and a lot of critics were not sure why. As rumors spread, it just happened. Sort of like Jed Clampet discovering oil by accident, while shooting rabbits. The media was attracted because other media found this case interesting. The "herd mentality" of journalism was at its finest.

Mordeci, who has patiently waited for his Editor to decide what the paper will print, found himself summoned to his office. They were joined by a stenographer and Richard Altman, the paper's Chief Legal Counsel, a grand title for a little man. Mordeci always believed the twerp suffered from the Napoleonic Syndrome, where short people demand big respect. Behind Altman was someone even more geeky looking, but was never introduced.

"Mort, Mr. Altman wants you to give a comprehensive run down on the Veins case. Start with the woman whom he's convicted of slaying and put the rest in perspective."

For the next three hours, Mordeci went through the files, one-by-one, with the evidence which linked Veins to the crime. He did not have forensic evidence, DNA or fingerprints. No one did. Mordeci couldn't go public yet, hence the reason for this meeting and C.P.D. was not about to remove their thumb from the dam and open a flood of scathing reports. If C.P.D. told the investigative agencies to check evidence found at these crimes to establish links to Eddie, then the secret was no more.

He reminded everyone that prior to his arrest, Veins had absolutely no record or even arrest, where fingerprints were taken. Therefore, he did not exist in FBI or state files. Even if they had found his fingerprints at the crime scenes, they had none of his on file to compare them to. Since Mrs. Kilponen was the last of the jurors to die, thus far, no one had thought to ask that his prints be checked for matching at other similar crime scenes. For one reason or another, the various agencies didn't suspect Veins.

In addition, the note at the Kilponen scene never took center stage of the trial. It was insignificant, really. The prosecution avoided it, so as not to cloud the "motive" element of their case. The defense had no reason to vehemently attack the physical evidence at trial. The defense posture was that Eddie was not the culprit, simply because he was in the area or could have committed the crime. "Reasonable Doubt," that venerable pattern jury instruction, took center stage from the beginning.

If a defense attorney attacks every piece of evidence, he detracts from the defense that his client was not around the crime scene. For instance, if the prosecution says, "the drug dealer," who was caught, is now cooperating in prosecuting his alleged supplier, and he says "Mr. X gave me the dope." If your defense is that your client barely knew this man or was someplace else when the transaction occurred which ensnared the dealer, it makes little sense to attack the chemical analog of the narcotics seized. An innocent defendant, given this scenario, wouldn't care what was in the packages. So, the defense did not subject every piece of evidence at Veins' trial to microscopic review. It just happened that no one really cared.

Mordeci described the discrepancies in Eddie's itinerary with records from job sites, gas purchases miles away from where he should have been and mileage on the company cars.

Altman was impressed with Mordeci's thoroughness and had to admit that the likelihood of Veins committing these slayings was fantastic in mathematical numbers. However, there was no physical evidence and without proof, it would be irresponsible for the paper to print mere innuendo. But, that was not his final decision, as the *Sun Times* could report links to these crimes and let the cops do the rest. But even the publication of that theory could scar the judicial system and undermine public confidence.

"In other words, you people want to see how many people would be ruined politically, and will assess the balance of harm to them against what these politicians could do for you later?"

Altman did not appreciate Mordeci's tone or attitude on this. "Mr. Habush, may I remind you that your job is to report news. While I grant you, it appears that Veins could have done these murders; you haven't got one iota of physical proof. If you print unreliable or presumptive articles, you not only subject this paper to civil litigation, but irreparably damage its reputation and circulation decreases. I am the legal expert in this room, not you. I said I would consider our options."

Mordeci never thought he could really hate someone, until now. "I'll prepare a draft for my next article, which will discuss the death of Mr. Veins. I'll leave open the ending, just in case we're going to release what we uncovered. In the alternative, we can support the Governor in his decision to commute his sentence, due to the circumstantial nature of the evidence. Give me as much lead time as possible."

Then Mordeci directed a comment at the Editor only. "When you have time, I'd like to see you alone." Mordeci did not wait for a response, but simply walked out. Politics and responsible journalism do not mix.

Chapter 35

Eddie was "hooked up" and moved to the visiting room for attorneys, where the Warden and Captain Greer were waiting. Once again, a thermos rested on the table and three mugs of coffee were waiting.

"Edward," the Warden began, "I received a call from Mr. Foreman this morning. He asked me if you had relayed your decision to me or have asked to use a phone to call him. I responded negative to both. The Captain and I are concerned."

The Warden looked at his Captain who said, "Eddie, tomorrow morning we'll be moving you to the observation cell. I'm really not supposed to tell you that, in case you wish to harm yourself. But, since you've been here, you've conducted yourself like a man and I respect that. Once there, staff will be outside your door at all times. Your approved visitors will be permitted to visit you from 8:00 a.m. to 8:00 p.m. in this room. We will provide them with meals. You will be allowed outside from 8:00 a.m. until 4:00 p.m. whenever you ask. The chaplain will be on call for you at any time. Any questions, Eddie?"

"What about the phones?"

The Warden answered this one. "The phone will be on a small table, outside your cell. Any time you wish to use it, just tell the officer at your door."

They were watching for a reaction from Eddie as the reality of it all would begin to set in now. Telling a man to prepare himself to die is no simple task. The enormity of it consumes everyone. You watch the metamorphosis from a man to wounded animal. They turn inside themselves, withdrawn, as their time approaches. Some cry, some shake, some turn to God for salvation, some become cold steel and a few accept their fate like gentlemen. Eddie was a gentleman. They expected that much from him and secretly hoped the governor would spare him, which had never been on their wish lists with others. The Warden knew there was exotic interest in this guy. He was quite special somehow. Perhaps because he had no prior record before this offense, an exemplary citizen?

"By the way Edward, Mr. Foreman would like to call you this morning."

An hour later, having sated himself on the fresh coffee, Edie called Foreman.

"Eddie, I see you got my message. There are two things I need to discuss with you. Have you made up your mind on what we've discussed? Remember, we can't talk too much on the phone, as it's recorded and monitored. Keep it simple."

"I haven't decided yet," was all Eddie would say.

"I need an answer pretty soon, Eddie, as others may act on this." Foreman knew that would get a rise out of him.

"What does that mean?"

"What it means, Eddie, is that a certain newspaper is going to authorize its legal counsel to file a petition in court on your behalf, as an *amicus*, or friend of the court."

"I have not authorized anyone to file anything in any court." Eddie was mad and said this loudly, startling the guard.

"As officers of the court, lawyers can always request *amicus* status. It happens in high profile cases and frequently in capital cases. They suggest different arguments on important issues or cases. Yours is high profile, in case you don't watch the news." Foreman enjoyed being flippant with Eddie.

"You mean that rag can have their attorneys file something against my wishes and create a story at my expense?"

"They aren't 'creating a story,' Eddie, they're trying to save your life because you won't." Eddie had to think about this. The newspaper could ruin everything.

"Eddie, you still there?"

"Yeah. Listen to me. You can inform all the agencies that want to talk to me that tomorrow is their big day at me. I want the stenographer, everything in writing that I requested before, and then you and I will meet. You can tell the Governor he can 'stay' this sideshow for seven days. If he doesn't like what he reads, then we won't file. There's my answer."

"Eddie, I think you're being smart now. If you live, something could change later and you could be freed. I'll get right on this. I'll have everything ready to sign when I see you."

Foreman hung up and began a landslide of calls. First, he called the Governor's counsel, who said the Governor would stay execution seven days, because "he was assured by credible sources that newly discovered evidence may affect his decision to grant clemency or permit the execution to go on." That would stave off reporters. His next call was to Mordeci, so that the *Sun Times* made no move to upset the whole clemency deal. Mordeci said he would take care of that, post-haste.

Foreman then called Benedict Ori, so that he could gather all the lead detectives on these cases and arrange for them to travel to Thames the following day. That required Ori to contact his Captain, who called the Chief and had him contact the Chiefs of the other jurisdictions to assure complete cooperation. Ben had the "greenie" arrange forty-five minutes for each agency, as that was ample time for a statement when the suspect was volunteering the information. It would be a full day, but everyone would know if they had their perp.

The last call was to Christian Schroeder, to get him up to speed. "Chris, Veins is meeting with everybody tomorrow. I'll be there with our stenographer. Then I'll spend the night and get him the clemency petition. It looks like we've got it settled. The Governor will stay the execution one week, to review everything, and that'll give us time to get things settled."

"OK, Ben, keep me informed about what's going on. If you need my help, call me. I'll leave word with my secretary to interrupt or find me."

Chapter 36

Some say that the Halls of Justice are lined with books and before leaving law school, the law student will read sixty percent of them. Law libraries are the lifeblood of studies and the theory behind the laws themselves. Students spend half their time in classes and the other half in these repositories for the thickest books known to man.

Where Kelly Rolland studies, at John Marshall Law School, the library is renowned for its completeness. It has state and federal circuits' resources. It has Federal Reporters, Supreme Court Reporters, etc., which consist of thousands of volumes of cases dating back to not only the United States Supreme Court beginnings, but to Admiralty, Maritime and Common Law, by such reporters as Cranch and John Locke. John Marshall's Library is the centerpiece to a well-rounded education. The library is huge and bustles with student traffic, judges and alumni, a constant tide of bodies shifting in and out.

Kelly came this particular afternoon to do some research on the "Blue Sky" laws, specifically one signed by President Jimmy Carter regarding government agencies and their records or files. It is commonly referred to as the "Freedom of Information Act," Title 5, United States Code, Section 552. Tests in law school are frequently the essay type, filling "blue books" with all of the knowledge possessed by the student on a certain topic, which the professor grades on composition and accuracy. Kelly had such an exam forthcoming and the professor advised them to pick three topics from the ten he provided and told them to be prepared to write about them in class. Kelly chose the "Blue Sky" portion of Administrative Law, because the mechanics of agencies and their policies fascinated her.

She arrived at about 2:30 p.m. on the bus. She carried her back-pack, which threatened to tear loose from the straps if she added any more weight. She found a table in the corner where she could study without interruption from friends or noise. She was in luck today, as no one else sat there and it permitted her to spread out books and really get into a receptive mood.

She started with the Smith-Hurd Annotated Statutes for Title 5. This book would direct her to precedent cases to support certain aspects and when she came across a point of contention, she would retrieve the volume or treatise referred to and open it on the table. Kelly removed a Brownberry muffin from a side pocket, a no-no in the library, and nibbled at it like a mouse, while studying. She became what she studied, lost in the Administrative Procedures Act and the penalties agencies face when they refuse to comply with the law. A man approached her table and asked if he could join her. She thought he was another alumnus, dressed in a smart suit and he had a professional appearance. What she noticed most, was how thick his glasses were. My gosh, they looked an inch thick.

The man carried a briefcase from which he extracted papers and a legal pad. He sat at the opposite corner from where she sat and looked as though he was researching some topic. Nothing unusual.

"Administrative law is difficult to comprehend sometimes, but not as challenging as criminal law," the man said.

"Oh, it's not an area of my choosing. I have an exam soon. I enjoy criminal law, particularly juvenile justice. I'd like to be a judge some day," Kelly responded.

"There are many quirks in criminal law. Sometimes the wrong people get off and sometimes the wrong people go to jail. Don't you agree?"

"For the most part, it's the guilty that go to jail, but I'll admit that guilty people sometimes get off."

"But what about the innocent who go to jail? Is that an acceptable price? Are we willing to let them pay the price for imperfections in our system?" the man asked.

Kelly thought about that, and then said, "I am not convinced that innocent people are convicted that often. I mean, they have to convince a dozen jurors that they're guilty. It's not like one person decides their fate."

"That's true, but don't you think that the law itself may permit a wrongful conviction?" the man inquired.

"Laws are written to protect and define what a citizen may or may not do. I don't see ambiguities in criminal law, in contrast to civil, let's say. If a person steals, either with a gun or bad check, it's still stealing. We just differentiate the degree of seriousness."

The man then asked, "What about protecting oneself or their family? Would someone be justified in using force to protect themselves or what if someone raped them? Would that fall between the cracks and permit someone to do something so out of character for them, as maybe kill someone?"

Kelly felt a little nervous about this question and it showed. "I don't believe citizens have a right to act like vigilantes. We have cops for that sort of thing."

"You sound like you've had experience in this area, young lady. Have you or a friend of yours ever had an encounter like that?" He looked directly into her eyes now.

"Not directly. Not as a victim, I mean. I sat on a jury once and it involved something like that."

"Oooh, that sounds interesting. How did the jury decide?" he said gently.

"Actually, we convicted her of shooting some scum-bag, but the law prohibits lynching and such summary death sentences. She left us no choice."

"What would you have done, if you were her?"

"First off, I wouldn't let myself get into such trouble. Also, I wouldn't take matters into my own hands. I would've let the cops handle it and put him away for life," Kelly responded tartly.

"People like that get short sentences or get off completely. They say the woman wanted it or consented. Or, some cop forgets to read him his rights and the case is thrown out."

"Who are you? Are you an attorney or a judge?" Kelly asked suspiciously.

"Sort of." was all he said, and then began to read the papers in front of him. He handed Kelly a document which she began reading.

"**People of the State of Illinois, versus Elizabeth Conly**," with "Indictment" below. Then, the man was no longer across from her when she looked up. She realized too late, that he was actually behind her now. Right behind her. She could feel his warm breath on her neck and a pinprick on her neck on the right side.

"Kelly, if you move or make one sound, I will push this into your neck. You see, Kelly, Elizabeth was my sister. She was a lot like you. Ambitious. Full of dreams. Hopes for a family of her own. That bastard destroyed all that when he took her soul. You could have returned her to us, where she could heal. You and your sanctimonious laws just couldn't permit that. You couldn't understand what she went through or feel her pain. All you saw was black or white."

Eddie's hand was on her left shoulder, next to her neck and whatever it was he held. She thought it was a knife most likely, and was just below her right ear, on the carotid artery. She knew a wound there would be fatal. "Kelly, didn't you see the agony my sister was in? You couldn't forgive her for shooting that thing that defiled her? Could you survive what she went through, Kelly?" Eddie whispered into her left ear.

"I'm sorry," was all she could muster as tears ran down her face, destroying her makeup.

"So am I, Kelly. So am I," Eddie said sincerely. The point left Kelly's neck and for that instant, she believed he had meant to scare her. Then Eddie's hand moved like lightening, from her shoulder to her mouth, her head clamped against Eddie's pelvis.

It wasn't a knife Eddie held, but an ice pick, about 8" long, which he slid into Kelly's ear canal and thrust it through the inner ear, the spongy area where sound vibrations register and directly into her cerebral cortex. She was dead, instantly, her eyes gazing up at him and only a slight trickle of blood from her ear. Eddie retrieved a note from his briefcase that said: "Justice is Silent."

He placed it in front of her. She looked as though she were asleep, the pick removed and stowed away in a zip lock bag in the briefcase. Her hair obscured the blood and she looked like she dozed off while studying. Students would be reluctant to wake her, as they had pulled all-nighters as well.

It would be hours before the depth of her sleep was discovered. By then, Eddie would be at home, making dinner, waiting for his sister to visit him. She visited more often these days, in his sleep and even during the day, when he wanted her to come to him. She would be happy with him today and thank him. He liked that. He enjoyed pleasing her!

Eddie walked out of the library, then the school and went to the company car in the parking garage several blocks away. He liked the weather and how the adrenaline rushed when he ended Kelly's life.

Chapter 37

The visiting area at Thames is not the same as where prisoners meet with their attorneys. Thames does not have "contact" visits for family and friends. Instead, it's a room slightly larger than a phone booth, where a concrete block wall and bullet proof glass separates the condemned from their visitors. There is a phone on the wall, which is monitored, that is the sole means of communication. One visitor at a time is permitted on the phone on their side, and an inch of glass between them and the visitor.

When he was brought in, Eddie's mother was sitting on the round metal stool, waiting for her son. The door behind him locked and slots opened so that a staff officer could unshackle and uncuff him. His mother watches as her son is unchained like an animal in a cage. Her heart wrenches at the sight, tears welling in the corners of her eyes. She tells Eddie they're tears of joy at seeing him, but he knows better. She's not fooling him for an instant, but he never lets on that he knows. It's tradition to tell people all is well, than to snivel and make your visitors feel bad. Visits are rough enough on everyone, especially when they have to leave. It's these last waves that crush a gut, but the thought of never seeing them at all, overcomes the good-byes.

On "the row," parents are sometimes carted away, kicking and screaming, as the realization hits that their son, daughter, brother, sister, dad or uncle, are going to be killed and the next time they'll see them will be in a casket.

"Hi Mom," Eddie says, ignoring her tears.

"Eddie, I want you to know that no matter what, I still love you. But, I have to ask you something and I don't need you to say anything. Just nod or shake your head."

Eddie knew what was coming. Foreman or Mordeci had to have approached his parents.

"Eddie, Mr. Habush and Mr. Foreman came to the house and told your father and me about some sort of deal. But, they said that you'd have to admit to some things first. Eddie, did you do these things?" Florence held her breath for the answer, her eyes searching his, back and forth like a railroad crossing, as if his eyes were the passage of truth.

"Mom, I don't expect you to understand. All I want is your forgiveness. I'm sorry I brought you more pain."

"Eddie, we all loved Betty, very much. But to do those other things, Eddie, I don't understand. It was that 'thing's' fault that hurt her, not those other people. Eddie, that was wrong." Florence's voice trailed off, sorrowful and bleating.

"Mom, I will not justify anything to you. It is what it is. I love you. That's all I'm going to say."

"Are you going to take this deal, Eddie?"

"Mom, I am meeting with everyone tomorrow, including Foreman. It's all part of the deal, as you call it."

Relieved, his mother let his father sit down to speak to him. "How are you, Eddie?"

"Better than expected. I get lots of fresh coffee, I can go outside whenever I want and play chess with the Warden. The Governor is staying everything, until I meet with everyone and he gets the reports."

"What kind of questions, Eddie? Have they indicated any knowledge of more than one person?" Clay asked.

"So far, what I'm advised by Foreman, is that they've got circumstantial evidence I did these things. What they want from me is to fill in the blanks on how I did these things. It seems a mere formality, more than an investigation. They've got records that show I was available for every one of them. Foreman says they have no other suspects."

Clay looked forlorn. "Eddie, it was an accident that they caught you. Now this…"

"Dad, it's no big deal. I clean up the books on these matters and it's over. Cases closed. I'll be all right with this."

"Eddie, your mother is scared. She's afraid that she's going to lose you and she's afraid that this will all come out and we have problems. When it comes down to it, she wants you to live. I do, too, son. You have to do what you feel is right."

"I'm meeting with everyone tomorrow. I'll let you know how it all comes out. Don't worry."

"I'll let your mother talk to you. Whatever you decide, I'm there for you."

For the next two hours, Eddie and his mother talked about books he'd read, the news and what was going on with her.

After his parents left, Eddie sat in his cell and prayed to a god he abandoned long ago, for the strength he'd need and for his family. What he did was on behalf of his sister, who guided his every move. He calls out to Betty now, as he needs her wisdom now. Although his crimes were righteous, they torment his every moment. For the first time in decades, Eddie knelt beside his bunk, folded his hands and bowed his head in silent prayer. Maybe he could answer the question, should he live for his parents and spend the rest of his life in prison, or let them kill him, which would probably kill his mother.

Chapter 38

The front gate at Thames was inundated with badges, guns, briefcases and anxious cops who wanted their turn at Edward Veins. The parade started at 7:30 a.m. when Foreman arrived with a woman with a steno machine and stacks of that little paper that feeds through it, ending up with dots and lines on it. The Warden had arranged for donuts and coffee, as he realized they had begun their trek to Thames quite early. Foreman and his stenographer were shown to the conference room, not the small visitor room where Foreman generally met with Eddie, but a much larger room, with an oak table and high-backed chairs. The Warden joined them at 8:00 a.m. and said he had arranged for Eddie to be brought there, as it would be more conducive for everyone's needs.

First up was a Trooper from Michigan, because he had a long drive back. His name was Corporal Charles Hedeman, a member of the State Patrol for seven years and a detective for three of those. He was told, as were the others, that he would learn the details from the admitted killer. It was to be a confession without the need for Miranda rights, as Veins was already sworn under oath, as this whole fiasco was part of a federal grand jury proceeding.

"Good Morning Mr. Veins. I am Corporal Hedeman with the Michigan State Patrol. I'm here to talk to you about Mr. Stolzenfeld."

"Sure, the guy I shot in the head with a nail gun and left floating in his aquarium."

"Can you tell me about it?"

"I drove there in a company rental. You can check the mileage, as it took four hours to get to Clawson. I arrived there late Friday night and drove past his home. I got his forwarding address from the Post Office here in Illinois. I realized he was alone, but was younger than me and may be quicker. I needed something, to help, so I bought an airless nail gun at the Lowes, about half a mile from there. It cost me over $600.00. I returned it to them later on, in its box, as if it never was used and I got a refund. I'll be on video there. The guy was working on a motorcycle in his garage and went back and forth to his house for beer and to use the bathroom. So, I entered the house through the back door and waited for him. While he was bent over foraging around in the refrigerator, I eased up behind him. When he stood up and turned, I had the nail gun to his forehead and pulled the trigger, sending a 10 penny nail into the front of his skull, dead center.   When he went down, I was not certain of him being dead, so you'll find nails at each temple. When I saw the tank with those miniature sharks, I dumped his upper body over the edge. I pinned the note to the left rear pocket of his jeans, "Justice if for Real Sharks." I returned to Chicago about 3:00 a.m. Sunday morning. Anything else?"

Just that nonchalantly, the guy admits to cold blooded murder, as easy as ordering pizza.

"Why did you kill Mr. Stolenfeld, Mr. Veins?"

Eddie leaned over so the Trooper didn't miss a word. "Because he killed my sister."

"You mean, because he was on the jury when she went to trial?"

"Yes."

"Thank you, Mr. Veins. Mr. Foreman, I will be in touch with you after I visit Loew's to see if he's on the video, or if they still have it. But, he knows too many details not to be the person responsible for the murder. I'm comfortable with his confession."

"Of course I know the details, Corporal. I did it." Eddie said, gloating. He had gotten away with murder in Michigan and they would never have caught him.

And so the day went on, with one cop after another. Eddie made the case for them, filling in details only the perp would know. He told how he burned people, electrocuted a corrections guy, slashed a man's throat and gouged out his eyes and injected insulin into a nurse. That was before lunch, which no one felt like eating now. The Warden, who had listened intently, was not surprised that no one had a clue who had killed these people. Eddie was the smartest man on death row now, and it was more luck than not that he was captured at all. In every interview, Eddie made the same rationale, "Because he/she killed my sister." People do bad things in the name of love but Barnhill didn't know how bad, until now.

They had a choice of coffee or soda for lunch. The BLT sandwiches sat untouched, for food was not important. Even the stenographer had never recorded such carnage or ever heard of such brutality. Of course, she was sworn to secrecy as well, so she could never relate what she'd learned. Besides, who would believe that someone had killed an entire jury and no one knew?

The afternoon session was done telephonically, with a detective from Sacramento, California. They heard how Eddie penetrated the United Airlines maintenance facility, fastened the jury's foreman to a blast shield behind a jet engine, questioned him about jurors and their roles in the verdict, then fired up the motor and turned the man to charcoal. It was all so easy for Eddie. He returned to Tahoe and enjoyed the rest of his vacation like he had done nothing more than squash a bug.

They broke for dinner, joining the Warden for bacon-cheeseburgers, fries and little cups of ice cream, which they ate ravenously. They had been going at it for 10 hours now and everyone was waiting for the grand finale.

Benedict Ori arrived precisely at 6 p.m. and was escorted to the conference room. Eddie knew he'd see his nemesis again. He had never admitted guilt for Mrs. Kilponen's death and because he had been sentenced to die, he was never charged with her daughter's abduction.

"Good evening, everyone. Mr. Veins, we meet again."

"Mr. Ori, we've made real progress here today. I believe it's safe to say that we have closed the books on ten cases so far. Eddie has kept his end of the bargain. Shall we begin?"

"Mr. Veins," Ben started, "you were convicted of murdering Catherine Kilponen. Did you in fact commit that crime?"

"Yes."

"Did you kill her because of her participation in WAVE or because she was on the jury in your sister's trial?"

"I took her because she took my sister."

"What do you mean 'took' her, Mr. Veins?" Ben asked.

"I did more than kill her, I took her soul. My sister wanted it that way." Eddie spat out. Then he continued. "She was against women and their right to protect their bodies. But, as we talked and I was slicing her flesh, she understood her error. She asked Betty to forgive her."

"Mr. Veins, why did you abduct her daughter?"

"The name. I didn't realize the mistake until Betty pointed it out. When I looked at her driver's license, I realized the mistake."

"So, you just let her go?" Ben asked with surprise in his voice.

"Betty and I had no problem with her. Betty told me to release her, unharmed. I told Betty that she'd identity me, but we finally agreed it was the right thing to do." Eddie seemed almost argumentative as to why Ori would be so stupid that he couldn't understand.

"Eddie, I am the official representative for the Chicago Police Department. You've been advised, I'm sure, that the Governor is contemplating clemency in your case. A critical point of contention is that you be completely candid, no misinformation or lies. You understand that?"

"Mr. Foreman had adequately performed his duties as my counsel, detective. I know what's going on." Eddie said defensively.

"Mr. Veins, there was another juror named Mundschau. Do you know anything about him?"

Eddie chuckled. "You don't know, do you? We threw him off an overpass in Ohio, around a city called Mansfield. Sonofabitch went right through the windshield of some 18-wheeler. Musta scared the hell out of the driver." A pronounced smile creased Eddie's face. He was proud of that one. They had timed it just right, so that when they let go of him, he'd meet the truck head on.

"And you did that for the same reason as the others, Mr. Veins?" Ben asked.

"Yes, Mr. Ori. He killed my sister."

Eddie had purposely saved that case for Ben. He knew Ben would come to this show. No one else asked about the 12th juror, but Eddie knew Ben would. He also knew he'd ask the most important question of all. During his trial, no one had asked him that question. Now was the perfect opportunity and Eddie enjoyed the suspense. Ben was trying to figure out how to phrase the question.

"Mr. Veins, I'm not an attorney, so I may not ask this delicately, so let me be blunt. Mrs. Kilponen was skinned. What did you do with it?"

"I'm not a surgeon, Detective, so it was a lot of pieces, really. I put it in a trash bag and took it out with me. I picked out a large piece which I removed from between her tits and threw the rest in the Chicago River for the bottom-feeders."

The stenographer was crying and was distraught at this vivid image, so they took a 15 minute break for her to compose herself. "I wish they had the electric chair or hanging. I'd pay to watch that sadistic bastard die. What kind of animal are we dealing with here, Mr. Foreman?"

Foreman, in a fatherly posture, said, "Janice, we are dealing with a highly intelligent schizophrenic, who also suffers from PTSD. He is not well. You've heard his testimony. His sister asked him to do these things. The world is full of sickness. Now, we only have a little more to go and you can scoot back to Chicago and start transcribing the day's work. OK?"

"God, I feel like I need a shower after being so close to that piece of shit."

Ben was back on track, wanting this whole thing behind him as well. "Mr. Veins, there were other victims who were missing body parts. Did you take those home, as well?"

"Of course, detective. We put them together, so Betty would have them." Eddie said sarcastically.

"Mr. Veins, we searched your home and office. We found nothing. Where are these items?"

"If you were real detectives you'd already know. Betty has them. She has the other things, too. We took something from every one of them. She even has the razor, not the phony from court, the ice pick and eyes, detective. She really liked those."

"Mr. Foreman," Ben said, "may I remind you that the agreement requires the truth, complete truth. It is unacceptable for your client to continue saying his dead sister possesses these articles. Please remind your client of the seriousness."

"Listen, I told you the truth. Look where Betty is."

"Are you telling us these items are at the grave-site, Mr. Veins?"

"There you go, Sherlock. Betty took them there so they can't escape from her. Don't you see?"

"Mr. Foreman, I have what I need. If the items are there, our agreement is complete. If not, I will recommend otherwise. Thank you, Mr. Veins."

Before Ben departed, he used a phone in the Warden's office and dispatched a team to Betty's grave and to contact the Ohio State Patrol to confirm Mundschau's death.

It was 8 p.m. when Foreman and his stenographer left Thames. Foreman went to a motel, exhausted and appalled at the statements his client made. He had never heard of such sociopathic conduct. He did not sleep well.

The next morning, Foreman appeared at Thames, ready to meet with his client. However, before being allowed to see him, the Warden requested to see him first.

"Mr. Foreman, I must tell you that the statements I witnessed yesterday are deeply upsetting. I am curious about this 'agreement' you referred to on several occasions. If it involves one of my prisoners or the security of this institution, I believe I have a right to know."

"Warden, I am not at liberty to advise you of any legal proceedings in which I may be involved in on behalf of my client. I will, however, advise you that nothing to which I am a party, poses any threat to your institution whatsoever. I'm sorry I can't be of any help to you. Is there anything else before I see Mr. Veins?"

"No, Mr. Foreman, but be advised, I'm going to rattle some cages to find out what the big secret is that involves Mr. Veins.

Thank you, Mr. Foreman! I'll have Eddie in the visiting room when you get there."

As Barnhill had promised, Eddie was already seated at the table in the visiting room when he arrived.

"Eddie, I got a call this morning at the motel, from Detective Ori. They were digging most of the night, one shovel-full at a time, but they found a canister made of PVC, which they x-rayed. They subsequently obtained a federal search warrant and cut it open. As you indicated, items were there which confirm your story. Ori is satisfied that you've complied with your end of the deal and has prepared the C.P.D. Attachment for our Petition to the Governor. It's done, Eddie. All we've got to do now is submit it and you're off the Row."

"Betty is not going to be happy that you took those things from her. She may hurt again!" Eddie said while shaking his head.

"Eddie, Betty is dead. It's all over. You're going to live. Don't you understand?" Foreman was getting a little red in the face now. He had put forth a lot of effort for this client.

"Betty is going to be mad at me for telling you where she hid those things." Like a little boy who had done something that would upset his mom, Eddie sat in the chair, head down and sad.

"Eddie, I need you to sign this Petition and I can overnight it to the Governor for his signature." Foreman laid the Petition before him, but Eddie made no move for the pen to sign the document.

"Look, Mr. Foreman, I am not going to rush into this. We have six days left, now that the Governor stayed this dog and pony show, so we have time. I'll go over this Petition tomorrow and let the Warden know. I am not prepared to decide today. I'm sorry."

"Goddamn you, Eddie! Sign that fucking thing right now! Listen, you crazy bastard. We've worked hard on this. Your parents have worked with us, too. We knew you murdered those people; we didn't need to hear it. We didn't need your little souvenirs from the graveyard to know you did it. Quit acting like some fucking celebrity, you piece of shit. Sign the Petition and go someplace where none of us has to look at you!" Foreman was about four inches from Eddie, face to face, when he finished. Here was one of the most dangerous men in the world, one who could kill someone like nothing had happened and he was in his face.

"My, my, counselor. You are not yourself right now. I told you, I will keep this and go over it. You'll have it by tomorrow." Then Eddie rose from his chair, started for the door, and then turned back. He leaned close to Foreman and whispered in his ear, "Betty just told me that she's going to pay your little house a visit."

Before Foreman could respond, Eddie went to the door and officers entered to escort him back to his cell. Foreman asked himself how he missed Eddie's psychosis before. How did his trial lawyer?

Chapter 39

"Good morning, Detective Ori. Go right in, the boss is waiting for you. Can I get you coffee?" the receptionist at the state's attorney's office said. The woman was always pleasant. Ben liked her.

"Yes, thank you. If you over tire of these abhorrent conditions," as Ben nodded towards Schroeder's door, "please come see me."

With a wicked smile she said, "May I quote you on that, the next time someone gives me a problem or denies my raise?"

"Of course," Ben said and then headed for Schroeder's office. This was going to be an interesting meeting.

"Good morning, Ben. Please sit down. I'm anxious to hear an update. I've already gotten calls from the Governor's staff. I understand it went well?"

"Well, sir, that would depend on your definition. If you mean, did Veins confess to all these murders and were his statements confirmed, then everything went fine. If you mean, did we encounter any problems, then it didn't. I'll tell you the problems." Just then his coffee arrived and Ben needed the moment to calm down.

"I have a problem listening to someone detail killing a dozen fine people, who I'm sworn to protect, without breaking his neck. I have a problem with having my guys digging up body parts half the night, not to prosecute the sonofabitch who mutilated those people, citizens I'm sworn to protect, but to let him live and cover the whole friggin' mess up. I have a major problem with politics getting involved in my profession. Now, I ask you, Mr. Prosecutor, do you have a problem with any of this? Tell me, did everything go well?" Ben's face was tinged and small beads of sweat were breaking out on his forehead. He sat back in his chair and sipped at his coffee, confident that he'd made his point.

Shroeder walked around to the front of his desk and sat on the corner, with one leg on the floor. Ben was not impressed with this pose.

"Ben, I don't expect you to understand, but politics, as you call it, was not a player in this agreement. It's the sanity of our justice system at stake. If it got out, Ben, that somehow our system failed to protect these twelve people, there would be severe and long-lasting implications. People will ignore summonses for juries, because they will be afraid of a person seeking revenge like this. We can't let that happen, Ben. I hope you see that."

"Well, then, I guess you'll call our grisly discovery a success in jurisprudence. I assume the agreement, deal, contract or whatever legalese you affix to it, is done? Has it been consummated yet? Has Veins screwed us?"

"If you're asking if the Governor has received Foreman's petition yet, Mr. Veins has it right now. He's expected to give it to the Warden there at Thames, today. By tomorrow, Ben, it should all be over and the U.S. Marshals will pick Veins up and transport him to the United States Penitentiary at Marion. I've already spoken to the Warden there and he assures me that the Bureau of Prisons policy on Marion will be followed to the letter. Veins will spend twenty-four hours per day in his cell, until he dies. I don't see that as a victory for him, Ben. I wouldn't call that 'life', would you?"

"Pardon me if I don't need Kleenex to dry my eyes for this prick, but he killed twelve people. I think we should starve him to death in that cell. It'd give him time to consider the pain that he inflicted. Yes, I would call it a victory for him. His victims didn't get that same option. Excuse me, but I have some bad guys to catch. Hopefully, you'll let them pay for what they did!"

"Detective, may I remind you who you are talking to? I am not one of your minions. Now, get out." Schroeder opened the door for Ben, who took his coffee mug with him to the reception area.

"That went as expected. You have a nice day," Ben said to the receptionist on his way out. He kept his coffee mug, too.

Chapter 40

It's a brilliant, sun-drenched day in Southern Illinois. A high pressure system from the Gulf has blessed the Midwest with 76-78 degree temperatures and light breezes to stir the leaves and transport those fragrances of farmland. Eddie is sitting on the concrete bench, the sun giving him internal warmth, as he rests with eyes closed and face turned up towards the sun. He heard someone approaching and figured that it must be the Warden, as he was the only one who would enter the cage with him like this.

"Edward, mind if I join you?" It was the Warden, who carried a carafe and two mugs. Eddie was getting used to all the fresh coffee.

"Certainly, J.D., since you brought the coffee. I tried to order some, but the room service here is terrible. The wait staff resembles cops and carries handcuffs. I wouldn't complain to the chef, if I were you."

"I must tell you, Edward, yesterday was quite disturbing. You must have cherished your sister?"

"I still do," Eddie corrected. "I still do."

"Foreman called me this morning. He wants to know if I've got the signed Petition. I told him that I'd check with you and call him back. Correct me if I'm wrong, but the agreement that was discussed yesterday, is that if you admitted these other crimes, you would not get executed?"

"I'm not supposed to discuss it with anyone, but since you were there, I don't mind. You're correct in that assumption. Good deal, huh?"

Eddie seemed more interested in the French Roast coffee reflecting his sad face back to him.

"Edward, after the meetings I had mixed feelings about you. I mean, the brutality and all, but then I considered the pain you must have felt, the anguish in your heart. I just don't know how to feel about you. Why didn't you sign that petition right away?"

"J.D. would you approve this deal?"

"Well," Barnhill started, then thought about how to word it, "from your perspective, I would save myself, but from the Governor's position, I'd never approve or even entertain such a ludicrous proposition. No matter how sour the medicine, I'd let the people know what happened and promise them it'll never happen again. So, no, I'd never embrace this agreement."

"Did they tell you not to tell anyone?" Eddie asked.

"Edward, I was told that if I discuss it with anyone, I'd be fired immediately, and Captain Greer would assume command. I'd have to resign, take my pension, then announce what's going on in the background and expose everyone involved. But, I'm no crusader, Edward. I work with the system, not against it. I didn't get where I am, being some rogue. No, their dirty laundry is safe with me. What are you going to do after you leave here? You won't be staying here after the Governor signs off. Will you tell your story?"

"J.D., you and I both know that they'll find a place for me where no one will get close and I won't be able to mail anything out. The whole thing will be buried alive with me."

Barnhill got up and advised Eddie to get the staff to call him when it was ready, as he had been directed to put a man in a car and drive it to Springfield to the Governor's office.

After the Warden left, Eddie pictured he and Betty at the park near their home. He asked her to help him, to reach down from heaven and show him what was right. Eddie asked for her forgiveness for telling them where her possessions could be found and asked how he could redeem himself. To Eddie's surprise, he heard Betty's voice, as if she were standing next to him. She told him what must be done, and Eddie relaxed. The decision made, he enjoyed the rest of the morning and the coffee Barnhill left behind. He wondered if he could get more coffee?

Eddie spent the rest of the day outside, except when he was taken inside for lunch and to use the commode. He was seen reading the National Geographics he had in his cell and something the staff had not seen for a long time; he was smiling.

Chapter 41

Not hearing from Veins for the rest of the day about the petition which would save his life, certain plans were manifested. Captain Greer, accompanied by two of his officers, appeared at Eddie's cell door. Eddie was hooked up, but instead of going outside, they went to "that" green door, which was opened from the opposite side, and Eddie was guided inside. Once there, he was stripped naked and a Physician's Assistant donned gloves, to conduct a physical inspection of Eddie's body. Every orifice was looked into and his rectum digitally examined, which Eddie endured quite well. He was handed a red jumpsuit and placed in the only cell there. His belongings, or what remained of them, arrived an hour later, after being methodically searched by officers. He was given a blanket, two sheets, a towel, a facecloth and the sandals which now served as his shoes.

The cell is smaller than his other one, which he left behind in a pregnant silence, as everyone on the Row watched "that door" consume Eddie and they knew that one day they'd disappear like that, as well. For two days after that, the other inmates would not speak and would be seen crying or unruly. That's why all recreation privileges were suspended until after Eddie's execution or clemency. Barnhill would not risk any problems by moving angry or scared prisoners. It was better to leave them be.

Eddie on the other hand, would be given the run of the recreation yard and have a phone next to the bars of his cell where he could call at any time and have visits all day.

There was no solid door here, just bars, with an officer eight feet in front of him. He had no privacy whatsoever. He would use the toilet with that officer watching, just in case he had swallowed something before being moved. Everything was security now.

"Edward," Eddie heard and looked up to see the Warden standing at the bars. "Sorry about having to move you here, but since you haven't given me the Petition yet, I must proceed as required. If you have it signed, I'll dispatch it immediately. By this afternoon, it'll be signed and we'll get you out of here."

"Thank you, J.D.," Eddie said, that smile still on his lips. "Let's talk about all this over coffee and a chess board, shall we?"

Ten minutes later, they were two generals at war with plastic soldiers and mugs of coffee. Normally, Barnhill would not be alone with someone who was scheduled to die in two days, but there was an unusual bond between him and Veins.

"J.D., Betty told me to join her in Heaven. I'm not signing any petition or authorizing anyone to try to stop this. I need to ask you something, man to man. Can anyone hear us right now?"

"There's only the one officer by the door."

"Would you send him for some coffee for me?" Eddie noticed that the Warden questioned the wisdom of sending his officer away and leaving him alone with him, but the look on Eddie's face must have convinced him that he was safe. The Warden turned slightly and asked his officer to get a carafe of hot coffee.

"J.D., as you know, I received the transcripts of our meeting and all the documents regarding the agreement to purchase my silence. I would like you to get it to the right people. Betty wants the story told, the truth of the cover-up and the politicians who would lie to people to save their jobs."

"Edward, that would cost me dearly. I'd lose my life here; my family would be upset with me. I'd be giving up everything. You ask too much, Edward."

"I have everything in a large, brown envelope. It's addressed to C.N.N. News. All you'd have to do is mail it." Eddie pleaded.

"Edward, they'd know. I can't."

The officer arrived with the carafe and passed it inside the fence to the Warden. For the next hour, it was just the two men playing chess and enjoying the weather. Both knew that there could be no more chess games or sitting outside in the beautiful weather. After this, it was all business. Betty liked him.

Eddie's parents came to see him later that day and got a motel room for the night, so they'd be close. Trying to find pleasant things to talk about, when one of the conversants is about to die, is an exercise in futility. No matter what Eddie brought up, his mother would revert into recollections and tears. When the Veins family parted that night, no one felt like sleeping. All they had was 36 hours.

Final Day

Eddie didn't sleep. He figured he'd have a thousand years to sleep after this day was over. He had scrambled eggs and bacon, toast and the endless cup of coffee. The Warden came to see him at 8:00 a.m. to see if there was a change of heart regarding the Petition and advised him that the Governor was standing by to stop the execution and sign the Clemency Order.

Foreman arrived at 9:00 a.m. and joined Eddie and his parents in the attorney's waiting room. The first order of business, as far as he was concerned, was to convince Eddie to sign the Petition and let him rush off to the Governor's Office for the eleventh hour reprieve. Suddenly he interrupted the colloquy between him and his client.

"Eddie, everybody's worked damn hard for you. What the hell is wrong with you? Why did we go through all this? Why meet with all those people and confess? Please don't tell me Betty thinks it's best. I don't care to hear about some dead girl telling us what to do. Do you hear me Eddie Veins?"

Before Eddie could respond, Eddie's father leaped from his chair, grabbed Foreman by the throat and then slammed him into the glass surround in a choke hold. Foreman's eyes bulged, his air completely cut off. Foreman was surprised at the strength and vise-like grip. There was a wild rage in

Clay's eyes, like a predatory lion. The two officers from outside the room rushed in and grabbed Clay, to pull him off of Foreman. They finally wrestled him to the floor and handcuffed him. A moment later the Warden ran in and demanded to know what went on. After hearing from his officers and asking Foreman if he wished to press charges, to which he responded in the negative, he ordered the officers to uncuff Eddie's father and to leave.

With order restored and emotions cooling down, he felt it safe enough to leave them alone once again.

After Warden Barnhill left, both men apologized to one another and to Mrs. Veins for upsetting her. Having failed to justify or persuade Eddie to sign the papers, Foreman advised him that he would go and wait with the Warden, who was also joined by the prison's counsel.

Eddie and his parents avoided windows or going outside to the recreation yard, as the media surrounded the institution and were clamoring for updates.

The Captain was holding a lottery with members of the press to see who would be permitted to witness the execution. He would draw numbers which corresponded to numbers that were issued to the reporters when they registered at the front gate. Only 10 reporters would be allowed in and would then hold a conference afterward where all the other media representatives could ask questions and statements of what they had witnessed.

The Warden's staff was inundated with calls from national celebrities in the news business. Larry King wanted to know if the Warden would appear on his show. The list included "60 Minutes," 20/20 and Geraldo. The Warden's official position was "no comment" at this point. What surprised J.D. Barnhill the most was that the secrets of the Veins case had been contained. "Damage Control" was the term that first came to mind, but if the truth ever reached these media sharks, political careers were finished.

Lunch was served for the Veins family, consisting of broiled chicken, mashed potatoes, corn on the cob and iced tea. They ate perfunctorily, each wanting to please the other and using the food as a distraction. Also, they used it to avoid looking at the clock. Eddie would have dinner with his parents at 6:00 p.m. and they would be required to leave at 8:00 p.m., giving Eddie time to compose himself. In a little over six hours, they would say good-bye to their son, forever.

"Eddie," his Father began, "It's not too late. Mr. Foreman is here and the Governor is waiting. If you want to change your mind, you have the time."

"I'm going to be with Betty tonight, Dad. We'll be waiting for you and Mom, but please take your time joining us," Eddie said with a boyish grin.

"They never understood, Eddie. You did well. I'll make sure they do. You have nothing to fear, son. We all died with Betty. Tell her we love her and miss her very much."

"I will. I'm not afraid. Betty will meet me right away."

The Chaplain stopped in and said a few prayers with everyone. He arranged to meet Eddie at 10:00 p.m. and would stay with him until the end.

Meanwhile, Foreman was burning up the phone lines between Thames and the Governor's staff in Springfield. The Governor would not sign the Clemency Order, unless properly requested by Eddie. However, he was on stand by at a moment's notice if the need arose. Also, at 12:30 a.m., the Governor had scheduled a press conference at the Capital building. He refused to travel to Thames for the execution, as his predecessor had done. He would simply wait by the phone, one way or the other.

Eddie and his parents spent the rest of the day playing gin rummy and making small talk. They had run out of real topics long ago. As the hour to leave grew nearer, the apprehension mounted. At 6:00 p.m., dinner was served on a cart like fancy restaurants use, with a white tablecloth and silver covers over plates of food. It wasn't the common fare Eddie had requested, but New York strip steaks grilled to perfection, with mushrooms, baked potatoes, baked beans, and French vanilla ice cream on lattice crust, Dutch apple pie and fresh coffee. They nibbled, but not much more. The minutes flew past.

At 8:00 p.m., four officers appeared at the door. They were accompanied by the Chaplain, prison psychologist and a doctor. Eddie's Mother fell to her knees, grabbed the legs of the officers and begged them not to make her leave so they could kill her son. The Chaplain knelt beside her, as well as her husband. They lifted her gently and placed her in Eddie's arms. She hugged him fiercely, as though she could save him, just by hanging onto him. Eddie walked to the door, carrying her as if she were a doll, cradled in his arms. He kissed her forehead and handed her over to his Father. Without a word, Clay carried her off, as streams of water rolled down his face. Neither looked back.

Eddie was taken to his cell, where his coffee awaited and a message from the Warden, that if he changed his mind, all he had to do was to call him.

Time seemed to stand still now. He kept watching the clock, but it refused to speed up for him. He started to gather his meager belongings. He placed the package addressed to CNN News, in Atlanta, on top of his bunk. He used the phone to place a call to Mordeci Habush at the *Sun Times*, but was connected to his answering machine. He left a message, thanking him for helping his sister and family. He also apologized for messing up his scoop about the jury. When he hung up, he was ready to join his sister.

A male nurse came to his cell at 11:00 p.m., to take Eddie's blood pressure and pulse. He also removed Eddie's right pant-leg, just below the hip, like gym shorts on one side. He shaved an area inside Eddie's thigh and applied some Betadine.

At 11:40 p.m. a number of solemn looking officers came to the door. The Chaplain, who had been talking with him about God and repentance since 10:00 p.m., walked with them. Eddie was cuffed and chained for the last time. He would soon be free of these buildings forever.

By 11:50 p.m., Eddie lay crucified on the stainless steel table with a large needle being inserted in his leg. It didn't hurt as much as he'd expected.

At midnight, the curtain next to him was drawn open and he could see the people who had come to watch him die. In the front row sat Melissa Kilponen with an older man next to her, which must be her father and the husband of the woman he had killed. They had eager looks on their faces, as if they would kill him themselves.

A moment later, Captain Greer appeared and read the Death Warrant aloud. He asked Eddie if he had any last words before the sentence was carried out. Eddie looked around the room for a minute, gazing into the eyes of the Kilponen family, wondering if they understood now, how he felt when his sister died and the loss he had felt. All he said was "no" and turned away from the witnesses. With a nod of the Captain's head, pumps began whirring and Eddie could feel a slight burning sensation in his leg. Then, he started to float, as if David Copperfield were performing his levitation trick. Soon, he was soaring through clouds and watched eagles circle around him. Then there was nothing and all was black.

Eddie was pronounced dead at 12:12 a.m. by the physician who took his life. His lifeless form was placed inside of a rubber body bag and transported to the rear gate where a hearse and police cars awaited.

At the exact moment Eddie was executed, J.D. Barnhill stood in Eddie's cell, holding the package for CNN News. He tucked the package under his arm and proceeded to his office. On his desk was an envelope addressed to the Director of the Illinois Department of Corrections, with his resignation and I.D. inside. He didn't bother to pack anything. They'd do that for him, for what he was about to do would label him a pariah. Along with Edward Veins, the political careers of a Governor, Cook County State's Attorney Christian Schroeder and the Mayor of Chicago, were about to die as well.

At the Veins home, police surrounded the house to assure their privacy and safety. Inside, Clay had given his wife her bedtime meds and carried her to bed. She was unconscious, either from grief or the double doses of her pills. Either way, she was not in pain.

Clay went back downstairs, where he poured himself a glass of Kentucky Bourbon and sat at his desk. Once there, the house silent as a vault, he opened the manila folder. He sat back, took a large swallow of the brownish liquid and started to read.

"Strayhorn, Earl, married, wife Elise, three children...two girls, one boy, all in college. Address is 2113 North Western

Avenue. Single family home, two levels, two doors. Detached garage…Employment, Circuit Judge…"

Epilog

While this is a fictional story, there is little doubt in my mind that somewhere, someone has taken vigilante justice into their own hands and punished a jury. Further, without question, I sincerely believe that prosecutors will make every effort to suppress those killings "in the name of justice" and to protect the families of those who paid with their lives after serving on a jury.

This is the first novel I ever put my hand to, so I was worried that it would not match up with my later works, except the people around me allayed those fears through their plaudits for the story, content and psychological twists.

I hope that I have caused you to wonder whether Eddie was "alone" or accompanied by someone of flesh and bone.

Sleep tight.

Daniel Storm